I0545968

Exploring
Normal - Paranormal - Supernormal

ALEC

Alexander Trilogy Book One
Originally published in part as The Princess

Followed by:
ALEXANDER
and
SACHA—THE WAY BACK

A novel by

Stan I.S. Law

IP

INHOUSEPRESS, MONTREAL, CANADA

Copyright © Stanislaw Kapuscinski 1997,
eBook 2010, Kindle Edition 2013
Paperback 2015
http://www.stanlaw.ca

All rights reserved. No part of this publication may be reproduced, stored
in a retrieval system or transmitted in any form or by any means
electronic, mechanical, photocopying, recording or otherwise, without the
prior written permission of the publisher.

Published by
INHOUSEPRESS
http://inhousepress.ca

Parts of the book was originally published under the title *The Princess*.

This book is a work of fiction.
Names, characters, titles, places and incidents are
either the products of the author's imagination
or used fictitiously.

ISBN 978-1-987864-07-6

Paperback Edition 2015
INHOUSEPRESS

SOME EXCERPTS FROM 5 STAR REVIEWS ON AMAZON KINDLE

...soon I was torn between reading as fast as possible to see what happens next or forcing myself to read slowly so that I could savor this book.

Diana L (TOP 500 REVIEWER, USA)

This is a novel that can be read by both young adults, as well as adults. Law has created a world of fantasy that is wonderfully fascinating. I can't wait to read the next book in the series.

Amelia Wallace (USA)

...parents of precocious teenagers will truly enjoy this story and perhaps become a little more enlightened as to how maturing children think.

Joan A. Adamak VINE VOICE (USA)

...Stan I.S. Law is a fantastic author and deserves to be read and appreciated.

Kevin Lintner (USA)

I am always deeply gratified when reading this author because he has the true gift of storytelling and then also elevates that story because of his deep facility with our collective experiences as humans, with myth, and with spiritual growth.
Stan I.S. Law is a balm to the seeker's soul, and ALEC is a fantastic read.

Alex Prosper (USA)

... a coming of age story and the method in which it is told by Stan I.S. Law is pure genius. Can't wait to read the next books in the series.

TrishFLReader (Florida, USA)

...I am a huge fan of this super talented author. ...I can't wait for more, this is beautifully written book that I highly recommend!

Mary Leckie (Florida, USA)

The writing is lush, sharply focused, vivid, exploratory and engaging. ...I finished the book lost in thought and eager to read more in the Alexander Trilogy, ...to sink my teeth into.

L. Collins (TOP 1000 REVIEWER, USA)

...I'm a huge fan of Stan I.S. Law's books... I simply cannot say enough good things about this book or this author. He has captured perfectly the essence of a teenage boy on his journey of self-discovery. Get this book, you will be glad that you did! I highly recommend.

M. Brown (TOP 500 REVIEWER, USA)

By the same author

ALEC (Alexander Trilogy, Book I)
ALEXANDER (Alexander Trilogy, Book II)
SACHA—The Way Back (Alexander Trilogy, Book III)
YESHUA—Personal Memoir of the Missing Years of Jesus
PETER AND PAUL (An intuitive sequel to Yeshûa)
ONE JUST MAN (Winston Trilogy Book I)
ELOHIM—Masters and Minions (Winston Trilogy Book II)
WINSTON'S KINGDOM (Winston Trilogy Book III)
THE AVATAR SYNDROME (Prequel to Headless World)
HEADLESS WORLD—The Vatican Incident
(Sequel to *The Avatar Syndrome*)
MARVIN CLARK–In Search of Freedom
THE GATE—Things My Mother Told Me
NOW—Being and Becoming
GIFT OF GAMMAN
THE PRINCESS
ENIGMA of the Second Coming
WALL—Love, Sex, and Immortality (Aquarius Trilogy Book I)
PLUTO EFFECT [Aquarius Trilogy Book II]
OLYMPUS—Of Gods and Men [Aquarius Trilogy Book III]

Short stories

THE JEWEL & OTHER STORIES
CATS AND DOGS
Sci-Fi Series 1
Sci-Fi Series 2

Non-fiction Books by Stanislaw Kapuscinski

VISUALIZATION—Creating Your Own Universe
KEY TO IMMORTALITY
[Commentary on the Gospel of Thomas]
BEYOND RELIGION: Volumes I, II and III
[Collections of essays on perception of Reality]
DICTIONARY OF BIBLICAL SYMBOLISM
DELUSIONS—Pragmatic Realism

Poetry in Polish
[with illustrations by Bozena Happach]
KILKA SŁÓW I TROCHĘ GLINY
WIĘCEJ SŁÓW I WIĘCEJ GLINY

INHOUSEPRESS, MONTREAL, CANADA
http://inhousepress.ca

Contents

Foreword

Epilogue

Introduction

In September 2010 part of this book had been published under the title *The Princess*. It received quite decent reviews but some of my readers claimed that it was principally suited to a younger audience. This was true, of course. It was a story about Coming-of-Age, although, at the time, I thought that the parents of young Alec would also find it interesting.

Since, I'd decided to make it part of a Trilogy.

With that in mind, I had to covert *The Princess* to a novel suitable for "mature audiences". The result is *Alec*, a novel that incorporates *all* of *The Princess*, but also adds elements that might be of greater interest for adult literary palate. It became more than just a Coming-of-Age story. The Trilogy, already available in ebook form, consists of:

ALEC + ALEXANDER + SACHA

That last name is Russian diminutive that is also derived from the name Alexander. Thus we have three generations of Alecs, or Alexanders, sharing with you their, I'm sure you'll agree, very unusual experiences. Briefly their stories deal with Normal, Paranormal, and Supernormal events. I hope you'll enjoy them all.

To whet your appetite, for the Princess, here are some of the reviews of the original version, which is retained in full:

> "...*The cosmic merging of Alec and Sandra is exceptional writing, even for this author from whom we can always expect the extraordinary...*"
> [Kate Jones, writer/editor, USA]

"...In many ways, this is a tale for us all, both young and old. It is a coming-of-age story high on life and hormones! It is a tale that breaks barriers and helps readers to realize that life's perspective is what we make it; we form our own realities..."
[T.D. Hollowell, author]

This is a story that contrives to blend normal and paranormal into a single reality.
[B. Happach, Publisher, Canada]

I trust you'll forgive this little subterfuge and enjoy my usual attempts to blend the three realities into a story that will tickle your mind as well as your heart. As I am sure you'll agree it is an extraordinary journey a boy takes within and without.

Stan I.S. Law.

1
Alec

"**O**nce upon a time,** a long, long time into the future, there lived a Princess. How can she live in the future? It is as easy as living in the past. To tell you the truth, she really lives in the Present. Only in the Present—though most people seem to prefer living in the past. I don't know why. I suppose they live in their memories. When you do nothing much, you don't create new memories, so you have to live in the past. But not the Princess. She has so much to do that a lot of what she does spills into the future."

Alec was sitting by the window, seemingly paying little attention. His mother was getting used to it. What mother wasn't? Perhaps Alec was getting too old for this? Not just this sort of book, but even for having his mother read to him. Alicia was reading aloud, in an attempt to inspire her son to read more books. Lately his interests have been limited to beating everyone at tennis. That's it. She had no idea what subject might excite him, but, she reasoned, there was no harm in trying. She cleared her throat to get his attention.

"But Mother," he stifled a yawn, "this is for children!"

At thirteen he considered himself very adult. She chose to ignore that.

"The story I am about to tell you," she continued, "all happened a long, long time ago, and it continues a long, long time into the future."

Alec's attention wondered off on a tangent. His mother's voice receded and then merged with the drone of a bee buzzing just outside the window. His imagination took over.

He pretended he was that bee. He almost felt the tiny wings flapping ceaselessly on his shoulder blades.

"Sometimes it all seems like a dream," he mused, "at other times it feels as real as the pink Christmas flowers on my windowsill."

This happened more and more often lately. His mother would read to him, and his mind would take over and spin his own story. She was getting worried about him. Didn't they call it attention deficit hyperactivity disorder? ADHD or something? Only Alec wasn't hyperactive. If anything he could sit for hours, seemingly lost in his thoughts.

Perhaps I ought to see a doctor, she mused?

"It all depends on what mood Alec's in..." she told his father that evening. She was close to tears. She thought she was losing her son.

Alex Baldwin Sr. was, in some respects, a fairly old-fashioned man. He was at a loss for words. Actually, he was thinking of his son's hormones, which were probably demanding their rightful recognition, but there was no elegant way to sharing his suspicions with his wife.

"It also depends on a great many other things..." Alex Senior replied.

But Alec Junior didn't know about great many things, until a long, long time into the future.

When Alec was a little boy, of two or three, both his and his father's names were Alec. Alec with a 'c' on the end. Alicia referred to them as Senior and Junior. Yet confusion persisted. By the time Alec was four, his father changed his name to Alex, with an 'x' on the end. Actually it was Alicia who had changed it. Alex Senior didn't mind. After all, it was closer to Alexander the Great than Alec could ever be. Nevertheless, the Senior and Junior qualifiers remained for some time. Just to make sure. On occasion.

Alexander, which the Baldwins liked to abbreviate to Alec, run in the family for six generations. He and Alicia were not about to give it up just to save some confusion.

***

One autumn day Alec woke up feeling rather queasy. His temperature was running a little high, and his mother, worried as most mothers usually are, told him to stay home. For most boys this would be a reason to be happy, but Alec liked his school. Perhaps not every subject, but on that day they were to have Geography, and Alec always managed to imagine that he was traveling to the places they were studying.

It first happened when the prim Miss Brunt, the geography teacher, was showing them a map of Peru. The large map had colorful photographs on each side, depicting people from a bygone era. On the slopes of a mountain that looked like cascading terraces, there were men and women and children all surrounded by strange animals she called llamas and alpacas.

Alec's mind was already beginning to wonder.

He thought Miss Brunt must be an old maid. She was probably mangled and hung up to dry, and then ironed into a crisp condition.

He saw himself turning the wheel of a clothes' wringer with Miss. Brunt coming out, thin and proper, at the other end.

Poor Miss Brunt, he thought. Shall I look like that if I never get married? At the same time the thought of getting married had left him as fast as it had come. Girls were not something Alec liked to think about. They were almost yuck. They giggled too much.

And yet...

Miss Brunt explained to the boys and girls that, although these were photographs of paintings, people still dressed in these same clothes, even more beautiful than a springtime rainbow. There were reds and crimsons, and rich blues and oranges and sunny yellows. They, Miss Brunt said, wove all their cloths themselves. Above the people on the green terraces, there rose a big stone wall upon which stood a man dressed in even more splendid attire. He was taller than the others, and he looked down on the men and women below him with a kindly smile. He must have been some kind of a king or ruler.

And suddenly Alec was an Inca prince, dressed in princely regalia, in colorful clothes spiced with gold thread. He stood next to the king and with him looked kindly upon his people from the top of the wall. He smiled down, and as the men and women approached, he distributed gold nuggets to them that he had collected on his many travels.

"Alec!" Miss Brunt's voice was even louder than the laughter of his people.

"Yes, Miss Brunt?"

"Are you paying attention?" she asked sternly. But not too sternly. Alec was her star geography pupil, even though his attention seemed to wander at times. "You *are* paying attention," she affirmed for her own satisfaction.

"Yes, Miss Brunt!" Alec agreed even as he handed another gold nugget to a youngster about his own age reaching up on his toes. "Would you like one, too?" he asked Miss Burnt quietly.

Luckily, Miss Brunt was already explaining how to make wool from Vicunas.

That same evening, on returning home, Alec read up all he could on the Inca Empire in the Encyclopedia. His dreams that night were filled with soaring mountains, their crags disappearing in mysterious mists while their bases seemed lost in deep, even more mysterious ravines. He pondered their mysteries while he traveled on a narrow mountain path, a stony trail high in the sky. Behind him, his people followed with a number of llamas carrying his tent, food and water.

He was only ten when he'd started having such visions. By the time he was twelve, he'd sat on the thrones of the Egyptian Pharaohs and the Czars of Russia. He'd slept in a Cossack tent in the middle of the Mongolian desert. He'd shared hot, sweet goat milk in cozy yurts surrounded by the inaccessible and forbidding Afghan mountains. He'd also crossed the Atlantic, the Pacific and the Indian oceans in a variety of ships, the powerful square-riggers, their sails billowing in the steady easterlies. Once, he almost died from lack of water on a raft that had strayed from the trade routes into the treacherous doldrums.

Later, or it could have been earlier, he'd lost track of time, he'd reached the North and the South Poles on foot, skis and sled. He'd climbed Everest and K2 in the perilous reaches towering over Kashmir. He'd sat at the feet of gurus in a somber Buddhist monastery, listening to the secret chant of Aum.

As time went on, his visions had become more and more real. He not only imagined the places he saw, he actually felt the cold air of the high mountains, he smelled the stale miasma of the subterranean caves, he tasted the thick black tea on the deck of original two-masted *dahabeahs* with their lanyard supporting their triangular sails, drifting majestically on the slow-moving waters of the Nile. He once woke up with bites from a scorpion he suffered crossing the Sahara on foot, only to find a tiny spider looking down on him from the ceiling.

Two weeks before his thirteenth birthday, his mother had taken him to see a doctor. Not a real doctor. A Ph.D., not an MD, she thought, not a psychiatrist; just a psychologist who, she's been told, specialized in children. He didn't deal with deranged minds. He just nudged them a little, now and then. He steered them in the right direction. She had no choice. Last week she had to call Alec's name five times before he came back from wherever he was in his imagination. It was just too much, she told her husband.

"Just too much," she repeated, herself drawing close to a nervous breakdown.

And now the nurse held to door for her and Alec to the doctor's office. Frankly, it didn't look like an office. More like a comfortable living room. Only a large mahogany desk in the corner suggested that, perhaps, some work took place here, on occasion.

"Do sit down, Mrs. Baldwin!"

Doctor Schmidthousen made a dive to offer Mrs. Baldwin a deeply upholstered armchair. She smiled in return.

The balding doctor displayed two rows of immaculately whitened protruding teeth, which instantly reminded Alec of some rabbits he saw last summer.

"Ah, eh, you too, young man..." he waved his arm at Alec who, for reasons he couldn't identify, took an instant dislike to him.

Mrs. Baldwin was a very attractive woman; slim, but not too slim, with all the right curves in all the right places. She kept her blond hair pinned up in a flamboyant knot atop her skull, reminiscent of Nefertiti. Or so her husband thought. She suspected that Alex Senior has long been in love with the Great Royal Wife of the Egyptian Pharaoh Akhenaten. She also thanked her lucky stars that Nefertiti has been dead for more than 3300 years.

She looked up at the good doctor with plea in her eyes.

What a pity she brought this brat with her, the doctor mused. He was about to send Alec to get some ice cream and suggest that Mrs. Baldwin might be more comfortable stretching out on the settee, but thought better of it. He remembered that he already had a case pending at the local magistrate for paying too much attention to one of his patients. Too much attention? You cannot pay too much attention to patient's comfort, he'd assured the judge.

"It's my job to make sure my patients are fully relaxed," he'd stated defensively at the preliminary hearing.

"On a settee with their clothes off, Dr. Schmidthousen?" asked the prosecuting attorney.

"It was a very hot day," the doctor pleaded. "Very, very hot day…" He tried hard to remember just how hot Mrs. What's-her-name was on that day.

"His mind seems to wander off to far away places," Alec's mother began.

"What… what was that? Ah, yes. Your son was wondering… Are you sure you wouldn't be more comfortable on the settee?"

"I came here about my son, doctor," Mrs. Baldwin murmured.

"Your… ah, what? It really was a very hot day…"

Only then the doctor remembered that the lady in question hadn't been his patient. She was a mother worried about her son… It's a small world, he thought.

Alicia Baldwin opened her mouth to say something, and changed her mind. Instead she shrugged, took Alec by the arm, and made for the door. It seemed to her, that the doctor was drifting into a reality of his own at least as much as her son. The blind leading the blind?

She wondered what sort of a bill she'd get for the consultation.

Late last year, on his thirteenth birthday, suddenly, most of Alec's imaginary trips had stopped. His father had given him a computer with a connection to the Internet. For a while the world opened its secrets to Alec, but… it wasn't the same. There was too much information. Alec knew too much, and places sort of became real on their own. Too real to visit in his daydreams. With his curiosity sated, overwhelmed, his imagination could not spring wings.

Mr. and Mrs. Baldwin relaxed. Alec was normal. A little obnoxious, temperamental, late for meals, but well, what thirteen-year-old wasn't?

For almost a month Alec did not 'travel'. Neither in his sleep nor in his daydreams. Instead, he grew restless, almost annoyed. Surely, he could not have seen all the places and moments of history. He was only thirteen, after all. There must be others. What other places would fire his mind, his desire, strongly enough to take him there? Even for a while.

Alec withdrew into himself.

His father tried hard to draw him into his own interests. Soccer, rugby, cricket... no, not baseball or Canadian football; well, not if any of the other sports were available. His father was born in Harlow, just North of London. Yes, UK, not Ontario. In Harlow he'd played rugger, which they called rugby on this side of the Atlantic, not some Canadian perversion of it.

His only son wasn't responding.

"He's a dreamer, just like you..." Alicia reminded him.

Indeed, Alex Senior had been a dreamer before he'd met his wife. Then, Nefertiti notwithstanding, his dreams had come true.

Alec tried hard to imagine the places he'd already visited, but it didn't work. It was as though he remembered them, as if they were real, very real, memories, but... well, it just wasn't the same. Reliving memory is a poor substitute for living in the Present. He had to experience his dreams in the Here-and-Now, not as some detached fragment of history. When he sat on the gilt throne of Russia, he sat on it in that very moment. He crossed the deserts, the wilderness of the Gobi, the unforgiving oceans, here and now.

***

2
Princess Sandra

At first he didn't see her. He felt her. Very gently. It was as though someone were watching him from very close, yet without ever touching him. On the second day, he thought he saw a girl's face smiling at him from the mirror. At first he was scared, but she was so beautiful. More beautiful than any girl he'd ever seen in his life. Not that he ever looked at girls very much. He had other things to do. But this...

The second time, he saw her image in the window when he was drawing the curtains. It was already dark outside, and the glass acted like a dark mirror. The face, a smile rather than a face, glanced at him and was gone. Alec pulled the curtains apart again, but to no avail. There was no one. In or out of the house. The room was quiet; there was no wind outside. The night was at peace. Alec was not.

He had to think about this. What was going on? Am I going crazy?

He almost went to tell his mother about it. She might explain it all to him. It was all very strange. It didn't make any sense. Yes, he mused, my mother would know.

Or… on the other hand, she might decide to take another trip to Dr. Schmidthousen and his teeth.

The risk was too great. He couldn't share his visions with a complete stranger. Even with mother it wouldn't have been easy.

He lay flat on his bed in a position in which, until recently, he enjoyed such marvelous imaginary travels. He

lay back and tried to think things through. He was pretty sure
he wasn't going crazy. Just relax, he told himself, as though
nothing bothered him at all. As though he didn't care.
Eventually he convinced himself that it had been one of his
daydreams. Slightly out of control, but a daydream. Slowly
his mind cleared and he thought of nothing.

It was then that he heard a voice.

"I'm sorry," it said.

Very slowly, Alec opened his eyes. There was enough
light in the room for him to know that he was alone. Anyway,
the door was closed, as were the windows.

"I didn't know how to contact you...?"

This time the voice was just a little more distinct,
although it wasn't really a voice. It did not come from
outside. Alec was used to hearing many voices on his travels.
He assumed that finally, after a month's break, he was finally
getting somewhere. Only usually he 'saw' the places first—
then he heard voices. Then he heard people talking. This was
the other way round.

"Can you hear me?"

The voice was definitely that of a girl. Maybe the same
girl he'd seen.

"Of course," he said out loud.

"Ouch..."

"What?" he almost shouted.

"Please, not so loud," the girl's voice said in an urgent
whisper. "I asked if *you* could hear me. There is nothing
wrong with *my* hearing."

"Sorry." Alec didn't know what else to say. "You're the
girl in the mirror," he added, mistrust still in his voice.
"Aren't you?"

"I am Princess Sandra."

"I am Alec," he said. What else could he say?

"Of course."

"You know me?" Slowly Alec was drawn into the
conversation. He was not traveling anywhere; he was neither
dreaming nor imagining things. His eyes were wide open, he

was aware of lying on his bed, of the ceiling above him. There was familiarity all around. Yet he heard her voice as distinctly as though she were sitting right next to him on the... well, on the chair next to the bed. Perhaps more so. More clearly, I mean.

Alec was too experienced a traveler to ask her how come he could hear her. What's more, after a whole month of doldrums, he was hungering for new experiences, new thrills, even if it meant talking to a girl.

"Why did you come?" he asked.

"Because you stopped traveling."

"I didn't want to..." He was instantly on the defensive. Then he interrupted himself, "You know about that...?"

He felt silly. Of course she knew. She'd just said so. He hated making a fool of himself, especially in front of a girl. Suddenly the passing image in the dark pane flashed before his eyes once more. A beautiful girl, he corrected himself.

There was a giggle. "You think so?" She giggled again.

"I think what?" He suspected what was coming. He cringed.

"That I am beautiful."

"How do you know?" Alec was trying hard to maintain his composure. He'd never, ever told any girl she was anything, let alone beautiful. There was another quiet giggle followed by a moment's silence.

"Where are you!?" His tone rose again.

"Shhhh... You know I can hear you. It hurts a little when you speak too loud. Anyway, you know where I am. I've been here for a long time."

"What?" Luckily the shout of surprise came out as a whisper.

"Well, I'm your... there isn't really a word for it. I'm sort of your other half."

Of course. What could be simpler? I am talking to my other half, who is not in the room but I can hear her every word. I must sleep more and give up the Internet for a while.

"Oh no, not on my account..." Sandra pleaded. Her voice was sort of diluted, as if she were drifting farther away. Suddenly Alec got scared.

"Don't go!" he said in a tone halfway between a plea and command.

He desperately needed company. Not of other boys who could only kick a football or swing their baseball bats, but someone to spend time with when he was alone. The moment he thought that, he realized that he was in trouble. How on earth can you spend time with someone if you're alone?

"You are now."

Her voice was like a caress. Like the beautiful smile in the mirror. Alec blushed even as the thought crossed his mind. He half expected another giggle, but happily none came.

"Yes, I am, aren't I..." he mused to himself. This was great! I mean it was nice, he quickly corrected his thought.

"Are you staying here long?" He tried hard not to sound too hopeful.

"Of course. I'm here all the time."

"What do you mean?" His voice rose again.

"I told you. I am your second half. I really don't know how else to put it."

"You mean that without you I'm incomplete?"

"Of course!" This time her voice smiled but there was no giggle. "We are like two peas in a pod. A single pod, but two peas."

Alec chewed that over. "How come we never met? Before, I mean?"

"I don't know." She sounded a little sad. "I suppose you never really wanted to, before, I mean.' It was funny how she echoed his words.

"You mean it was up to me?"

"Oh, yes. It always is."

Now this needed thinking over. There she was, true, a girl, but this couldn't be helped. Anyway, as long as nobody else saw her, there wouldn't be any snide remarks from the guys. They always had to make jokes about girls. No matter what they did. Girls were this, they were that. Always something. If girls were so bad, how come they could never stop talking about them? There were other subjects? He couldn't tell them about his own fantastic voyages. They were his and his alone. Not even his mother or father knew about them. He'd tried to tell them once or twice, but then he overheard them saying that it was his overactive imagination. They said he would soon grow out of it.

That last thing they said really hurt him. Really hurt...

He did not want to grow out of it. Never. His journeys into the unknown were the most wonderful times he had. They were better than anything. He would rather die than give them up. Sure, he liked school, but he had few friends. Not really close ones, but still. None he could tell about his trips. They would laugh. Or call him a sicko. Or worse.

Perhaps it was his size. He was shorter than most boys in his class. Not very good at sports, the team sports, that is; he'd learned early to keep to himself. He could hold his own in chess or other games that did not require physical ability. He liked walking by the river, but others preferred to play. Together. Always together. In a crowd. He hated crowds. The very same boys in a crowd behaved differently. It was as if they were continuously in competition. As if they always wanted to outdo each other. What for? He never discovered. Alec had no desire to do anything better than anybody else. He only wanted to do his own very best. Regardless of what anybody said.

And now?

And now he had a chance not to be alone. To share his innermost thoughts and not be laughed at. Well, perhaps a little giggle, but not really a laugh.

"Can I see you?" he thought out loud.

"Yes and no."

"What sort of an answer is that?" he wanted to know. He wished she wouldn't talk in riddles.

"I'm not. You can and you can't. Or can, depending on... Oh, I don't know! This is the first time we are talking like this."

Alec didn't want to hurt her. Least of all lose her. Girl she might be, but she was here and now. In the Present. He didn't have to travel anywhere to meet her. And, well, and she did appear to be beautiful.

"I didn't mean to offend you." He really was contrite.

"Thank you."

"What for?"

"For still thinking that I am beautiful."

"Oh..."

Alec was exasperated. The boys talked stupid, but girls weren't all that easy, either. Why were they so obsessed with beauty? His father once said it was only skin deep. That was after his mother spent two hours in front of a mirror making herself nice for him. Alec remembered he thought his father wasn't nice that time. Well, what if they are obsessed with the way they look? There are worse problems in life. Even if you're just thirteen years old.

For a little while there was silence.

"Why is it so important to you?" he asked.

"How I look?"

"Yes."

"It isn't."

"But..." Girls were *always* exasperating.

"It is not important to me how I look. It is important to me what you think of me," she explained, and even as her voice formed in his head, he grew closer to this very voice. It was almost as though he were talking to himself, only much, much better. There was an intimacy that he'd never experienced before. Not even with his mother. Close, but not the same.

Alec supposed that she might well be right. He was never really concerned how he looked. His mop of unruly hair giving him the appearance of a precocious absentminded professor, his relatively big head, the object of some school-time ridicule, all seemed of little importance. His mother always told him that his blue eyes looked like the bluest sky on a late summer day. He always found the skies on late summer days on the gray side, what with all the pollution that Dad always talked about. Still, he seldom saw his own eyes. A mirror was something only girls used. Or so he thought.

And this brought him back to Sandra. Princess Sandra? He got up from the bed and walked out to the mirror in the hall. He looked and looked, but no beautiful girl stared back at him. In fact, she seemed to have disappeared.

"Sandra?" He whispered.

Silence.

"Damn." He knew it was bad to swear. "Damn and damn again," he thought.

He clenched his teeth. "Damn!" he repeated out loud. But Sandra was nowhere to be seen. Nor heard. She was gone.

***

"This," Alicia thought, "this," she repeated aloud with even more determination in her voice, "just isn't good enough. No, sireee, not nearly good enough!"

There, she felt a little better now.

It was hardly surprising. With Alex Senior apparently determined to make sure that all towns and cities north of the 60th parallel had airfields with melting equipment embedded in concrete runways, heated by geothermal energy, and Alec Junior spending endless hours hitting a tennis ball, she was destined to stay alone.

At home, alone.

"While both my husband and my son are having fun!"

She didn't actually say all this, but as far as she was concerned, both men, well, men-and-a-half, in her life, must take it as said. "So there," she added, this time examining herself in the mirror.

Not bad, she thought, not bad...

And then she added, "What a waste..."

Yet in spite of her appearance over which she was taking great care, she was determined to find herself a hobby to compensate for being a grass widow. Except for winter, when both her men stayed more at home, she was spending endless hours trying to determine which dress to wear, what to cook for dinner, or what was the latest gossip stimulating the lives of her lady friends who, more often then not, were in the same soup as she was, so to speak.

She had her books, of course. She'd read them all—some twice. Mostly on art. Sometimes she thought that she'd already read all the books that were worth reading.

And then it hit her.

Since she was a little girl, in school, she had been told that her little sketches and drawings, colored with her crayons, had been good enough to be published. Not that anyone had offered her an actual contract, but still…

"You should get a job as an illustrator of children's books," she recalled her bespectacled teacher telling her. Perhaps she had bad eyesight, she mused.

No. She really meant it. So long ago…

"I'll do it," she said aloud. She got in a habit of speaking aloud when she was alone at home. Somehow it made her less lonely. "I'll do it!"

She did it.

Starting that same day she went out and bought some tubes of watercolor paint, a number of sheets of artist's paper, a collapsible easel, and some brushes.

"Sable, Madam?"

She had no idea what sable was.

"Of course, these five," she replied, with a straight face. So that's sable, she smiled. Of course, she repeated, this time to herself.

The moment she got home, she set the easel up. Next she had to find something to paint. She had no idea what. There were no children's books to illustrate.

And then she remembered the aquarelles she saw at Joan's house, in Westmount. She had a number of paintings, mostly oils but also a few aquarelles. The watercolors were all of flowers in full bloom. They were light, in color and texture. They captured light that seemed to sit on the leaves and flowers in a magic garden.

She opened the window.

It was a bit chilly.

She went out again, and drove to the nearest flower shop. An hour later she was back with a two pots of amaryllis almost in full boom. One was salmon the other tending towards red, still unfolding.

This was the first time that she got nervous. Nevertheless, she spread a newspaper on the table in case she'd spill some water, squeezed some pain on her palette, and picked up a brush.

That was when time stopped.

The next thing she heard was her son slamming the front door. Not loud, but enough to break her trance. The painting was virtually finished. The two plants seemed to embrace each other, with the blooms on the verge of a flowery kiss. She smiled.

"They are as happy as I am this moment," she said, still to herself.

Alec charged in as though chased by wild boar.

"Mom, that's beautiful!"

She had no idea if her son was referring to the two pots of amaryllis or to her painting. She didn't care.

Why did I wait so long, she asked herself? This time quite silently.

***

3
The School

The next morning as Alec walked to school, his head was full of remorse. He was really annoyed with himself.

Walking to the mirror had been very rude. One doesn't walk away in the middle of a conversation without saying a word. It just isn't nice. He must have offended her. Suddenly he stopped dead in his tracks. A man behind him only just pulled up short of falling over his heels.

"Sorry, sir!" he said quickly. "I forgot something," he lied.

The man didn't say anything and walked on. Alec hated lying. He never did it on purpose. Sometimes it just popped out. "Sorry," he repeated under his breath, this time to himself.

What stopped him in the middle of a busy sidewalk was something he'd just remembered from yesterday's conversation. She said she was Princess Sandra. *Princess!* For crying out loud!   He walked out in the middle of a conversation with a Princess. Without so much as a beg your pardon.

"I walked out on a Princess... How could I have been so stupid?" he asked himself. "How could I have been *so* stupid???" He shook his head from side to side as he walked on.

And then his parents went on holidays. For the first time Alec was left alone in the house.

Actually, this wasn't quite true. There was a neighbor across the street that kept vigil over Alec's welfare. She was a retired widow, who liked nothing better than to pick up a pair of binoculars and keep a keen eye on Alec. Alicia had asked her not to butt in, but if there was any suspicious activity to contact Pete's parents. Pete was Alec's tennis partner, and also lived next door. But under no circumstanced was she, the widowed Mrs. or really *Madame* Ouelette, to let Alec know that he was being watched. On the other hand, although in many ways Alec was a precocious boy, and although his father thought such precautions quite unnecessary, Alicia felt better knowing that, if need's be, Alec can get all the help he might need.

As far as Alec was concerned there was no supervision, no babysitters, no neighbors looking in on him to make sure he didn't set the house on fire. He was alone, free. He was the master of the house, the master of his time. He was the master of himself. That was when Sandra came.

***

"Do you think he's over it, darling?" Alice asked. Her voice did not exude excessive confidence. She needed reassurance.

With spring offering but a smidgen of sunshine, she liked the cabin her husband had rented on Singer Island. It would be a nice diversion. They'd arrived at noon. She was just learning to love her painting, but as yet, she loved sunshine more. Alex Baldwin M.Sc., P.Eng., not to mention a member of the *Ordre des Ingénieurs du Québec* and half a dozen other affiliations, having spent some weeks up north consulting an a new hydro project, deserved a break. They wanted something different than yet another hotel. This was a brand new development, with prices cut to attract new customers. It consisted of a largish living room with a loft upstairs, just for an oversized bed.

Alice was half-convinced that the computer her husband had given their son cured him, the son, not the husband, of all the chimerical shebang. Yet, for some reason, she wasn't totally convinced. And after almost a month of Alec acting like a distraught juvenile delinquent, these last few days he turned nice again. Nice, and sort of dreamy?

"What did Doctor Shmousenhopper say?" his voice emerged from the innards of a substitute armchair. He was looking forward the sunshine, but he was already missing his favorite armchair.

He meant Dr. Schmidthousen. Before Mr. Baldwin went away on business last week, she'd agreed that if all else failed she'd see the doctor again. Actually she'd never had any intention of seeing him again, nor any other quack but, at the time, she'd given in to her husband, to avoid an argument. Alex Senior liked to insist, as though she was part of the team he commanded at the office. He was used to giving order. She hated that.

"I decided not to see him," she confessed.

Alex looked up over the top of his newspaper.

"Why?" His voice was quite relaxed.

"Because he's a sex-maniac."

"Fridlehooper? I thought you told me he had rabbit's teeth."

"That was Alec," she smiled. "He'd said that. Alec thought of taking some carrots with him, if we ever retuned to his office."

"So if there was no need to go, why do you ask me?"

Why must men be so damnably logical? It wasn't a question of thinking. It was a question of how she felt.

"Because Alec is so nice, lately," she replied, her voice trailing to a whisper.

"I see," Alex replied, his face perfectly straight. Nevertheless, he lifted up his newspaper to hide the smile he couldn't quite contain. There was little he could add to the conversation.

"Look at page seventeen, that's right, in the bottom right corner…"

Alex flipped the unwieldy pages of the Montreal Gazette he'd brought with him. He'd missed it for a whole week. Then, even as she watched him, his eyes grew larger.

"Well, I never!"

"You did lots of time, darling, but only to your own wife," she murmured.

"What?" he still looked amazed.

The article claimed that Dr. Schmidthousen has been cleared of any charges of abusing his patients. He was, however, sentenced to 160 hours of community service, 40 hours for each of the four mothers whom he'd seduced in his office under the pretext of psychotherapy. He claimed that the ladies had been willing participators in the curative measures he'd administered. Apparently, it was at least partially true— hence the light sentence.

"Son of a gun…" Alex's tone was a mixture of admiration and incredulity. "Four of them!"

"That's not funny," Alicia's voice changed it timbre.

"It would be if you… never mind. You're quite right, dear. Shall we go upstairs?

"You've only just come down." She was in no mood when her husband was in an artificially invoked mood. "You want to play doctors, don't you?" By now her voice has softened. "Finish the Gazette. You might find other games to play…"

She wondered why did such cases and that of Dr. Schmidthousen have the opposite effect on men to those they had on her. Yet, an hour later she'd changed her mind.

"Same time tomorrow, Miss Baldwin?" her husband asked.

"Do you think we ought to wait that long, doctor?"

The funny thing was that all this transpired only because she'd glanced at the paper Alex had brought from Montreal. She looked at it early in the morning, before her husband came down for breakfast. Now, that they were back in the sitting room downstairs, she regarded him with grateful affection. He was taking a well-deserved rest after a four-day visit to a site over the frozen tundra up north, let alone from performing his medical duties upstairs. She wondered why was it that we invariably accord members of the medical profession with their professional titles, while her husband, who she felt sure was a much better engineer than they were 'healers', was never shown equal respect. God knows, he deserved it.

No matter, when the building collapses on their heads they might think about it, she mused.

Alex picked up his paper again.

"So you've decided to forego another visit to the rabbit?" he asked innocently.

***

There was no Geography today, but history was almost as good. It was History that gave Alec the chance to travel not only to different places, but also to different times. He could do that also with Geography, but History was better. He learned, relaxed, and waited for what might happen. Before, he usually succeeded in taking a trip about once a week, and the trips were followed by at least three nights of vivid dreams. They were almost identical, only sometimes he did not have such a good recall of the dream. Sometimes, he could recount them minute-by-minute. Only there was a different kind of passage of time in his dreams. In an hourly daydream he could go all the way to the North Pole and get back in time for supper.

It was funny how it worked.

He smiled to himself. He remembered when he told Miss Brunt some things about Egypt that he saw on one of his travels, which Miss Brunt had never told them about in the classroom. She was taken aback and grilled him how he knew such things. She only let him be when he told her that he read about it on the Internet. This was the first and only time he ever lied in school. From that moment on he never, never volunteered any information. He answered questions when asked, and stuck to the subject he was asked about.

The classes dragged on and on and on. Alec had just one thing on his mind. The Princess. She was not a thing, obviously, but he was completely preoccupied with all things concerning her. Would she come back tonight? Ever?

"Yes!" he said half-aloud and quickly cleared his throat. "Sorry," he half-whispered.

He decided to pay more attention. During the afternoon he had Math and Geometry. To him they were both one, really. It all had to do with logical thinking. He was really quite good at that. But his heart wasn't in it. He still preferred Geography and History. He wondered why, now that he hadn't traveled for a month, Math did seem more interesting.

Finally school was over for the day. He was prepared to run home practically all the way. And then he heard a vague giggle. For the second time today, he stopped dead.

"Sandra?"

Nothing. No more giggle, not a word. "Are you there?" He tried again. Where was 'there', anyway. That's right, where was there?

He slowed his pace. Maybe she wanted to see the school. He walked to the parapet and sat down. It was an older building, put up probably some 150 years ago. All stone, smoother higher up and rough at ground level. The original side-hung wooden-frame windows had all been replaced with aluminum, for easier maintenance. Or so he supposed. He wondered how he knew those things. The eaves overhung about two to three feet, with copper gutter and down-pipes, all green from the pollution. Probably acid rain, he thought. And then he wondered again: "How do I know these things?" He'd never read up on the school buildings, never even read an introductory pamphlet. His parents did that. It was of absolutely no interest to him. Yet now...?

He walked around the building discovering details that had never before entered his awareness. There was a carved stone portal over the heavy, ornately carved main doors. Almost like a castle he'd once visited...

The boys and girls didn't use these doors, except on festive occasions. When some ceremonies were held with the parents present, the heavy doors were opened directly onto an impressive entrance hall. The Headmaster would stand there and shake hands with the visitors. The parents, of course, not the pupils. The boys and girls never touched the Headmaster. Not until they finished school and got their certificate. Alec would shake the Headmaster's hand next year.

There were many other details Alec noticed until he felt tired and slowly walked home. Funny how he'd completely forgotten about Sandra. The school building was really interesting, he thought. It was almost like traveling...

Almost.

When he got home, he went to the fridge. His mother had left him exactly twelve of them. One for each night of their holidays. He wondered why he'd never had any brothers or sisters. With two or three of them, there wouldn't be enough room in the refrigerator, and his parents would never be able to go on a holiday. That was probably the reason. Of course, they could buy a bigger fridge. But then the kitchen would be too small. He didn't really feel like another TV dinner.

He switched on his computer instead and clicked to open the Internet. He looked up some buildings from about two centuries ago. They did look fairly nice though also rather somber. He wondered if people were also somber in those days. The older buildings looked even more interesting. He read about two of them, then quit the Internet and stretched out on the settee. A minute later he woke up in the darkest, scariest, dampest dungeon he could imagine. Only he wasn't imagining it. He really was there. Right in it.

4
The Castle

Sitting on the beach and watching the gentle easterlies fill the sails of the idle-rich was fun, but not as much fun as being aboard a yacht.

"I wonder what it would be like to be filthy rich…" Alice mused, sipping her second Bloody Mary just to kill boredom. She had no idea what sailing was like, but Alec would show her. He was a sailor once.

It was only the beginning of the afternoon, but it must have been 5.00 p.m. somewhere. After the problem they had with her husband's aunt, Alicia had promised her husband not to touch a drop before five. On the other hand he must have long forgotten. His aunt had died in England from cirrhosis of the liver some five years ago. Apparently women have smaller tolerance for alcohol—or so he'd said at the time.

Alicia wasn't used to doing nothings for hours on end. With nothing to clean, nothing to cook, no shopping to do, she seemed lost. The Baldwins were, what is known as, comfortably off, but hardly rich. They never really needed money for its own sake. Alec liked his job, and lately Alice fell in love with painting; together they enjoyed walks in the Mount Royal, good friends, and an occasional game of Bridge with his business associates.

"I should have taken you to the Virgin Islands. There are all sorts of people looking for crews out there", Alec said, pointing towards the east with his chin.

There was a magnificent schooner seemingly frozen in space silhouetted against the blue horizon. Then he snapped his fingers for another Bloody Mary. Alec Senior enjoyed a good capacity for all things that pretended not to be alcoholic.

For a while they both closed their eyes.

It was hot, really hot, but coming from Canada, it just couldn't be too hot. After our bloody winters we need not only Bloody Marys but also sun, he mused. Lots of sun. And a gentle breeze to make it tolerable, if necessary.

"For my old bones... just for my old bones," he murmured.

"What, dear?" Alicia asked, but didn't wait for an answer. "I shouldn't have done it," Alicia said, interrupting his meandering thoughts.

"Of course you should have..." Alec had no idea what his wife was referring to, but preferred to play it safe and be affirmative.

"No, I shouldn't have," she insisted.

"What, dear?" He was treading on dangerous ground. For all he knew, he may have been supposed to know what she was talking about.

"The story I read for him. I told you about it," she said, taking a deep swig of the red liquid through a long straw. "About the princess."

Alec cringed. He knew he was guilty.

"I guess you are right, dear..." he tried agreement for size.

"You have no idea what I am talking about, do you darling?"

The word 'darling' was a good sign. He might get away with it. Just then the pool-boy brought his next Bloody Mary. He signed the chit and gave Alicia his most disarming smile. It seemed to have worked.

"To encourage Alec to read more books, I began reading aloud for him. It was a charming story about a Princess. I quite enjoyed it, but then I thought that he might use it as a sprig-board for his own musings."

"Cheers!" said Alex, raising his glass.

Alec took a sip. The drink smelled good. Almost too good. He suspected they used moonshine rum instead of vodka. Still, it also tasted good.

Alicia shrugged, smiled, and closed her eyes again. They said one shouldn't read in the sunshine, by the time they got to the pool, all the umbrellas were already taken. Anyway, they came here for the sun; she could read at home. And her husband was too tired, even to read. He deserved this short break in the routine.

***

Alec had absolutely no desire to travel to the murky innards of a medieval stone castle. He really wanted to meet Sandra again, rather than resume his travels. And if he had to travel, well, there was plenty to see of a stone castle without having to end up in a dungeon. And then his heart almost stopped!

He was sitting on a stone bench, about a chair's height. Around his wrists and ankles he saw metal rings with chains leading to great rings anchored to the wall behind him. The wall was just close enough to lean against if he lifted his legs off the floor. The room was about eight by twelve feet, no more than six feet high, with a slot of a window just below the ceiling. There was no way anyone could escape through that slot, even if he could free himself from these chains.

"What on earth am I doing here?" he wondered, half aloud. "What on earth am I doing here?" he repeated, listening to his own voice. He imagined he'd heard a slight echo.

The walls remained absolutely silent. There was no sound of any nature anywhere. He felt, and probably was, completely alone.

For a moment he panicked. "I'm going to starve to death." Then he calmed himself, remembering that this was only one of his trips—unpleasant, but only one of his trips. "But why the dungeon?"

There were footsteps behind the wall directly in front of him. In the darkness, he thought he saw a door in the wall. If you could call it a door. It was little more than five feet high. A door for...

A door for a fairly short thirteen-year-old boy.

The door didn't open, but a slot at its foot swung into the cell and a plate was pushed in. Someone pushed it along the floor with a stick until it was within Alec's reach. The chain on his left wrist was longer than the one on his right. Alec bent down to retrieve the plate. There was an odd-looking sandwich on it. It was some kind of meat on a soggy piece of crust with another piece of crust lying on the edge of the metal plate. Lord Sandwich obviously hadn't been born yet.

"Supper?" he wondered.

And then he heard a quiet sob. He would have paid more attention if he hadn't been so hungry. He put down the 'sandwich' in short order and looked around for something to drink. At this very moment, the hatch in the door swung towards him again and a metal jug was pushed along the floor.

"Room service..." he remembered his father saying last winter in a Florida motel.

Room service it was, only by now his eyes had adjusted to the murk of the dungeon and he saw that the water didn't look that clean. There was an easy way out. What you can't see can't hurt you, he mused, closed his eyes and drank avidly. Wiping his mouth on his sleeve, his spirits improved somewhat. Just then he heard it again. The sobbing. This time not just one catch of breath but a series. Someone was crying. Close. Very close.

Even as he asked himself the question, he knew the answer. The Princess needed his help. His Princess. His Sandra. This would make up for his rudeness last night. But he was cast in irons, hand and foot. There was a heavy wooden door straight ahead, but he was sure it was locked. And his Sandra needed help. Alec was torn between the desire to break the chains with his meager strength or join Sandra in her sobbing.

He did neither.

For a moment he sat to consider his situation. He relaxed as best he could and closed his eyes. The idea came to him with vivid clarity. He remembered how he got here. How he got anywhere on his travels.

He closed his eyes and imagined that his irons were falling off. He expected the clang of metal... Alas, nothing happened. Nothing except for another plaintive sob. He looked at his arms in desperation. There was a peculiar sheen on his arms and legs. As if he were sprayed with just a little silver dust. Just a little. Very slowly he pulled his hand against the metal bracelet. Even before anything happened, a smile brightened his face. The bracelet had been made for adults, not for thirteen-year-old, rather small, boys. His left hand slid quite easily through the irons, as did his other hand. The legs were a bit more difficult, but the sound of quiet weeping from nearby gave him the fortitude to bear a little pain. Well, quite a lot of pain, but he was free—except for the heavy door reinforced with iron bars, and the unknowns of a strange castle. Not to mention the unknown whereabouts of his Princess.

"Sandra... Sandra... where are you?" He listened for an answer. None came.

Then... an agonizing shriek broke the silence. There was no doubt about it. There were other people in the dungeons. There were the masters and the minions. The torturers and the tortured. Alec shivered. A cold sweat covered his whole body.

"Where on earth am I?"

This was not at all like his old travels. On previous trips, he experienced extremes of cold and heat, and even the lack of air at the top of the Himalayas, but this? This was scary. This was not at all like a dream, waking or not. All his previous experiences had been real, but in them he was a sort of... spectator, while he was also participating. Here he was right in the thick of things. The dampness was too damp. The stone walls too forbidding. The feeling of being alone in his predicament simply too oppressive. This was much too real, even for his liking.

Another shriek followed by a whimper propelled him to his feet. In three steps he was at the door. The door was not even bolted. 'How come?' he asked himself. Is this a dream after all? And then he remembered that until minutes ago he was tethered hand and foot in heavy irons. They, whoever *they* were, never imagined he would free himself. An adult evidently couldn't. For the first time Alec was really happy that he was small. Small even for his age. With a sigh of relief he left the dark chamber.

Outside, the corridor sloped upwards, ending in a flight of steps; funny, rather small steps. As though designed by or for people as small as himself. At the foot of the flight he stopped and listened. Nothing.

He had to do something.

He climbed the stairs and arrived about eight feet higher up at a landing which extended to the left and right, only to end in two flights of stairs, each leading down. Immediately in front there was a door leading to...

There was no time to speculate. Again he heard gentle sobs and a sleepy yet painful whimper. Then silence again. Total, absolute silence.

A 50/50 chance. On instinct, he ran down the steps on his left. The door at the bottom of the flight was latched shut. At least he wouldn't need a key he didn't have. He raised the latch quietly. The dungeon inside seemed even darker than his own. Lying on the stone bench under the slot window was a man. A very large man. There was blood on his face, and his left arm hung loose from his shoulder. He cringed when Alec came near him.

"Easy now," Alec whispered. "I'm a friend."

The man looked at him half with fear, half with mistrust.

"I've come to get you out of here," Alec assured him, having absolutely no idea how he would go about this salutary mission.

The man looked at him again.

"Who are you?" the monster asked.

"Never mind that. We must get you out of here." The man did not look as though he placed much faith in Alec's words. "My name is Alec, if you must know." And then he added as an afterthought: "I've come here to free the Princess."

"They got her, too?" The man seemed even more desolate than before.

The man knew the Princess. This might help. Of course, it might not. "Can you walk?" Alec thought they'd wasted enough time.

As the large man got up, he was half-bent at the waist to fit under the low ceiling. He staggered, sat down, and got up again. He obviously was much weakened by his ordeal but almost obediently moved, albeit slowly, towards the door.

"Do you know who your torturers are?" Alec asked over his shoulder.

"Of course," the man talked with a rasping voice. "It was them little ones. It always is. They can't stand us big'uns. They're jealous. That's what them is." Then he added in an even quieter voice, "I thought you was one of them, at first." The words, albeit not very grammatical, came at a flood. He seemed to feel better after they spilled out.

"This way, up the steps." Alec led the way.

"They gave me that drink to drink and it was poisoned. They tortured me, an' there was nothing I could do. No strength. I fell down them steps. No strength at all—the little bastards."

"Why do you keep saying how small they are?" Alec wanted to know.

"They are no bigger than you's." The man nodded to himself. "Only uglier. Much uglier."

Alec preferred not to ask how ugly he was himself. His mind was already working on saving his Princess. She must be down the other steps. There was no other way he could have heard both, the man's whimpers and the Princess' sobs. At the top of the landing, he told the huge man, still doubled up to fit under the ceiling, to wait. That's how he must have fallen down those steps, by hitting his head on the ceiling. Poor sap, Alec felt genuinely sorry for such a big man with so little initiative.

He ran down and pushed the door. Sandra was lying on the stone bench, rather like the man had been, but she hardly covered half of it. Her face was hidden in her hands. She was crying quietly.

"Princess...?" Alec was sure it was she. As sure as he was that he would save her. Whatever the cost. Even if it cost him his life.

***

"Thirty!" Alex Senior announced, making sure that most people plastered to their deckchairs around the pool could hear. His tone sounded as though he'd just conquered Mount Everest. This probably also accounted for him being considerably out off breath.

He looked down on his wife stretched out on her stomach, her bra unpinned, her body allowing the sun to caress her sinuous back.

"And I didn't even raise a sweat," he added. He continued eyeing his wife who hasn't stirred since she'd finished her second Bloody Mary.

He leaned over the edge of the pool, and grabbed a handful of water in his cupped palm. Then, without another word, he began dripping it on her back. Alicia's shriek raised the heads of a dozen guests.

"I'll get you for this," she hissed, her voice halfway between amusement and annoyance.

"Now or later?" Alex asked.

She rolled over on her back, nearly forgetting about her unfastened bra.

"I see it's right now," he bent over her.

"Don't you dare touch me with those wet paws," she warned. Then her tone changed. "Would you fasten me, darling?"

He did.

"Good swim?" she asked. All seemed forgiven now.

"Why don't you try for yourself?"

"I can't," she replied, a wistful expression on her face.

"It's that time of the month coming?" he asked in a whisper.

"Don't be silly, darling. You forgot last night?"

"Then…?"

"It's my hair, sweetheart. I couldn't possibly get it wet!"

Her previous patrician hairdo, or had it been Nefertiti's, disappeared. Instead her hair was hanging loosely, straight down as was popular among the select 90% of women. She only just had it straightened out.

"Of course," he sounded humble. "How silly of me…"

He beckoned a boy for another Bloody Mary. He'd earned it. Their cabin might have been small, but after all, the pool was an Olympic size pool.

***

Very slowly, Sandra raised her face. The tears ran down her cheeks, yet the smile of recognition illuminated her face. The whole dungeon seemed brighter.

"Alec, oh, Alec!" she cried, running into his arms.

Now this wasn't funny. Thirteen-year-old boys do not take girls into their arms. Never! It is an unwritten law of boyhood. So Alec just stood there, only gently pressing Sandra to his meager chest.

"Now, now," he tried to console her.

He knew this was the right thing to say because he'd seen it in a TV movie only last week. All too quickly Sandra recovered. Alec was prepared to suffer her embrace a little longer, for her sake, of course. Nevertheless, she pulled back.

"How did you find me?" she asked.

"Later," he admonished in his most masculine voice, which wasn't very masculine at all. But Sandra obeyed anyway. "Follow me," he added in a loud whisper.

He led the way to the door and then let Sandra pass him. He needed time to think. What on earth was he going to do? He had two people to save and no idea how to do it. The little ones, whoever they were, might be back any moment. A second later Sandra was back in his arms.

"What happened?" he asked in a whisper.

"There is a monster up there. A very large monster!" She pressed herself into Alec's body as though trying to get to the other side of him.

"He's a friend." Alec smiled for the first time. "I got him out of his cell, too." The look of admiration in Sandra's eyes was more than Alec could hope for.

"You freed *him*?"

"Well, he was drugged and couldn't walk. I think they expected him to sleep for a few hours yet."

The monster's face cracked in a hideous smile.

"Princess!" he rumbled.

He tried to stoop even lower to pay her homage and almost fell down the stairs. He would have pinned the both of them to the stone floor. Probably broken all their bones.

"Igor?" Sandra asked incredulously. "Is it really you?"

"Yes, Princess. A bit worse for wear."

Suddenly his heavily accented speech had become completely normal. Almost refined. Alec supposed that one must speak well in front of the Princess. It is only proper.

Sandra ran up to Igor, for that was indeed his name, and fell into the huge man's massive arms. She was good at falling into men's arms, Alec thought. Maybe a little too good? And then he heard the familiar giggle. He bit his tongue.

"Do you know the way out of here?" Sandra asked. "Alec saved me, but I'm not sure he knows the way...?"

"Yes, Princess, right through that door."

"Hold on!" Alec commanded. "How do you know that there are no bad, ah, little ones out there?"

"Well, there may be, but I'm not drugged any more. I'm not afraid of them when I'm myself."

"Let me go first, then." Alec was still in charge. Igor obediently took two steps back down the other staircase to allow him access to the door. Alec pushed the door's heavy metal handle but the door hardly moved.

"Here, let me. After all, you did save me," Igor said behind his back.

And as Igor reached over Alec's head and pushed the thick wooden door, Alec literally fell through. He caught himself on the very edge of the settee. Igor and, what was worse, Sandra were both gone. He was alone in his living room. He looked around just to make sure he was really here and alone. He didn't know whether to laugh or cry. He decided to lie back a while and think about his adventure. Dream or not, he had saved Sandra. Or so it seemed.

***

5
Hello Again

It seemed like only yesterday. At the time Alex Baldwin was still living in Harlow, just north of London, UK, of course. Having passed A-level exams in a number of subjects, he and his buddy George Sims, shared digs close to the QMUL School of Engineering on Mile End Road, where he'd eventually obtained his civil engineering credentials.

England is, or at least was at the time, deprived of her fair share of sunshine. Each summer he and George waited patiently to hitchhike south, to the French Riviera. More precisely, to Mandelieu, just west of Cannes. East of Cannes, sequestered in their voluptuous villas overlooking the Méditarranée, were the fat cats. Cap d'Antibes, Juan-le-Pins, all the way to Monaco was the rich people's playground.

He and George stayed in tents, on canvas cots with straw mattresses. An array of showers and toilets offered necessities some hundred paces off. They ate outdoors under a thatched roof, where wine was cheaper than orange juice or coca cola. To get to the seashore, the beach, they walked about three or four kilometers, often running part of the way.

At the time he had been only a little older than his son was now. About seventeen? He thought the Camping offered the peak of luxury. He wondered if his son would agree with him. Alec Junior has been brought up to expect a swimming pool right at the doorstep, and an oceanfront he could get to in two minutes flat. Without running. It wasn't that his son was spoiled. Times have changed. Times and geography.

There and then, in Mandelieu, they would lie down on the sand and got up only for a swim, or to go back to, what used to be called, *Camping International de Cannes*. It had nothing to do with Cannes, of course. Cannes was for the wealthy. Still is.

After dinner they would go hunting.

Lots of game was ready and willing right there, on the spot, in the female portion of the Campground. With luck he or his buddy would score. Such successes were at the expense of the fellow who shared your tent. The poor bastard had to spend the night outside, or at least wait until the fair sex sneaked out to her own domain. More often then not, however, the hunt proved fruitless. Those were strange times when most of the girls thought that sex was something one enjoyed only after the wedding ceremony. Luckily, some did not.

Times change.

And now, Alicia and he were resting on very comfortable, padded deckchairs, sipping Bloody Marys, and getting very close to being bored stiff.

He wished Alec didn't have to attend school; that he could have come with them. They would have played some games, kicked a ball perhaps, thrown a Frisbee. Or even just played together on the oncoming waves to see who could surf closer to shore on the breakers. That's what they did last year, during summer, but coming here during summer was not the same. And in summer he was really busy at work.

Actually, this year there was a near permanent black flag displayed, denoting a shark warning, and the Portuguese Men o'War made even walking on the beach on the risky side. Their venomous tentacles could well deliver a painful sting.

Pollution, they said in the hotel. Too much pollution.

Nevertheless, he did take a walk, alone, along the shore. And… he did get stung. Back at the pool he went to the public washrooms and tried peeing on his sore toe. It had absolutely no effect, other than making room in his bladder for yet another Bloody Mary.

That helped a lot more than the pee.

On his return to the deckchair, this time he kept Alicia company a little longer. Yet, after being fried in the Florida sun for some twenty minutes, he got up and plunged into the pool. Alicia followed him, slowly, at the shallow end. She had to be careful. As ever, she couldn't get her hair wet. It just wouldn't do. Hanging straight down, half-blinding her left eye.

Noblesse oblige, her husband mused, but he couldn't understand her qualms. He realized there and then that in as much as he loved his wife more than ever, he also loved her not just for but also in spite of a number of things. Her hair rituals, her shoes, even her insistence on treating his son almost like a baby. Or was it a number of quirks? Whatever anyone might call them, he couldn't imagine life without her.

But mostly it was for her smile. No matter how tired he was, her smile set him at peace. Always.

***

Alec Junior must have dozed off for a few minutes. When he came to, a whimsical smile was playing about his lips. He was reasonably happy with his performance. He remembered every detail. He had been afraid, but he had overcome his fear. He hadn't run to save himself but had risked his freedom, perhaps his life, to help others. So what if it had only been a daydream? It takes just as much guts to act in the real as in the imaginary world. He remembered waking up covered in sweat after some of his previous adventures. And today was no different. But what was most important, he had actually met Sandra. Sandra—his Princess. He couldn't think of her in any other way but as his. Of course he had no claim on her, none whatsoever, but... he had saved her.

He was her knight.

She was more beautiful than he ever imagined. That is, than when he half-saw her in the mirror and the dark pane of glass. Her hair was long and golden. Pure gold. Perhaps all Princesses have golden hair, but it didn't matter. His did, and that was enough. She was just a little shorter than he, but just tall enough to fall into his arms comfortably. He blushed at the recollection. And then he tried to remember what her tiny, lithe body felt like against his. And then he did remember, and he blushed again.

He went to the kitchen and got himself a glass of water. He came back and sat in dad's favorite armchair. It swung to and fro, it spun around, and you could lie completely flat on it. It was quite a chair. He sat down, released the back support and relaxed. He wondered if Sandra would ever come on another of his jaunts. Gosh, she was beautiful. Her eyes shone like little stars. Her face and hands seemed to fill the dungeon with an eerie light. Like moonlight from a full moon. Alec desperately tried to think of other things. Not a chance. His thoughts made a loop and came back to Sandra. He wondered why.

"I told you." He heard her distinct voice. He fought the desire to sit up and look around and managed to keep perfectly still. "It's all right," her voice smiled. "I'll stay a while. After all, you did save me."

For some unknown reason there was a chuckle at the end of that assurance. A chuckle much too close to becoming a giggle. Alec was a little hurt.

"I'm sorry," she assured. "I really am very grateful." And when Alec still remained gruff, she added, "You behaved like a real gentleman. Like a knight in shining armour. Really!"

Alec relaxed again. "Thank you, it was nothing."

"Saving me was *nothing*?"

"That's not what I meant!"

He really had no idea how to talk to girls. They always twisted everything and got the better of you.

"Did you enjoy the adventure?" she asked innocently.

Alec had seldom, if ever, enjoyed anything more in his life. It wouldn't do to admit it, though. She would be bound to laugh.

"No, I wouldn't. I would be flattered."

"Can you read all my thoughts?" Alec was becoming exasperated again.

"Pretty much," her voice smiled again. "Only if they are not bad ones. Those I can't, but I can sense them all."

"Is that when you go away? I mean when I have bad thoughts?" he asked.

"I never go away."

"But..."

"I never go away. Sometimes you lose contact with me. I am always there, or rather here, with you."

"I'd never lose contact with..."

And Alec blushed again. I must really stop this blushing business. It's embarrassing. He prayed she couldn't detect these last thoughts.

For the next little while, even without uttering a single word, Alec was acutely aware of her presence. He was still tired from his ordeal, but he felt contented, relaxed, complete. As if two lost parts of him had found each other and become one. Alec realized that, although he couldn't read or sense Sandra's thoughts, he could, in a way, sense her emotions. He sensed her smile, her worry, her concern. Even gratitude. It had nothing to do with the actual words. Yet it was there, unmistakably. It was like playing the piano. There were no words, but the emotions were all there. As plain as could be.

He also knew, just knew, that she always spoke the truth. He couldn't imagine her lying. He wondered if she could lie, ever.

"No." The same smile.

"Not even not to hurt someone?" Alec pressed.

"Not even not to hurt someone." Quite definitive. Since Alec couldn't quite figure it out, she continued, "What you hear, when I talk, are things that you really want to hear. In your heart. Not what you were taught by your parents, or in school, or read in books, but what is really at the very depth of your..."

"I know what you mean." Alec sensed her meaning. "I know that I can always trust you. Always!" He added again as though defying anyone to contradict him. Then he changed the subject. "Who was Igor? Have you known him long?"

"I met him before. He has a problem with his size. He thinks that anyone who is half his size is against him."

"That's about half of the world's population," Alec quipped.

"Exactly." Her tone wasn't smiling. After a moment she added, "There are some people who think that those larger than they are also against them."

"That's different!" Alec was adamant.

"Is it?" He sensed her smile again. "Does size really matter that much?"

Alec did not answer. He remembered the feats he performed in his dreams. Size had not come into it. Not at all. He knew she was right, but it wouldn't do always to admit that a girl was right.

"Can't you help him?" He changed the subject.

"I do. I always show him that although I'm little he has nothing to fear from me. Not just physically but also in any other way. He never fears big men because he's bigger than most, so he channels his fear toward the 'little ones'. But I also never laugh at him. Never ridicule his apparent clumsiness. But he must overcome his opinion of himself by himself. That's what the dungeons are for, mostly. To help people overcome their fears."

"You mean my saving him might help to restore his faith or trust in, ah..."

"...in people much smaller than himself. He's already learned to trust individuals. He must still learn to feel comfortable in a crowd."

"A crowd of little people?"

"Next to him, everybody is 'little people'."

There was another moment of silence. It seemed to Alec that we all had things to learn. Regardless of size, or age or anything else. Life was a continuous lesson, or a series of lessons, if one chose to treat them as such. We could learn and move on, or refuse to learn, and, sort of, keep walking in circles. He wondered if all people knew that; if they knew that life was a continuous lesson.

"Unfortunately, no. There are many who seem to refuse to learn."

"What happens to them?" He felt sorry for such people.

"Their lessons become more and more... persuasive."

"You mean they are forced to learn?"

"No. You can't teach anyone anything. All learning comes from within yourself."

"Then what are schools for?" Alec asked triumphantly.

"Schools are there to convey to the pupils what the consequences of other people's thoughts, ideas or deeds in various circumstances are. Whether the pupil accepts the lessons contained therein is up to the pupil. No teacher can force anyone to learn."

"She can fail them at the exam?"

"Not really. It is the pupil who fails the exam. Miss Brunt, or any other teacher, can only affirm this fact by allotting the pupil an appropriate mark."

The Princess was right again. Gee, she's clever! Alec felt incredibly proud that such a clever (and beautiful), and kind, and courageous Princess would choose him to be her knight. He was the luckiest boy in the world.

"Do other boys have Princesses? I mean know... I mean hear..."

He felt very embarrassed. He didn't own the Princess. He did not *have* her.

"I know what you mean." She was kind again. "Yes. All boys will discover, sooner or later, their... other halves. And the girls, too. They will find their Princes."

"And adults? My mom and dad?"

"For them it's harder. They are set in their ways, and it is harder for them to free themselves from the evidence of their senses. They believe only what they see and touch and smell, and so on."

"But I do the same...?"

"You do the same, but you also accept what you see with your eyes closed. For them it is harder."

The Princess seemed to search for the right words.

"There are some adults," she resumed, "who still accept the reality of the imaginary world. Mostly they are the artists. They create from what they sense within themselves. They sort of bring it out. From within to without."

"I thought artists had models, or painted what they saw."

"They do, but only up to a point. A moot point. The object or the person they are looking at acts as an inspiration. They use what they see to focus their attention. Leonardo da Vinci didn't paint the face he saw. Not even the smile. What he painted was the secret thought, the mystery, the enigma..."

He thought he understood what Sandra was saying, although he'd never really looked at the Mona Lisa in quite such a deep way. But really, it was not the painting, as such, which had made such an impression on him; it was the smile on the lady's face. What was she smiling at? Why was she smiling? Was it something Mr. da Vinci had said? No, he'd never thought of a painting in this light.

"So artists can travel?"

"There are some who do travel on the wings of their imagination, just as you do. But what is more important, many of them can translate what they see within for others to share on the outside, or in the material world. That way they expand the awareness of the people among whom they live."

He felt, again, that he had so very much to learn. Alec was looking at artists with a new respect and decided to investigate the books on art his mother kept in the living room. He was sure that Sandra would be a great help to him. Of that he was very sure. He wondered if one could ever learn enough to know everything. Not to have to visit the dungeons any more. Not to have to...

"There is always more to learn. Always, no matter what you already know. Remember that every new day is the first day of the rest of your life. Think of it—of life—as going on forever. Think of having so much to learn that you could never, never get bored. Not if you lived for a million-million years. Nor even longer. Think of life being fun..."

But Alec wasn't thinking at all. His head was leaning slightly on his left shoulder, his heavy eyelids shutting out the remains of daylight. He sank into a dreamless sleep, resting his imaginary body before the next taxing exploits. He was sure they would come. What form they would take, he had no idea. But it was the fact that they were ventures into the unknown that made them so fascinating. So enticing.

And then, there was Sandra... her voice still reverberating in his youthful heart.

***

6
The Far Country

It's been a three days since the Baldwins stepped aboard the Catalina. Catalina 42, the biggest yacht Alex had put his foot on. The British expatriates considered it unpatriotic not to love the sea, with sailing their first love. It all started quite by accident. Tomorrow they would be back in Palm Beach, and then on Singer Island for the rest of their holidays, and then fly back to Montreal.

It all began quite by accident.

Walking along Worth Avenue, her eyes peeled to the shop-fronts evidently designed to attract the fair sex, Alicia had bumped into a man. He gave Alicia a curious once-over. Before she could even apologize he nodded towards an outdoor café immediately behind her.

"Keen Ah buy you a cup o' cooauffee?" he asked, his eyes peeled on Alicia. Only then he'd noticed Alex. "You too, Ah preeesume, Sir?" he added with a lot less enthusiasm.

He was a Texan, and he wouldn't take no 'fer' an answer. Alex shrugged, Alicia managed a slight blush, and the three of them settled at an outdoor table right there. They've been walking for more than an hour, and a little rest wouldn't do any harm.

The Texan was as Texan, as can be imagined. He spoke with a Texan drawl, talked mostly about oil, cows, money and his collection of pistols, double-barrel guns, and three, that's right three rapid fire Uzis.

"You nevah knowah when you might need'em," he assured Alex who wouldn't touch a gun for fear of shooting himself in a foot.

After exhausting the subjects   mentioned above, he mentioned causally that he also owned a li'l boat, and kept it in a marina in Palm Beach. He didn't like hotels, he'd said.

"Jist a li'l west from heere," he added. He meant his boat.

Suddenly Alex's ears perked up. "Just a little west..." That would be Lake Worth?

"You nevah knowah whoo you might run intaw," the Texan drawled on, only just managing to avoid dropping the ash from his oversized cigar into his bourbon. It seemed that his 'cooauffee' had miraculously metamorphosed into Garrison Brothers oversized Texan bourbon on the rocks.

"You just neav'r knowah, these days," he repeated to make sure that Alicia heard him. He paid little attention to Alex.

It seemed that Don, the Texan, didn't know quite a few things, but it transpired that he certainly knew a beautiful boat when he saw one. As Baldwins finished their 'cooauffees', Don left his bourbon half-finished, put a $20 bill on the table under his glass and got to his feet.

"Peerhaps you'd like a li'l look at my li'l boat? Got two bouys runnin' 'er," he added, "I wouldn't know which eeand is heed and which is the other eeand..." he assured them of his growing ignorance.

This was the second time that Alex actually listened to his drawl. Don had referred to his boat as ''er' meaning 'her'. He couldn't be all-bad.

It also transpired, a little later, that Don was anything but ignorant. He just liked to create an impression of a country yokel, in case people took him for a rich Texan. Neither the rich part—with the boat, not the Texan part—with his accent, could be avoided. Alex thought Don was just bored, and did things to enrich the monotony of a lonely Texan on the East Coast. Actually, it turned out later, that he thought that if he'd exaggerated all that stuff about oil and guns, no one would take him seriously. It was a form of protection.

It was a fairly short walk. They stepped on board.

"You nev'r knowah whom you might meet in Pielm Beach these days," he repeated his previous sentiment. "There's all keends of riff-ruff," he said. "Why, only the other day they asked me how much I'd charge them fer a day trip on my lady here," he added, lovingly patting the fiberglass curve of the bow. "Ah told'm to geet lost…"

The next thing, in seeming contradiction to his previous reservations, Don had asked them if they'd like a li'l run to Nassau.

"That's a li'l town on a li'l island they call New Providence, right next to Paradise Island where they used to keep pigs, and now serve the best and biggest lobsters in the Caribbean…"

Don seemed ready to expound further about the mysteries of the Bahamian cuisine when he noticed that Alex's eyes have doubled in size. Also, as he talked sailing, his drawl seemed to diminish somewhat. Alicia, on the other hand, noticed that everything was li'l in Don's eyes except for the lobsters. And Texas, of course.

Don didn't have to ask twice. It took Alicia and Alex about two hours to get their swimming costumes, and an overnight bag with toiletry essentials.

By sunrise the next day they'd set sail.

On the second day aboard, Don dropped his drawl. He was soft spoken, yes, still a Texan, but no longer acting as protection against "riffraff".

***

Alec woke up in the middle of the night, his mind telling him that something about Sandra had changed. Then he got it. Last night, before he went to sleep, she hadn't been talking like the little girl he'd first met. She hadn't giggled as much, not even really laughed. There had been no jokes, no verbal sparring. Obviously, what she'd been trying to tell him was important and... he'd fallen asleep.

"I've been rude again," he thought. "I must stop being rude to Sandra."

With this thought still fresh in his mind, he ran upstairs and went to bed. The good thing about being alone in the house was not having to wash himself. At least, not every time. Not even his teeth. Just dive into his bed and sleep.

He woke up at seven, washed, made his bed, ate a bowl of Cornflakes and ran to school. He felt elated as though he'd accomplished something great. Something he'd never done before. At the back of his mind he knew what it was. He had saved his Princess from a fate worse than death. He'd never understood what that meant, but he'd done it anyway. He was a knight in shining armor.

He almost tripped as he remembered a detail from last night. Was it last night? Time got funny when Sandra was around. Anyway, he recalled his arms and legs down in the dungeons having a slight sheen. Was that the shining armor? Was he really a knight? A real knight?

For a moment he was in danger of falling off his steed.

He continued on his way with hops and leaps, parrying the thrusts and lunges of his imaginary adversary. Carried away, he punched his sword right through an old lady's fruit basket. He pulled back, saluted with his invisible blade at his nose, and beat a hasty retreat. The lady was still scratching her head when he turned the next corner.

School kept him busy for the next six hours. He was happy—cracked a few jokes. The boys *and* girls actually laughed at them. Was he becoming popular? Life was becoming more beautiful by the minute. He actually enjoyed *all* his classes, and afterwards he hopped and skipped practically all the way home. It was good to be... To be what? He didn't care. Just to be!

An hour later he made himself a TV dinner that didn't taste bad at all. Not after the soggy crust with the long-dead meat on a metal plate yesterday. He smiled at the recollection. Could it have all been just his imagination?

Frankly, he would never believe it. Nor would anyone who had taken part in last night's exploits. Then he had an idea. He rolled down his socks and looked at his ankles. There they were. The red welts he'd made pulling the irons over his heels. They didn't hurt any more, but the telltale signs were still there. He'd been in the castle, he'd been there, and he *had* saved Sandra and the big, big man. He wondered if Igor was becoming more sure of himself. It was really strange that a man that size could be afraid of anything. He was so strong. And yet?

He had so much to learn.

He wished Sandra were here. Of course, he already knew that you do not command a Princess to your presence. You can save her, you might even hold her in your arms for a while—if you're really lucky—but you do not command her. She would come when she chose. All he could do was to be ever ready to welcome her. To wait upon her every whim. If he so much as heard her laughter, or a sigh, or even a giggle, he would be ready to drop everything and be at her disposal.

A deep, tremulous sigh escaped from his young, lonesome heart.

It was not easy being a knight.

By ten o'clock Sandra hadn't come. He worked on some schoolwork, took out the garbage. All the things a man must do around the house. And then he did brush his teeth, wash his face and hands, and behind his ears. Then he hesitated for a while and decided to wash his feet as well. The red welts were gone. Funny that, he thought, and went to bed. After another few sighs he was fast asleep.

***

Don, in ridiculously oversized swimming trunks, stood at the wheel. His legs astride, he practically oozed confidence. His recently confessed ignorance about sailing seemed to have vanished the moment he'd stepped on board.

Alex couldn't help but to ask him how come he'd invited them.

"I've been sailing since I was a little boy. I can tell a sailor when I see one," he said, grinning from ear to ear.

"You mean you needed a crew?"

"Do you mind?"

"Do I look as though… You're very kind, Don. We are both very grateful." And then Alex looked puzzled. "Just where are you hiding those two boys you'd said…"

"They stayed in the Marina. Why is the boat dirty somewhere?"

"It's Bristol fashion," Alex replied. "Shipshape," he added, his eyes filled with admiration.

"Well, you have the boys to thank for that." And then he gave Alex a curious look. "I cheated," he added.

"You…?"

"I was watching your eyes when I mention my 'li'l bouat'," he slipped into his previous accent.

Alex could only smile. He'd underestimated his newfound friend, in more ways than one.

"So you intended to take a forty-two-foot boat across an open sea singlehanded?"

"Francis Chichester was 65 when he took his Gypsy Moth IV around the world in 1966. I'm a lot younger and marine technology has advanced a lot since that time."

Don grew in Alex's eyes by the minute.

"And…" Don added, making a minute adjustment to the fores'l without letting go the wheel. All lines had been brought into the cockpit and were within reach of the helmsman. "And Gypsy Moth IV was 54 feet, not a mere 42."

Alex's mouth dropped still lower. Don knew about his childhood hero.

"But it's a lot more fun to do it in company…" Don added wistfully.

Alex had learned later that neither Don's second nor his third wife liked sailing. Not unless it was a motorboat. Don called them noisy stinkpots; the motorboats, not the wives— although Alex hadn't heard anything particularly complementary about them either.

"So you know Sir Francis…"

"Not exactly. He died before I was born. But I know what you mean. I admire the guy, although I don't have the guts myself."

And, Alex mused, you're not really a loner… You've just had bad luck with your wives.

Alex wondered if he could ever sail the seven seas solo. The most he'd done solo had been Folkestone to Calais, across the English Channel. He remembered when the wind had died on him. He'd spent half the night drifting in utter silence.

He'd never forget that trip.

An unearthly calm descended all around him. Not even a slightest whisper of a breeze disturbed the mirror of the sea, stretching in all directions. He'd felt suspended between two sparkling universes. The stars were above and below him.

The stars were everywhere…

***

The stars were everywhere. The sky wasn't blue; it was as black as the velvet dress his mom once made for a ball on New Year's Eve. Black and deep—deep beyond imagination. There was no end to this blackness. And suspended in this soft velvet were those innumerable diamonds. Sharp, crystal-like; some shimmering, some fixed with the coldness of broken ice.

"The Far Country," he heard a mere whisper. In this cathedral of the Infinite, one could only talk in whispers. Even Sandra.

Out of the corner of his eye he saw one diamond chip expand and then explode like the purest silver and gold firecracker. He had no idea how far it was from him, but it did not seem to get any closer.

"A Nova. An exploding star. She'd run to the end of her purpose in her present form. Many planets will get their raw materials from this event. Isn't it beautiful?"

He sensed, more than heard, her voice. It was as though she were right inside him. As if she occupied the same space. "Two peas in the same pod," he remembered her saying. Gosh, this is just marvelous! He wished he could show it to his mom and dad. Especially to mom. She liked beautiful things. And this...

This was beyond beauty...

Anyway, here was the greatest silence he'd ever heard. If you can hear silence. The only other thing to be heard was the regular beat of his heart and vague cracking sounds—rather like the electric sparks when he combed his hair in the winter. In winter he had to comb his hair or his hat wouldn't fit.

"The hydrogen atoms falling right through you," she explained. How come she knew so much? She looked about his age... "Here, you're mostly empty space. Only a weak electromagnetic field keeps your body together."

He had no idea what this meant but thought it best not to ask.

"We'll talk about that later." She sensed curiosity and added, "I promise."

His body was very slowly spinning about its own middle. Both ways, lengthwise and about his waist. The Nova, still growing in size, was drifting over his left shoulder. Coming into his view was a ball of fire with some round, much dimmer but more colorful balls moving slowly around it. They all moved in the same direction but at different speeds. He wondered what...

"A sun with its planets...?" she whispered. "Not the Earth's sun, but a sun about five times bigger. We are two galaxies away from the Milky Way."

He looked around, trying to understand what it all meant. "Why here?"

He sensed her amusement. For some reason she would not tell him. He already knew her well enough to know that there was a reason for her silence. Perhaps he wouldn't understand. Yet. Already that last time she had not treated him like a little boy. Perhaps after he had saved her, she had decided that he was quite mature. For his age, of course.

"Do you remember nothing?"

What was there to remember? He'd never been here in his life. Not even on his wildest travels. Suddenly a large block of ice was falling straight at him. It came out of nowhere. Out of total darkness. He panicked. He shut his eyes and saw himself sleeping in his bed. This same instant, he relaxed. The stars were still there, the missile was gone.

"Thank heaven," he sighed.

He was doing a lot of sighing lately. But you should see these stars. Zillions upon zillions of them. Everywhere.

"That was a comet. It missed us by about thirty thousand kilometers."

So he had made a fool of himself. In the Far Country all things were measured with a different yardstick. You might call it a divine yardstick. It was a different ball game altogether.

"What am I supposed to remember?" He returned to her last question.

"This solar system. Look at the fifth planet from the sun, the one on the left."

The planet on the left grew larger even as he looked at it. It seemed perfectly round. As he got nearer to it, or was it the planet getting closer to him, he counted seven moons. All different sizes, some dark, some reflecting light. Most were silverish, but one was perfectly red. It was just beautiful. Like a great big red ball. All smooth and shiny. "I remember that ball," he thought, but the memory was no more than a vague whiff of a dream. His attention was distracted by the main planet. It was like the Earth, only it seemed much, much bigger. There was a beautiful, clear blue halo around it, and suspended in the halo were myriad clouds. There were levels upon levels of them. They must have reached an incredible height. They almost seemed to reach the nearest moon.

"Why does this place look, sort of, sort of...?" He couldn't quite say it.

"...familiar?" she prompted.

"But it can't be!? It just can't!" he insisted.

She didn't say anything. Alec hung or floated in space, his mouth slightly open, his eyes wide. "Familiar?" he thought. "This world, this moon, moons, these clouds..." And then images formed in his mind. "These oceans, these mountains piercing many layers of clouds, these forests where the trees were as high as the tallest building on Earth, these..."

His head spun. His mind couldn't contain the pictures and memories crowding into his mind. The planet receded, the sky grayed a little, and the zillions of stars seemed to rush away, swallowed into the ever-expanding grayness.

Alec slept. He was overwhelmed by the mounting memories. He slept until his wristwatch beeped repeatedly seven o'clock. For the first time in a long time he didn't remember much of his dream. He thought he'd seen Sandra, but he wasn't sure.

Next time... he smiled. Next time I will not let her go so easily. And he jumped out of his bed and ran to the bathroom. He had to take a shower. The first in three days. A long shower. It felt good. He decided to shower more often. Even if he was perfectly clean. Just for fun.

**

7
Home

Although he couldn't remember most of last night's dream, or perhaps because of it, Alec's mind kept returning to that night in the castle. Five days had passed since that night, in or out of a dream. A sleep-dream or a daydream. Not that there was so much difference. He didn't really care. What he did care about, and couldn't help, was not seeing the Princess. Once or twice he thought he heard her voice, but then… but then he was again quite alone. No mother, no father, no Sandra. Just Miss Brunt and a bunch of noisy boys and girls.

He counted the TV dinners. There were six left. In six days his parents would be back. Why didn't they call? He spent most of his evenings at home. They could have called. Only six days, but it felt like a year. His sulking was interrupted by the chime of the telephone he had just relegated to eternal silence.

"Mom?" he virtually shouted into the mouthpiece.

"No, son, it's me. Your father," his dad added unnecessarily. "We called you twice, but the rest of the time we were offshore, and our cellular couldn't reach you. How are you doing, ol' man?"

"Oh, I'm fine, Dad. Just fine. How's Mom?"

"We're both fine. I wanted to ask you how you are coping. Are you sure you're OK? Not feeling too lonely, are you?"

"Who, me? Dad! I'm thirteen years old. I can take care of myself."

"Good! Now listen. I've left two hundred dollars in the left lower drawer in my desk in the study. That's in case you need it. To tell you the truth..."

"Ali, darling, this is me. I love you. We both love you," Alec's mother interrupted. "Darling, do you think you could give us a few extra days? Say till Wednesday. It's just that this man has this..."

"Mom..."

"...this marvelous yacht and he offered to take us to the Bahamas, all the way to Nassau, and back in a week or so. We wouldn't be able to get back by Sunday. But we won't go if you need us. You must be honest with me..."

"Mom!"

"Yes, darling?"

"It's all right. Stay as long as you want. Dad just told me where he left me some extra money. I won't starve. Enjoy yourselves!" he lied. He already missed them something awful. He hadn't thought he would. But he did.

"Thank you, sweetheart. Say so long to daddy. I love you..."

"Bye, Mom. Have a good time."

"Bye, son. Be back soon. Don't forget about the money. The bottom left drawer. Use as much as you want. Bye!"

And the line went dead.

Alec's dad was the best dad a guy could hope to have. How many dads would give their thirteen-year-old access to two hundred bucks? He was kind, generous, even not bad to play chess with, but he saw the world as numbers. He put a dollar sign on just about everything. "Give him a few bucks and he'll be all right," was his motto. And the trouble was that, more often than not, he was right.

Alec supposed that just such a father, a husband rather, was precisely what his mother needed. She was the very opposite. Money was of no consequence to her, not that she had any idea of its worth. She chose her friends from all walks of life, regardless of their financial standing. She once dragged out their 'cleaning lady' to the Museum of Fine Arts, on the day on which the girl was supposed to do the cleaning, just so that the poor girl would get a taste of a little culture. Creative impulse, she called it. His mother, not the girl. Then his mother did the cleaning herself but paid the girl anyway. Somehow, this made mother laugh in unrestrained joy. Alec always envied his mother for her facility in dealing with people. She was just herself, perfectly natural. People seemed to accept her for what she was, without conditions or expectations. But, at the same time, dad could not really trust her with the domestic finances. Left to herself, she would find a thousand worthy causes on which to empty their bank account. For dad, two and two always made four. For mother it depended on the circumstances.

So now they would be back on Wednesday at the latest. Not Sunday. The house was sort of empty. And silent. He liked the silence but not the emptiness. Yesterday he started listening to his own footsteps, just not to feel so alone. And now even Sandra appeared to have gone.

"I must *do* something."

He started by making a grand tour of the house. He never realized that it had been years since he was in his parents' bedroom alone. Or in his father's study. If I am the master of the house, he mused, then I'd better know what is what. Or what is where. Just in case. Never mind in case of what. People in charge have to know things.

He didn't find anything exciting in either the bedroom or the study. Funny how the 'forbidden' always seems fascinating. Not that he'd ever been expressly forbidden to enter certain rooms; but, well, he always knocked before he did. Now, being in charge, he had the right to go anywhere.

This took care of most of the day. The following day loneliness returned. Somehow, just hearing his parents' voices filled the void that was growing deeper and deeper. There was only one thing to do. That evening he went to his own room, sat in front of the dark window, and waited.

"She will know that I am lonely," he murmured. "Why am I whispering?"

No one would hear him. He could speak as loud as he wanted to. "I'm a man. Men don't get lonely," he said out loud. The lie didn't work.

There was always TV, but he thought TV was for the old folks who had nothing to do. Like me? He chuckled. It wasn't a pleasant chuckle. And he needed a break from the Internet. His eyes were beginning to hurt.

He got up and returned to the living room. He sat in dad's chair and tried to figure out what to do next. All he needed was a little company. Surely, even men need that, don't they?

And then he caught his breath.

"She heard me! Sandra heard me," he whispered. It wouldn't do to actually tell her out loud. It wouldn't be manly.

Yet even as he leaned back in dad's chair, trying to decide what to do with the rest of the evening, her voice came to him with the usual softness, almost hesitation, as if she weren't sure she was welcome. That's ridiculous, he shook his head from side to side. The Princess not welcome???

"Thank you. It is nice to hear you, too, Sir Alec."

Alec's chest got about two inches bigger. He knew he was a knight, but it was nice to hear it from somebody else.

"At your service, my Princess," he replied in kind. They both laughed.

How was it that whenever I'm in touch with Sandra I don't care what happens to me? How come she makes me so happy? She doesn't have to do anything, just be there. That's all I'll ever need.

"But I'm always here," she whispered as though a little hurt.

"Then how come I can't see you or even hear you?"

"Hearing and seeing are only two ways of being aware of my presence."

"But..."

"Alec. It is only a few days since you first heard me. Don't you think you have a lot to learn?"

Did he ever! He was again embarrassed by his possessiveness.

"It's not that. It is just that you are here, on Earth, to live your life. Not to escape into dreams. It is all right to dream, in fact it is very good, but not all the time." She sounded quite adamant.

"But I don't dream all the time." He felt offended.

"But wouldn't you like to?"

Of course, he would like to. He would like to spend all his time with Sandra, even if it meant saving her from a dozen dungeons. Or from anything or anybody anywhere else, for that matter. No matter how hard, how difficult. He needed to be with her.

"But we are together all the time," she admonished.

"...like two peas in a single pod," he remembered.

"Exactly!"

"So how come I *feel* alone?"

"It's an old habit. You just don't know how old. All people think that they are alone all the time. In fact they never are. Not one of them. It's just that they don't know it."

Now Alec wasn't sure he liked that. He could just about tolerate other boys having their Princesses (whom they probably never saw or heard), or even girls having their Princes, but everybody? Everybody—that's an awful lot of people. There would have to be millions and millions and millions of Princes and Princesses all over the place. They would be virtually... virtually... He couldn't quite say the word 'common'. His Princess would never, *never*, be common. No, sir. Not as long as he was her knight.

"It doesn't quite work like that," she spoke in her kindest tone. When Alec didn't react, she continued, "You now begin to understand how you and I seem quite different and that only together do we form a complete unit. Two peas, one pod."

She stopped. She seemed to be waiting for a response. None came. Alec was churning the idea of zillions of Princesses gallivanting all over the world, being chased by zillions and zillions of boys.

"Sorry," he said, finally. "Sorry, I just thought..."

"...that you are unique." Her presence smiled. "You are, Alec. You are quite unique. There is no one the world over who is anything like you," she assured him, her voice full of conviction.

Alec recovered most of his composure. Even if there were zillions of Princes and Princesses, none were likely to be as beautiful as his Princess. Nor as clever, he suddenly realized. She sure knows a lot for a girl!?

There was that giggle again. He blushed, the first time in four days. He was getting better at controlling his emotions but not yet his thoughts.

"Well, even as you are an individual different from anyone, anywhere, and yet you and I are sort of... one, so it is with other people. But all the Princes and Princesses also fit into a... into a... pod. All together they form a... a King and Queen."

Now this was more than Alec could stomach. He had spent three days waiting for her. And before that, all his life. That's right, all his thirteen years and seven months. That was a long time to wait. And now he discovered that she was... well, she was...

He was filled with very mixed emotions. He couldn't help holding Sandra in the deepest chamber of his heart, but he refused to let other people in there. Something was going very wrong with this setup.

Hey, maybe Sandra doesn't know everything. Not everything?

But the other side of his heart told him that Sandra cannot lie. Not even if she wanted to. Not even to him, so as not to hurt him.

This time it was he who left his daydream. He was a little angry, terribly disappointed. Almost cheated. All he ever really wanted was a real friend. A secret friend. Someone he could count on. All the time. Always. Someone with whom to share his dreams, his travels. To go where no man has ever been before... With those words Captain James T. Kirk had sent him on many of his jaunts.

Now he learned that his Sandra was sharing some other pod with others of her kind. This wasn't fair. He had a right to keep her.

"She is mine!" he almost shouted. "Mine and mine alone!"

But at the same time he knew in his heart of hearts that no one ever owns a Princess. It was the Princess who owned him. Entirely. Lock, stock and barrel.

***

The Baldwins were back on board that same evening. With Alec being OK they could afford an extra day or two. And this time they really would go to Nassau. The first outing was a try out. Not just how well Alex and Alicia could crew— Don could handle the boat alone—but if they would stand each other for a whole week.

Life on board is different. At home, if you don't like somebody's company, you just leave. Here it would be a very wet experience. And, of late, sharks have been reported not just in Florida, but also in the vicinity of the Leeward Islands. Well, around Puerto Rico, some thousand miles away, anyway.

Still, neither Alicia nor Alex felt like walking the plank, here or anywhere.

At first light, they were already on their way. Once in the open sea, Alex took over the wheel. Way back when, he'd had plenty of practice. Now he made up in chutzpa for the dwindling experience. Although even the last day's he'd already spent at sea restored a lot of his previous confidence.

Don trusted him to take good care of the boat. Last night, when the Baldwins returned to Singer Island to call Alec and collect some more of their stuff, he had been invited to a party in Palm Beach, which lasted till early hours. Now he went below for a quiet nap.

Alicia looked at Alex at the wheel.

He hasn't change a bit, she thought. He looks just like the man I fell in love with some fifteen years ago, she thought. Perhaps a little heavier, with grey just touching his temples, but that made him look more distinguished. She liked that.

Also, the first few days in Singer Island, and then the wind and the sun on board the Catalina, had already turned his skin to dark bronze. If his hair were to be just a tad darker, he'd make a splendid Latin lover. Or French?

No matter, he was all the lover she'd ever need. He always was. Is.

Don emerged from the quarter berth rubbing his eyes.

"Are we there yet?"

He didn't specify where 'there' was.

"Naah, we're well past it," Alex replied in kind.

The Catalina, beamy as she was, healed considerably when beating into the easterlies. It gave the impression of great speed, possibly around 7 knots, but is felt like 12.

Don sat next to Alicia.

"How's he doing, young lady," he asked. Don may have been ten years older than she was.

"He rammed a few broadsides, but apart of that, he fired only the two rounds," she replied with straight face.

"Which reminds me," Alex joined the nonsense talk, "where do you keep all your artillery?" After earlier assurances, he expected at least a dozen firearms to be stashed on board.

"Artillery? Ah, yes. You believed my story, I see. Most Americans do, but I thought you were a Canadian?"

"Yes, but you are not."

"I stand corrected," Don said, stretching on the side bench. "Well, to be quite honest, I have some firearms. That's mostly why I keep away from Texas. Too many of them out there. But on board..." he left that hanging.

Don seemed to look slightly embarrassed.

"Back home," he resumed, "if you don't tell people about your firepower, they think of you as half-a-man. It's as if you had no," he stole a quick glance at Alicia, "as if you had no *cojones*," he finished in a loud whisper.

Alex spoke some Spanish. *Tener cojones* meant the same in almost any language. And they spoke a lot of Spanish in Texas—mostly with illegal immigrants.

"You don't carry protection even in the open sea?"

Don rubbed his chin thoughtfully. He then looked Alex in the eye. "Did you ever have a SOS distress flare fired into your stomach?"

Alex was beginning to put two and two together.

"I guess it would be quite a hot experience?"

"You've got it my friend. I don't need anything else. And we've got two of them. You can reload one as you fire the other... never had to use either," he added, with just a trace of ruefulness.

It was a superb run, with the easterlies filling the sails set mostly in broad reach, easily clearing 7 knots. By late afternoon they left the Little Bahama Bank on their port side, and with the dying rays of the setting sun, they dropped anchor in the lee of Grand Bahama Island, south of Freeport. They were careful to avoid frequent shoals that pepper the ocean all the way to Turks and Caicos Islands. After all, the Commonwealth of the Bahamas consisted of more than 700 islands, cays and islets scattered over a vast area.

It was clear from Alicia's facial expression that she had absolutely no intention of sailing during the night. After all, this was her first outing into the open waters of the Atlantic.

Alex's seconded the motion, which allowed him to take a swim.

Being a retiring macho, Alex had to dive in, of course. Alex wouldn't dream of entering the water from the steps at the stern of the boat. That would be much too easy. He was determined to dive from the side. Don, a Texan gentleman that he was, reached over Alicia who was taking in the last rays of the sun on the port side seat, and undid the lifeline to allow Alex a free and easy passage for his dive.

Alex thanked him, stepped over Alicia's legs and dove head first into the crystal clear waters. As he'd obviously climb on board through the stern steps, Don, once again a gentleman, reached over Alicia to reattach the lifeline.

And that's when it happened.

Alex's dive splashed water on the edge of the seat on which Don placed his hand to reattach the lifeline. His hand slipped and landed on the upper portion of Alicia's naked thigh. If that weren't enough, in an attempt to restore his balance, and as the fickle finger of fate, or in this case the whole fickle palm, would have it, his other hand grabbed her right boob. Quite unwittingly her thigh jerked upward unbalancing poor Don who, just as unwittingly, followed Alex into the drink.

There was a momentary confusion when Alicia realized that she was alone on board. Forgetting that the anchor was down, she gasped, screamed, wailed and, in an attempt to be as close to Alex as soon as she possibly could, rather than being left alone on board she followed both men into the water.

A very refreshing interlude, they all agreed.

Back on board, Don treated them to superb single malt that tasted older than Alex was himself. In fact, such as Alex hadn't tasted since he was toasted at his fiftieth birthday at the Beaver Club in Montreal. They leaned back, reminiscing, with the stars twinkling above them and in Alicia's eyes.

There was peace in the air.

Alex had to smile. It seemed to him that after a single day Alicia was sold on sailing. Her reservations evaporated into the clear sea air. Finally she looked totally relaxed, as though christened by the beneficial if unpremeditated swim. Whatever the dive did to her, she looked even younger than she did that very morning.

Later Alex examined the flare guns, just in case he'd have to use them. Unbeknownst to Alex, American Coast Guard and other local authorities usually require that boater carry at least three signal flares. Don carried two-dozen that he could fire from two flare guns. After all, he often sailed solo, and might have been in need of help from afar. Don didn't like firearms, but he was not foolhardy either.

"A flare gun can save your life at sea," he murmured, almost as if embarrassed for taking such precautions.

They'd spent the next five days on open seas, without firing a single shot. The pirates must have retired and were tucked away on some desert island living off their old age pension. It didn't really matter. At each anchorage around the Bahamas Alex dove overboard, flexing his muscles on return. Don was careful to leave the lifelines alone. In fact, while Alex swam, Don preferred to concentrate on Alicia, checking first if her surrounding were perfectly dry. He did so with such charm that Alicia didn't seem to mind at all.

Nor did Alex—while swimming.

***

8
Home Again

He slept until ten. Actually, the last hour or so he wasn't asleep, but stayed in bed trying to work out yesterday's discussion with Sandra. After careful negotiations with his ego, he decided that what Sandra did when she was not with him was her business. After all, when he went to school, or anywhere, he didn't ask Sandra for her permission. Sandra was as old as he was, and she seemed to know tons more than he did. Maybe she had to attend classes in some kind of a school of her own. Who can tell what Princesses do with their time?

And he had seen her quite a few times. Well, seen and heard. He couldn't really accuse her of not sparing him enough of her time. For all he knew, she might have to hold court, or something, every day. Princesses could be very busy.

Only she'd said she was always with him. Trust girls not to make sense. She couldn't possibly be in his 'pod' and some other pod at the same time. Could she?

Could she...?

***

Alex would remember those few days for a long, long time. The intrepid trio spent the second night in the lee of Berry Islands—three times almost getting stuck on a shoal. With a badly hidden embarrassment, if not actual disgust, Don had to fire the engine to get them free. Neither Alex nor Alicia shared his apparent discomfiture using the occasions to get yet another swim. On the last such occasion they actually dragged poor Don overboard, which broke down his mortification in an explosion of laughter.

By early evening of the third day, they came into the Paradise Island Club Marina, where apparently Don was already well known.

The lobster was everything Don had promised. Not as large, perhaps, but beautifully delicate, and delicious as only that Bahamians can do it. The *Pouilly Fuissé* complemented the feast to everyone's delight.

"They think they know it all, about lobsters, I mean," Don put in after sucking on the final claw. "But I strongly suspect that all the Caribbean nations know all there is to know about *frutti di mare*. *Fruits de mer*, I think you call it, don't you?"

Alicia's appreciation of Don grew in hops and leaps. He was not just rich, generous, and friendly, but also knowledgeable.

"My second wife was Italian," Don put in as an afterthought.

The return trip was an ongoing frolic, in which Alicia took active part. No longer worried about her stylish hair, she dove overboard each time they dropped anchor in the lee of the tiny islands. The starlit nights were just as enchanting with not s single drop of rain marring their pleasure.

All three had splendid time. On return to Palm Beach, they exchanged cell numbers and emails, and agreed to repeat the same in the future.

Less Alex diving from the side of the boat.

Alex soon discovered that he was right. Alicia was sold on sail. Body and soul. He wondered what would be next.

***

By ten o'clock Alec decided that, whatever Sandra did today, he had to take a shower and then have breakfast. This afternoon he had promised to go to a tennis match with Pete who lived next door. Pete was his good buddy. If Alec ever went anywhere, it was with Pete. Or with mom and dad, of course. Pete was his tennis partner, and they played twice a week. Once after school and once on the weekend. Normally, on weekends, and weather permitting, Pete and Alec would play singles for an hour, and then they would face any other two guys for one hour of doubles. They never lost a match against anyone their own age, and they often beat boys seventeen and older. The gym teacher, Mr. Grimm, who doubled as the school tennis pro, told them that they could play doubles at the junior pros, but Alec resisted. He preferred to play in friendly matches, where he could serve as Laver, or McEnroe, or that Brazilian guy with as much hair on his head as Alec himself. He'd learned to copy their style of serving. So much so that Mr. Grimm would shout from the sidelines, "Show me AB, for a change." AB stood for Alec Baldwin, which was the name Alec had inherited from his father, and his grandfather before him. There was also some film star of that name, but absolutely no relation. There were also over two-dozen other Baldwins in the telephone book; and as far as he knew, they were no relations, either. Except for Aunt Martha, but she died last year.

They would have played today, but Pete's dad had got them tickets for the pro match final. A chance too good to miss.

His own dad always preferred cricket and soccer, and Alec thought both games a bit dumb. Dad only looked occasionally at baseball as it was the nearest he could get to cricket, and football to rugby. For Alec the Canadian pros were just a bunch of guys dressed up in funny tight pajamas, who did a lot of spitting and patting each other on their rear ends. Alec would never allow anyone to touch his behind. Never.

In the shower, he stood at the helm of a large sailing vessel, a brigantine, his strong arms firmly on the wheel, his mother and father cringing below deck, while he fought off the waves. His jaw set in defiance, his face awash with the sea spray. By the time he was finished, there were pools of water all over the bathroom floor.

Later he made himself a boiled egg with toast and a glass of milk. The egg came out much too hard, but a little mayonnaise took care of that. He had four eggs left and some TV dinners. He had to do some shopping if he was going to survive till his parents returned. Unless he resigned himself to eating only food wrapped in plastic. He was already seeing himself stranded on a desert island, bereft of food and drink, casting a long, thin, emaciated shadow on the sand, when he remembered that he still had six Minute Maid orange juice concentrates. Well, bereft of food, he at least would not die of thirst. Two hours later his shopping was done and, armed with a twenty-dollar bill in his pocket, he knocked on Pete's door.

After the match, he invited Pete home for an orange juice. They played some games on the computer, tried to play chess, but it was getting late, and Pete still had to do his English essay. By six Alec was alone again. By six-thirty, he couldn't get his mind off Sandra. By seven he gave up trying. By seven-o-five, he heard her voice.

She sounded different.

Her voice was friendly, but, well, it sounded a little guarded. As if she weren't as spontaneous as before. As if she'd decided to choose her words a little more carefully. Alec didn't like that. He wished they could get back to the old trust. He'd already forgiven her for not being with him all the time, at his every whim, even though, he reminded himself, he'd never had any rights in that department to begin with. That it was she who was essentially the giver. He, the taker, the recipient of her gifts. Except for his saving her, of course. Suddenly an idea struck him.

"Am I forgiven?" he asked.

In that instant the tone of her voice changed to the old familiar, almost conspiratorial intimacy. "I was never angry," Sandra replied. "I just didn't want to hurt you again."

Alec breathed deeply. Wasn't she something? He was nasty to her, and *she* didn't want to hurt *him*. The Princess was definitely something else.

"Do you remember our visit to the Far Country?" she asked.

"Of course. The big sun, the big, big planet, the clouds, the mountains, the..."

"That's the one. Do you know why I took you there?"

He had no idea why Sandra had taken him to the Far Country.

"I thought so." Her voice smiled. "Do you have any suspicions?"

He thought for a while. "Well, there is one thing. The place, the planet and the moons, I mean, well... they looked familiar. They looked as if I'd seen them before."

"Just seen...?"

What was she trying to do? What else was he meant to say? They looked familiar. That's it. But—just a minute. How come I remembered the planet from the top down *and* from the bottom up? I really remember looking up at those soaring mountains disappearing into the clouds above, reappearing again, and again hiding their crowns in even higher clouds. How could I possibly have seen that from below? But, for that matter, how could I have seen them from above! That's even more ridiculous.

"Not if you obey the laws of that reality."

"Reality?"

Alec's pulled his thoughts back from the mountains. One of the most beautiful sights in the Far Country, Sandra knew.

"Yes, Sandra. It did look familiar. But that's not possible."

"It was your home for many years." Her voice came as a mere whisper, as though she thought that the idea might be too much for him.

He knew, intuitively, that Sandra couldn't lie.

"I am thirteen years old," he said, nevertheless.

"Yes, you are."

Well, why didn't she explain? Was he supposed to figure it out himself? How can I be thirteen, actually thirteen-and-a-half, and have lived somewhere for many, many years? Come on, Sandra...

"Were you there with me? I mean on that planet?" he asked instead.

"Of course, I am always with you."

She had said that before. The pod.

"How old was I then?" The question didn't make any sense but had to be asked. There are some different rules out there.

"On that particular occasion we stayed there for one thousand three hundred and twenty-three years."

"What! How long? And we were together?"

"It's always we. It cannot be otherwise."

This wasn't getting any easier. One thousand three hundred... for crying out loud, I'm only thirteen! And suddenly Alec remembered the shadow he'd cast on the sand on the Desert Island. The place he had been going to starve to death on before he went to the grocery store. It was a long, long shadow cast by a tall, lanky man. He must have been at least as old as his father. Only taller and much thinner. Were all things so flexible?

"You are whatever you think you are."

"You mean I could be any age, right now?" There was just a pinch of doubt in his voice. He did trust Sandra, but *any* age?

"You must also obey the rules of the world you live in. If you want to change certain things, you must change your reality."

"Like using my imagination?" He was beginning to catch on.

"That's how you start."

"There is more than imagination?" He should have known better. He knew now by his own experiences that other realities were just as real.

"Some realities you just imagine. Others you create with your mind. They are not quite the same."

"That's it?" As if that weren't enough!

"No. There is more. But the next step is harder to explain."

But Alec was busy digesting. He'd never imagined that there might be different ways to travel. On the inside, he meant. Not just imagination, but—what did she say, mind?

"How can you imagine worlds without using imagination?"

"You did it when you were outside our Home world."

"What do you mean?"

"Don't you remember?"

In an instant Alec felt suspended in the middle of nowhere, in total darkness, surrounded by zillions of stars. This time it all looked sort of familiar. This was exactly where he had been on his first visit to the Far Country. Far Country? Home planet? Somehow these terms sounded right. How come he thought of that? Home planet, he repeated again, and it appeared before him, suspended in the glory of the Universe. "My Home planet..."

He felt a smile coming from Sandra. No words, just a warm smile.

Alec was suspended in a place he'd never imagined. He couldn't have imagined. Surely, you can't imagine what you've never seen, can you?

"This is what you have created in your mind, instead."

He heard her voice, but his heart was filled with such wonder, such gratitude, that he was speechless. There was a beginning of knowledge formulating in his consciousness. Knowledge he never suspected existed. For now, he was imbued with beauty on such a gigantic scale that even his mind could hardly embrace it.

But that was quite another story.

***

They took a taxi to the Palm Beach International airport. In spite of the superb weather and the unexpected yacht cruise, Alicia's mind was already home, hugging and kissing and generally mangling little Alec. 'Little' in her eyes, of course. By now Alec, who must have shot up almost six inches in the last few months, was almost her height; and most likely stronger, particularly in his tennis arm, than she was.

They say that your children remain your children forever, regardless of size, age or prowess. This was certainly true of Alicia's attitude. While his father accorded Alec his Coming of Age dues, for her he remained li'l Alec, as Don would say. She smiled when she recalled how Don referred to his thousands of acres farm as li'l spread. Perhaps Alec really was growing up, only she wished he didn't do so quite so quickly. She dreaded the thought that one day he'd move out and she'd hardly see him again.

"He might move out to Toronto, or Vancouver or even farther away," she whispered to herself, once they were airborne.

They took the last minute Expedia flight. For a mere five hours they didn't need to book in advance, and were free to sit anywhere.

"What was that, dear?" Alex's ears were still pricking.

"I was thinking of Alec..." She didn't elaborate.

"Me too," Alex Senior confessed, surprisingly. "You know, even last year Alec was company. We played games, climbed Mont Royal, went for bike rides along Lachine Canal, and now...?"

"And now our li'l boy is growing up."

Alicia was finally beginning to face the truth. Her little boy was no longer so little. Soon she'd no longer be the only 'woman' in his life. He'd find a girl friend; he'd spend his free time with her. He'd go for walks with her... sit around and chat... even as he had done with her not so long ago.

"Why must children grow up?" she asked her husband. Her voice implied that it was all his fault.

"Don't look at me," Alex was on the defensive. "I had nothing to do with it," he added triumphantly.

"If it hadn't been for you, he wouldn't even be here!" she replied in kind.

Alexander Baldwin let that pass. It was too easy to counter. He smiled, and patted her hand.

"I was under an impression that we've adopted him together..." he said softly. "It won't be long now. We're almost there."

They were, about four hours later, plus another hour from the Dorval Airport to home. Actually, it now was Pierre Eliot Trudeau Airport, also International. It amused Alex to think that the Federal Government had renamed it only to annoy the Quebec separatists for whom Trudeau, the name of the late Prime Minister of Canada, was a dirty word. When asked what he might do to the separatists during the so-called October crisis way back in 1970, he replied: "Just watch me." The October Crisis had been triggered by two kidnappings of government officials by the FLQ. The *Front de liberations du Québec*. No one knew from whom they were trying to liberate Quebec, as the Prime Minister and most of the ministers of the federal government were all French Canadians. Perhaps they wanted to liberate Canada from Quebec?

For Alex that crisis forever remained a mystery. Yet the politicians used Trudeau's phrase "Just watch me", to this day.

"Do you think you can ever make him into a little boy again," Alicia asked, tiny tears swirling in her eyes.

It seemed that Alicia's mind was entangled in her motherly heart.

"Just watch me," Alex Baldwin replied, deep conviction in his voice. "Just watch me," he repeated, just to make sure.

Only then he realized that he had absolutely no idea what his darling wife was asking him.

***

9
The Parents

He spent Sunday walking through the park, skimming flat stones over the canal, trying to chase squirrels, as they played peek-a-boo around the tree trunks. Pete invited him for a Sunday lunch that his mother had prepared with her usual excess. If Pete wasn't careful, he would grow up as fat as his father. Not that his mother was a lightweight. She kept her pounds down, though not quite successfully, by constantly bouncing up and down, prancing to and fro, passing this and that, making sure everybody was happy. Happy, in her definition, meant having your mouth full of food.

The next three days Alec was quite busy at school. The end-of-the-year exams were approaching, and Alec was used to scoring quite well. He really liked learning. Almost anything. He did have his favorite subjects, but he found, early on, that the more you know about anything, anything at all, the more interesting it becomes. And he was still slowly working his way through the leather-bound collection of Shakespeare his father had given him last Christmas. His father thought it was important for Alec to read the best of the best, as he called it.

At home he was catching up on his reading. Not just schoolwork, but the old classics ranging from Dickens to Conan Doyle. After his mother attempted to stir his interest in books with the story about some imaginary princess, he quickly got down to *real* books. He had his own Princess and didn't need any funny stories for children.

"I am thirteen, for crying out loud," he said out loud for all to hear. The fact that he was alone didn't matter. "I don't read children's stories. At least... not any more," he added, his tone a lot quieter.

Nevertheless, his reading always resulted in short but very real exploits, in his imagination, on the subjects just read. He visited old London, dodged the drunks in the East End, stole apples from the carts in the Covent Garden market. It was unfortunate that some of his exploits occurred when he was supposed to be paying attention in school. Miss Brunt was not amused. When she asked Alec to describe what was the architectural style of the Notre Dame Cathedral in Paris, he jumped up and screamed, "I only took one and it was full of worms!"

Miss Brunt was about to remonstrate with him for his inattention when he was whisked away from danger by the ringing of his cell phone. It was dad, confirming his parents' return on Wednesday.

"What did we say about the cell phones ringing in the classroom, Alec?"

"Sorry, Miss Brunt. It's my father, he's away and..."

"Yes, I know. Now put it away and pay attention."

Thanks, Dad, Alec whispered. In the process, the worm-eaten apple had been forgotten.

And Wednesday was here. In about three hours his parents would be back home.

Alec excused himself from school at three to return home and clean the place up for their return. Miss Brunt knew about his parents' being away and trusted Alec's judgment. Since Alec had touched neither broom nor vacuum cleaner in almost three weeks, he had plenty to do. It wasn't that the place was dirty, or messy, but it didn't look fresh. He took care of that. He wondered if either mom or dad would notice.

Then he returned to his room, quickly got rid of his homework, and returned downstairs. The place definitely looked cleaner. He suddenly remembered that he hadn't done any dusting. The kitchen dishcloth did the job in ten minutes. Then he lay back in dad's favorite chair. He knew he would lose it the moment dad got back. His father seemed quite unable to sit anywhere else. He promised himself that when he grew up, he would have his own chair, with his name on it. It would be his spaceship, his base of operations for his jaunts and frolics. He really hoped he wouldn't grow out of them, as his parents suspected. And then he heard footsteps on the front porch.

"Darling!" his mother screamed for the whole neighborhood to hear. "Darling, how I missed you!"

Alec felt himself swept off the floor, his feet dangling, the air squeezed out of his lungs. Motherly love can be a frightening thing.

A good minute later, he shook hands with dad.

"How are you, old man?" he was asked the usual greeting. "You look great! I told you, darling, that he would be just fine. That's my boy. Ha!"

The final "Ha!" was proof of the pudding. Alec felt like dad's project had come to a successful conclusion. He wasn't exactly displeased.

He picked up one of the tote-bags and carried it inside. Dad took the other two, shut the door with his foot, dropped the bags and made a beeline for the fridge.

"What I really missed was good ol' Canadian beer. That stuff down South is more like water than water. Only too cold to swim in."

By the time he stopped talking, the bottle was at his lips. After three drags, he walked to his chair. "I missed you, too," he addressed the armchair fondly. "They don't make them like you down South. No, sir, not like you." And with that he settled into his private haven. The fact that his chair, like most things, had been made in China didn't seem to matter to dad.

"Darling, you must tell me all about yourself. I want to know everything. Every minute detail," his mother said as she ran upstairs to change. For the next ten minutes Alec and his dad were alone.

"So how was it really, son? Bit lonely, eh?"

"Not really, dad. Maybe in the beginning. But later..."

"Well, I know I would be. I like having you and mother around. I reckon that's why I married her. Ha, ha, and that's why we had you, eh, old man?"

Alec didn't think dad's attempt at wit required a comment.

"Tell me about the boat trip."

"Yacht. A big, beautiful yacht. A Catalina 42. That's a real ship. A sloop but with a cutter rig. She's gorgeous in the Trade Winds. Just eats up those waves. Next time I'm taking you with me. Only don't tell mother. She was a bit scared, now and again."

"Where did you get on board?" Alec liked to know the details. They invariably served as material for his future exploits. Of the Inner variety, of course.

"On Lake Worth. That's the Intracoastal Waterway between the Florida coast and Palm Beach County. We actually stayed on Singer Island, but mother wanted to go shopping on Worth Avenue—that's in Palm Beach—and that's when we met Don. The fellow is filthy rich, and lonely. A cattleman before they found oil on his property." And here, Alec's dad put on his best Texan accent. "Big daddy hand'd me down a li'l spread, 'bout tieen thousan' hieed of cattle. Was doin' all right tieell some boys found oil on mah patch. Been a poor millionaire eever since." Mr. Baldwin reverted to his Canadian accent with English overtones. "He asked us, there and then, if we would like to go for a sail with him. About ten minutes after meeting us. I think what he really wanted was to see mother in a bikini! Ha, ha... good that, eh, son?"

"And you sailed..."

"From the Lake through Freetown all the way to Nassau. That's the capital of Bahamas, I suppose, on New Providence.

Of all the seven hundred odd islands. That's Bahamas Archipelago, son."

"How fast did you go?" Alec really dug in.

"A lot faster coming back than going, I'll tell you that. The Easterlies made us do some tacking on the way out, but coming back was a dream. Just plain sailing all the way back, it was!"

This time, Mr. Alex Baldwin Sr. couldn't contain himself. He laughed with a mirth he normally exhibited only after his third beer. Perhaps he'd had a few on the flight back.

"There you are!"

Alec's mother flew down the stairs wearing a new, airy frock that served to show off her beautifully tanned arms, legs, shoulders, back and just about every other part of her body that decency allowed her to exhibit. Alicia Baldwin had married Alec's father when she was hardly nineteen.

"Did dad tell you all about our trip?"

"Sail," father corrected.

She again took Alec in her arms and smothered him with kisses. "There, that's better!" she affirmed after she'd had her fill. Alec was equally grateful for being set free. He preferred to cuddle up to his mother on the settee after dinner, in front of the TV, rather than be part of her main course.

"It was marvelous, just marvelous!" she beamed. "You simply must come with us next time, Ali, you simply must!"

No one raised any objections though Mr. Baldwin was a trifle surprised that mother was willing to expose the apple of her eye to the dangers of the cruel seas. Still, you never can tall with women, he mused, not for the first time.

"It would be nicer if you waited another month, when the school year was over," Alec observed judiciously.

"No can do, son. By then we'd be into the hurricane season. Not funny. Those gusts go up to 250 miles an hour. Or is it knots? Don't want to be caught on a ship in that sort of a breeze!"

It was nearly seven, and Alec wondered if, for the first time in eighteen days, he would be spared a TV dinner. He didn't have to wonder long.

"Darling, we already ate on the plane. Do you think you could rustle yourself something up this one last time? I promise to cook you the best dinner you've ever had tomorrow. Really." His mother beamed her promise with those perfect white teeth, looking twice as white against her bronzed skin.

"Yes, mother. No problem. No problem at all." Alec actually managed a smile.

His parents were back.

Things were back to normal.

He preferred a sandwich to a TV dinner. In fact, he made a sandwich for each of them. In truth, in spite of mother's buoyancy, they both looked tired. Half an hour later, after the sandwiches, his father was snoring gently in his private armchair. Alec and his mother went upstairs and stretched on the bed. This was his favourite way of talking to mother. Relaxed, uninhibited, away from the TV dinner or the box itself. Here, her love was almost palpable. In her every action, every move, every look. That was probably what he missed most when he was alone. Not the food, the physically being looked after, but that intangible, unspoken feeling of being loved.

He did love dad, too, of course. He was also aware of his love. But it's not the same between men. It's more a sense of friendship, of such rapport that only comrades can truly experience. And, yes, definitely of respect. He wondered if things like that would change when he grew older.

Mom and he talked well into the night. When not stimulated to make an impression, even on her own family, his mother was an easy person to talk to. They talked at random, about almost anything, interrupting each other as new ideas crossed their minds. Alec described his first stint as the master of the house. He was quite happy that nothing dreadful had happened in his parents' absence. His mother shared with him her own concerns. She said she resisted going on the yacht for a whole day, knowing that she wouldn't be able to call him.

"In the end dad and Don, that's our host, darling, gave in, and we turned back early to have supper on shore. Also a lobster. But not as good as in Nassau, later."

Alec had absolutely no interest in lobsters. He'd never eaten one. He had no idea what was all the fuss about some stupid creepy-crawly bug.

"So we'd decided to come back early and call you before we took off again, this time all the way to the Nassau. Oh, darling, how I'd wished you were there!"

This was followed by a serried of hugs and squeezes.

"I really wished you were there, Ali. If we ever get a chance, I'll fly you in, even if it is in the middle of the school year. Only don't tell daddy, he's bound to say it's too dangerous. He was a bit scared, now and again."

She left Alec sleeping on top of the sheets. Covering him with a spare blanket, she tiptoed out, switching off the light. Sailing was great, but it was good to be home. It was good to see Alec, after all this time. He seemed older than she remembered.

It had taken Alec almost two weeks to get used to being alone, but it took just one day to adjust to having his parents back. Sure there was a bit more washing-behind-everything, a bit more sitting-up-straight, and make-sure-your-bed-is-made before he came down for breakfast, but breakfast was ready when he did finally come down, and the dinner, as his mother promised, consisted of all his favourite dishes. His mother may have had an artistic temperament, but she did keep her promises; and, well, he knew that she loved him.

***

10
The Next Step

Three days passed before he really missed Sandra. He'd been so busy with school and the return of his parents. Of course, he thought about her when going to bed or when just playing on his computer; but he didn't feel that hunger for her company. However, as he'd already learned, Sandra didn't have a cell phone. Perhaps she only came when she was needed. Really needed. Like last week. Or perhaps she was holding court somewhere.

But she did come back.

She came when he least expected her. It was Saturday night. He was sitting alone, in his room, on his bed. He was tired from a hard match against Pete; it went to a tie-breaker in all three sets. Eventually Alec had won. It was, like all the others, a friendly match, but they each gave their best. Always. To do otherwise would be insulting.

Sandra came back with a song—a melody, really, that wasn't really a melody. It sounded like blades of grass rubbing against each other, like tiny bows on tiny violins, millions of them, perhaps swaying in the wind, and producing a swelling and receding harmony. Just harmony. Long, elongated chords, interlocking with each other. He didn't really *hear* the music, if music it was. He was in it. And, in a strange way, part of it.

"The music of the spheres," he heard a distant whisper. Quiet, as though not to interrupt the sweet strains.

His heart beat just a little faster. A phrase from *Twelfth Night* flowed across this mind, "If music be the food of love,

play on; Give me excess of it..." Yes, since that first time
mother had read to him, he's already tasted a little
Shakespeare from the volume his father had given him. This
is what he wanted. He wanted to be filled with this music to
excess. Completely. To be lost in this food of love. Never to
come out.

"Perhaps I do all things to excess, he mused?

For a moment he couldn't say anything. It was almost as
though he'd grown shy. Then he swallowed his pride.

"I missed you," he said, finally.

"I know."

"Then why didn't you come?"

"I never left."

So we were back to this again: "I'm always with you
only you can't see me or hear me, or be aware of me in any
other way." He cut his thought stream short when he heard
the old, familiar giggle.

"I'm sorry," she smiled.

He knew she wasn't apologizing for her absence, only
for the giggle.

"I suppose I deserve that," he acknowledged. The strange
music seemed to rise between them, smoothing over the
instantaneous anger. It swelled, then ebbed like a gentle tide
lapping on a shore. After quite a while, he emerged with a
question. "Will I ever be able to hear you all the time?"

"You would grow tired of me," she quipped.

"Seriously...?"

"Yes. I promise you, here and now, that a time will come
when you will be unable to tell the difference between you
and me."

"WHAT?"

"Shhhh..."

"Sorry, I know you can hear me. It's just, well, you and
me... You're not kidding, are you?"

"I very seldom kid. But I like listening to your jokes."

"I've never told you any."

"That's true. But I've heard them, anyway. And jokes, to me, are not just funny words. In fact, more often than not, they are expressed in actions. And you are very good at those."

Alec wasn't sure what she was talking about, but he took her words as a compliment. Perhaps he should try harder to amuse her? After all, he was still her knight.

"Oh, but you do, Alec. You really do. And you don't have to try. Just be yourself."

After a moment's silence, Sandra's tone changed. "Would you like to take the Next Step?"

He had no idea what she meant, but agreed immediately. "Yes, please..." Any step she wanted him to take, to anywhere... Any...

The next instant he was again suspended in the middle of the Universe—stars all around him. His first reaction was utter panic. The immensity of the Universe seemed much larger than on his previous visit. The Far Country became the Infinite Country. Not enormous: infinite. There was one difference, though—Sandra wasn't there. She was nowhere to be seen, or felt. He was all alone.

Alone in the whole wide Universe.

He strained his hearing to detect any echo of her presence—he grew afraid. He was as alone as anyone can be. Much, much more alone than when his parents went away. For a moment his panicking mind strayed, wondering if his parents' absence had been an exercise, a forerunner of this experience. He almost laughed at himself.

That was child's play.

In that very moment he realized that he didn't feel like a child. Like a boy. It's not that he felt old or mature, it's just that age had nothing to do with his present condition. He seemed to hover in a realm where the difference between time and non-time, whatever that was, seemed hazy. Blurred. He could never describe, for instance, how long he hovered there, a mere speck in the vastness of space.

He tried to see himself, but it was too dark. He couldn't even see his hand in front of his face. Wherever his face was. And then another wave of panic gripped him with renewed force. He lost awareness of his body. He was an observer observing only that which was outside himself. His own physical being seemed to cease to exist. Oh, he knew he was there. He knew he had arms and legs, but this knowledge was, in a way, theoretical. Not backed up by the evidence of his senses.

Like that feeling of falling just before you get to sleep. You did not feel the wind rushing past nor hear things nor feel anything solid. He would just see the land moving faster and faster, and feel with total conviction that he was falling.

He blinked several times in disbelief.

And yet he could see. He was observing it as though watching his own thoughts. As he directed his attention in any particular direction, the stars in that segment of Everywhere became clearer, brighter, perhaps nearer. And, yes, if he concentrated, they approached him as if he were looking through a powerful telescopic lens.

"Home..." his thoughts directed.

And the Home planet loomed almost instantaneously before him. There was neither time nor motion involved, no way to be sure if he had zoomed to the planet or it had zoomed to him. They were just simply closer, instantly. This was like nothing that had happened to him before. No matter, the planet was close, beautiful, familiar. Oh, how very familiar. His previous waves of panic vanished. He was Home.

"Sandra!?"

"I knew you could do it." Her happiness was palpable. He sensed it with his whole being. He was filled with it to overflowing.

"Where am I?"

"Don't you know?"

"I don't mean above my Home world." He smiled. "I mean here…" There were no words he could find to describe his present whereabouts.

"We are in the no-man's-land between the two worlds. The world of imagination and the world created by your mind." The concepts she fed him came slowly, as though giving time for them to sink in.

"Created…"

"…by your mind," she confirmed.

He was fully aware that he couldn't possibly *imagine* the Universe with its endless worlds, worlds within worlds, the zillions of stars. Was there really no end to them? Miss Brunt never talked about such places in her geography lessons.

This was bigger, vaster, more fabulous than anything he'd ever dared imagine. The Home world was where his feet were, but all around him… the enormous sun and the many planets were all mere dots in the endless ocean of forever. He lost all sensation of time, all feeling for the enormousness of space. This was also true of the world of his dreams, but not like this. Here *he* had to give it reality. It did not exist in its own right. This didn't evolve, this happened. Somehow, inexplicably, he made it happen. All around him, all of it came out of his mind. Of his will.

"It's like being Merlin! The greatest Wizard of all time!" The thought flashed through his mind.

She didn't say anything. She waited for his reactions to find their own ground. The silence was all-encompassing. Alec attempted to reconcile his sense of power with a strange feeling of being terribly little. As little as he was in that cathedral, in Paris, on the way back from the Middle East, when he was only five or six. Only much, much more so. In this vastness, the gigantic stars were little more than candles flickering on the altar of Infinity.

"I made it happen," he thought, hardly believing his own words. "It's almost like being a god," he whispered, "yet so very insignificant…"

Back in his room, spent and exhausted, Alec collapsed on his bed. The images remained vivid for hours. For a while he seemed to oscillate between the physical and the world of his mind. The factors that determined his reality were unclear. Overlapping. He felt tired, yet didn't want to let go of the freedom the black Universe had offered. Black? Black with the countless stars, suns, with the light energy pouring at him from all directions...

He'd experienced something that had nothing to do with his many travels, his many jaunts into the imaginary realities. This was as different from those exploits as the inner worlds were from the physical surroundings. They were all as real. Yet the scale, the sense of freedom, even the sense of power, were incomparable.

Just before he sank into a deep, dreamless sleep, he knew that he had taken the Next Step. To where? To when, for that matter? This he had a lifetime to discover.

Perhaps much longer.

***

Alicia had other problems than just coping with her son's vivid imagination. Now that that her ladies' painting group had grown to seven semi-professional artists, it was time to think about a joint exhibition. Alicia raised the subject once or twice before, but she didn't detect particular interest. Perhaps they didn't have enough canvases to be proud of, at least not in public.

Even as she was trying to trace the contours of the slightly overweight model with charcoal onto her paper, she mused how would her partners react if she were to present them with a *fait accompli*.

As though the matter that has been already arranged.

The seven of them were sitting in a three-quarter circle, changing places ever half-hour, to try different angles. It was amazing how different the model looked from every side; not just the contours of her body changed but the lighting made all the difference.

"Light is everything," mentioned pontifically a visiting professional artist. It just so happened that he was right.

Alicia peeked over the edge of her easel. On her own, she preferred landscapes. Here she learned to control other media. She was a quick sketcher and invariably finished before most of her colleagues. Immediately on her right was Pat. Pat was plump, nice, what is normally referred to as *still* pretty. Although only in her late fifties, the signs of a *bon vivant* were beginning to catch up with her. What she lacked in talent she made up in good disposition.

Next to her was Joan. In her early forties, Joan was the only one Alicia could count on to help her organize the show. She was tall, energetic, pretty in a vaguely inaccessible way, well spoken though not very tolerant when it came to abject stupidity. She spoke her mind out and "to hell with Burgundy", as she liked to point out when people objected to her opinions without grounding their opinions in facts. Her canvas displayed her character. Even in charcoal her lines were sharp, confident, without hesitation. She would be good at etching in metal—an unforgiving but permanent medium.

Judy? Well Judy had a chip on her narrow shoulders. She never had enough room.

"Move over a bit, Mary!"

Or… Jean, Pat, or whoever was encroaching on her real or imagined territory.

Alicia often wondered why the others tolerated her. Actually herself and Joan were the only two whom she'd never attempted to bully. It all wouldn't be so ridiculous if Judy would be a bit bigger physically. As it was, she hardly cleared five feet. To respond to her complaints one had to look downwards, and then try hard to hide a smile.

As for Jean and Mary, they displayed quite amazing lack of distinguishing characteristics, except that they both came from Westmount and thus were well bread, well behaved, and well supported by their husbands.

And then there was Zaza.

Zaza was definitely talented. She could probably break out on her own and make good money. Only, it seemed, that she didn't need it. What she needed were nudes. Lots and lots of nudes. Even when others were trying to catch the models poses in charcoal she, with but a few stokes of her beloved acrylic immortalized the various aspects of their pulchritude in vivid color.

Alicia had to admit to herself, that there had been moments when she'd suspected that Zaza might harbor latent lesbian tendencies. And then, on just one occasion, they had a male model. Alicia noticed how Zaza's breathing quickened the moment the model threw off his robe. And then there was no hiding the passion that that was visible in her eyes.

For now, Zaza remained an enigma.

***

11
The Enigma

The day after the Baldwins got back from the vacations, Alex Senior received an invitation to attend a conference in London. That's London, England. Just three days, but all expenses paid. Considering he was only a consultant, as against a partner, he felt flattered that the firm had chosen him to attend the annual meeting of The Society of Professional Engineers in UK. Although the Society was established only in 1969, it combined the engineering societies of the whole Commonwealth under a single umbrella.

It was a singular distinction to be invited.

He'd only just got back from Singer Island and now he'd be off again—the day after tomorrow.

While Alicia didn't like missing him for a few days, there was so much to catch up on. She made a whole list of her friends to whom she wanted to recount the experiences Alex and she shared in board the Catalina. And about Don, of course, with his imaginary artillery, his li'l patch, and li'l oil wells. Considering that Texas invariably laid claim to have everything bigger than anyone else on the North American continents, if not the world, she found it amazing how they liked the word li'l to describe considerable size.

"You simply wouldn't believe, daaahling! His boat, I mean ship, really a ship, with sails and motor, and cabins and a fully-fledged galley. That's kitchen, daaahling, aboard a ship. I mean a yacht, of course, but really a ship. Why, she was wider than this room, daaahling. Really, wider than this room!"

She meant that the Catalina sported a beam of almost 14 feet. She wasn't sure about the overall length, but was sure that it was a lot longer then her friend's house.

She practiced in front of a mirror for the command performances she'd perform in her husband's absence. According to her hastily put together list, she'd have to deliver this li'l speech at least seven times. She could have called all her friends together and told them the story all at once. But, surely, it wouldn't have been as much fun. Just watching their faces, one at a time, and hearing the oohs and aahs, was worth repeating the same story a dozen times, let alone seven.

But first the beauty salon. After the li'l experience with Don's thrusting hands and the consequent swim in the ocean, and the then repeated dips in the Bahamian waters, her hair needed all the love and attention they surely deserved. François would do them justice. *N'est-ce pas?*

Alicia was happy.

***

The pace for a thirteen-year-old is quite different from that of an adult. He did not have to save the world. He didn't have to decide whether or not they should increase or kill international trade with China. Or bomb some godforsaken country just because they were harbouring some terrorists. His problems were of a more practical nature. They dealt with what this or that girl said to him in school, or would she laugh at him if he asked her something. Or how to beat Pete at tennis. He also had to decide if he could grow taller faster, how to broaden his shoulders, or expand his chest, and how to solve the problems with his voice. He talked normally, and suddenly his voice would rise into a frustrated chicken's lilt, only to drop lower than before. These were serious problems for a normal thirteen-and-a-half-year-old.

The more he thought about last night's experience, the more it didn't make sense. Was he no more than an observer, or did he have something more to do with the reality he visited? The first time Sandra took him there, well, almost there, he supposed, the world was, let's face it, already there. Wherever *there* was! It could not have had anything to do with the activity of his mind. What did she mean, "world created by your mind"? That's crazy. He couldn't create a spec of dust, never mind a single world. But that? The endless Universe???

Things always happen for a purpose, he was told; he forgot by whom. His parents had gone to London. He had a lot of thinking to do. Thinking he couldn't share with anyone. Except Sandra, of course. But Sandra, well...

Sandra kept her own hours.

The day was sunny, the first sunny Sunday in a long time. A walk along the canal wouldn't do any harm. Sometimes his mind cleared when he walked. Outside, that is. Away from the traffic, or crowds, or even the sound of TV. He'd used that footpath along the canal before for that very purpose. To get away, to feel the change of pace.

He sat down on a tree stump and watched concentric circles forming on the water, caused by some gnat being scooped up by a hungry fish. The circles grew and grew, rather like the scale of his inner worlds. Why did the physical world seem to remain the same size, while what happened inside him was expanding at such an incredible rate? He did not doubt for a moment that what he'd seen or really felt last night wasn't real. He could describe every detail, recount the exact order in which events unfolded. They were real, all right. A little too real for his liking.

A little too scary.

The Universe responded, well... it responded to his every whim. It contracted and expanded at his bidding. It changed the proximity of stars and nebulas. It brought into his vicinity his Home planet. This last he couldn't think of in any other terms. He knew with utter certainty that it *was* his Home planet. Even if he didn't really know what it meant.

But if he did command the Universe, then why did he feel so very, very insignificant? So puny. Was he really that small, that inconsequential? The bug the fish swallowed had more use than he. He just moved stars around, but why? For his amusement? Out of curiosity?

What was the purpose of life, anyway? He had to go to school, pass his exams. Grow bigger, eventually meet a girl, get married, have at least two children, feed them, clothe them, educate them. Then grow old and die. And the children, in time, would do exactly the same. Isn't that what life was all about?

He refused to accept that.

Alec thought of himself as a conqueror of the unknown. He was more scared by the prospect of a dull class in school than of being on the receiving end of a herd of charging elephants. In his dreams, of course. Actually, he never had a bunch of elephants charging at him in any type of dream; but he still preferred it to the doldrums of an average life.

Every fiber in his body rebelled against being a cog in a biological wheel. There had to be more to life than being a self-reproducing biological robot.

Alec came back home no wiser than when he left. His head was much too full of possibilities for any of them to take precedence. Somehow he felt that Sandra could provide all the answers; but he was equally as sure that she wouldn't.

"You have to live your life, not just escape," she'd said.

Was living just walking in circles, he asked himself again. Just doing what his parents did, and their parents, and their parents before them?

"No!" he shouted. "No! No! NO!" he repeated, through his teeth. "If I can live so fully in the Inner worlds, why can't I do so here also?"

Columbus did not have a dull life. Nor did Marco Polo. Nor did, surely, many great artists, not if what Sandra had said was true. And Sandra never lied. Could it be possible to live a life as exciting in the... the physical world, as he experienced in his travels? As in the Far Country?

He knew instinctively that it was not. No matter what you did here and now, it could not possibly match the There and Then! Never! There simply was no comparison. Why did Sandra say that he must live his life here and now?

***

The night before leaving for London, Mr. Baldwin had decided to cough up for an extra ticket and take Mrs. Baldwin to London with him. The hotels invariably offered queen-size beds, and food would cost as much there as here.

"But, darling, there's Alec. We simply can't leave him alone. Not again."

She'd also have to postpone the stories she wanted to tell all her friends. Of course, the stories would keep and, well, she hasn't seen old London Town for ages and ages

"You want to take him with us?" He hoped she'd take it as a rhetorical question.

"He's got his school," she countered, evidently taking his offer seriously.

"Darling," he tried again. "It's only three days. It's ages since we've been to London together. Think of the shopping..."

Alicia looked in the mirror. François had done his usual excellent job. Her hair was hanging loose, straight down, straighter then before the rinse in the brine. She smiled. She was thinking about shopping on Oxford Street. From Oxford Circus all the way to Marble Arch.

"Well," she said softly, "if you think that he'd really be all right..."

***

Alec's parents came back as happy as always. There was the usual hugging, squeezing and inquiries if he was sure that he was all right. Finally they let him go. They both seemed tired. Really tired.

"We'll tell you all about it tomorrow, darling." His mother smiled sadly. "Now, I rely must get some sleep. Window-shopping is very exhausting."

For a moment young Alec wondered what was it that made his parents so tired. Sitting in First Class 747? And what was so tiring about window-shopping anyway? He'd never shopped for any windows, and if he did, he certainly wouldn't go to London to get them. He also wondered why his parents seemed so contented. His father, a structural engineer, had some interesting problems to solve, but even those problems, except for the details, seemed repetitive. His mother was content with just about everything. How lucky she was... A single look at a fresh rose sprouting in their small garden seemed to fill her with joy to last the day. Was that the secret of life? To be happy with the minute things in life? To expect nothing from life, and then rejoice in every *something* which came your way?

Somehow he felt that this wasn't for him.

He went to bed early, but his poor brain was still in turmoil.

And then there was the problem of the Home planet. He had an idea what it was; Sandra had told him that he, or *they* she'd said, had been there together over a thousand years! What on Earth did she mean by that? People didn't live that long. And if he could get bored by a single dull lesson, what in heaven's name would he do for a thousand, or for that matter, one thousand three-hundred and twenty-three years? Did children remain children there for, say, three hundred years before they grew up? Did people change jobs every hundred years or so, when they couldn't stand doing the same thing, over and over, any longer?

"Sandra!" he sighed. "Sandra," he whispered with resignation. "Please help me. I am only thirteen..."

It was too much for him.

"Please..." he repeated, as the sound of grass rubbing against other blades of grass produced a sound more caressing than a thousand violins could do with a thousand bows. The gentle sustained chord massaged him.

"Please..." he whispered again. As his eyes closed, his lips curved in a joyful smile. He was going Home.

***

12
Zooming In

"Don't you know** that you can come here whenever you want to?"

For the first time Alec did not react immediately to Sandra's evocative voice. He was still torn by turbulent thoughts, concepts playing havoc with his mind. The music helped a lot, but it took time. Even though time did not exist here—not in the 'real' sense.

"Thank you," he managed. He couldn't find words to say how glad he was that she'd heard his plea. He really was at the very end of his tether.

"Take it easy," she whispered. "There is no rush... not here."

He knew. Slowly he took in the now familiar stars, the embracing darkness, the unrestricted freedom. The velvety darkness didn't seem quite as frightening. It was more like a womb. At least he thought so. Who knows what a womb really feels like? But it offered a sense of security he had not detected before.

There seemed no "must" or "have-to" or anything here. There was nothing pressing, commanding, or requiring any effort on his part. He practically just was. Sandra was right. This could be relaxing if he could only accept this unimaginable infinity as home. Down there, on Earth, he was preoccupied with action. With *doing* things, no matter in what reality. Here... here time didn't count.

"Why am I not bored then?"

Her smile washed over his body. It was the nearest thing to a giggle that wasn't a giggle. But definitely a smile.

"You are never really bored, Alec. Occasionally, you just think you are. It is a sort of stimulus to action people use on Earth."

"But don't I have to *do* things?"

"Of course you must. But not here. Here you are learning to essentially just be."

"Be?"

"Yes, just be. To experience action, to be active, you descend to lower levels of consciousness. The lower worlds *are* the fields of action. There," she almost giggled again, "there, if you're not active, you'll die of starvation, soon enough!"

Suddenly Alec realized that, although he had eaten occasionally in his previous escapades, he'd never actually felt any hunger here. None at all. In fact, he didn't have any physical desires whatever. Strange, he thought. But then again, just about everything he was doing with Sandra was strange.

"Your body, here, is not the same body as on Earth, or in the realm of your imagination. It is always the body you occupy which is the seat of desire. It is a personal expression of the reality you select to live in. In a way, it is your reality."

Seat of desire? What was she talking about? He had no desires. He just wanted to... what did he want? In here he wanted to listen to Sandra. What he wanted was knowledge. That's right. What he really wanted was to know the thoughts...

"...the thoughts of God?" Sandra smiled again.

"What do you mean?"

"Nothing. A very wise man, on Earth, once said that. His name was Einstein. Albert Einstein. You will be studying his theories in about three years."

"You know the future?"

"It is not exactly knowing, nor exactly the future. You will learn about it when we take the next step."

"There is a Next Step?" Alec would have sat up had he been sitting. "When?"

"It may be tomorrow, it could be in a million years. Is time still so important to you?"

On this occasion it was his turn to laugh. He stopped short when he realized that her tone wasn't joking.

"I'll be very dead and eaten by many little bugs," he said wistfully. "Like the bugs by the fish in the canal..." he added pensively.

She said nothing. She knew he would work it out for himself. The more he worked out himself, the more real it would be for him. It would be his reality. In a very short time he would become the master of his own perceptions. Here, that is, he would only allow into his thought-stream ideas or concepts, stars for that matter, which he desired. And it would all be his alone. His contribution to the Whole. It would also give him confidence. Maturity. And most of all, it would prepare him for the next step.

For the next segment of eternity they just hung there, suspended in the vastness of the Womb. Alec experimented with moving stars, closer and farther away. He found he couldn't move them sideways, nor up and down. Just to and fro... And then it hit him. The stars remained where they were. It was he, or the body he now occupied, that moved farther from or closer to the stars.

"Body? What body?"

He tried to look at himself. He remembered trying to see his hand and thinking it was too dark. Well, he began to suspect he didn't know what he was looking for. Sandra did say he occupied, here, a different body. Was it really a body? He must be something. His consciousness must be somewhere. He tried looking at his hand again. Slowly, very slowly, he became aware of a blue-violet outline. Even as he looked, he was creating a hand. More and more of it was coming into focus. He tried it with his other hand. The same thing happened. As he looked closer, the outline became filled with countless moving pinpoints of light. Pinpoints with little halos around them. He looked closer still. The pinpoints became fiery miniature suns, the halos resolved into individual planets swirling around them. He was looking at the Universe concealed in one of his hands. Even as he thought of sharing his discovery with Sandra, the ethereal outline began to waver and fade. His hands and arms were dissolving before his eyes. That is, if he had any eyes.

"If I need them, I'll just make them," he thought to himself.

And his invisible, non-existent mouth formed a smile. It was as real to him as the stars all around. "How come the stars remain when I dissolve so quickly?" His ethereal lung heaved with yet another sigh. There was so much to learn. Maybe that's why one didn't have to do anything here. There was so much to think about. Yeah, so much to learn.

Sandra's voice interrupted his thoughts. "It is time we said hello to some of our friends."

"Friends? Here?"

"Not here. At Home."

For an inexplicable reason he knew exactly what Home she was talking about. The Home away from home. She intimated it was his, or their, *real* home. It must have been, if they spent so much time there.

"Lead on, my Princess. I am at your service." He waved an invisible hat sweeping an invisible floor with its feathers. He loved being a knight, even if he confused the part he played with one of the three musketeers.

The next instant they were hovering just above one of the peaks that pierced the multi-layered clouds. The tallest peak was surrounded on all sides with other crags, showing their inaccessible crowns through mysterious mists, even as their lower regions seemed lost in misty, mysterious emanations of some hidden gods. Though they were still much too high to tell, Alec could sense the pure mountain air awaiting them. The main peak, towards which their attention brought them, was more like a plateau. Looking still closer, he saw some buildings there. And people! People moving about!

"There are people moving there!" he repeated to himself.

"I know, Alec. I can hear you."

People on top of a mountain about ten times higher than Mount Everest. How could they breathe? For that matter... what am I breathing here? Yet I must be, he smiled. And he could not contain his happiness. He zoomed down to the clouds, punched a hole in their puffy whiteness with his fists, bounced, and arrived exactly back where he had started. Just for fun.

"Let's meet our friends, Sandra."

The moment they landed on the plateau, he saw her. Here, on the top of the highest mountain, she became visible. She was more beautiful than ever. Anyway, than the last time. It was good to be able to see his own body. Even better to see hers! Evidently, they were back in the world of imagination— only much, much larger than any imaginary world he'd ever visited before. It was also by far the most beautiful world he'd ever seen.

"Is it Machu Picchu?" he asked, not really expecting confirmation. None came.

As they neared the plateau, the city revealed itself in some detail. Almost immediately, Alec became aware of his lungs and took a deep breath. And then he held it. He had to. It just felt so good!

"This is my Home?" he whispered, apparently to himself.

It was not really a question. He knew the answer. He felt it. It felt right. It felt as full of memories of the past as, in a strange way, memories of the future. This is where he had learned to dream. This is where he had learned to create reality in the depth of his heart. Although his knowledge was limited only to his feelings—no details were familiar. They seemed almost fluid, as though in a constant state of flux of becoming—he knew he was home.

"Let's go down," she said softly. "Here, hold my hand."

And then Alec looked at Sandra again, and once more he caught his breath. This was definitely Sandra. But she was no longer a thirteen-year-old girl. She was tall and slim. She was a young woman. And she was still some six inches shorter than he was. I wonder how she sees me now, he mused, what I look like in this world. Life had become more beautiful than he ever dared to imagine.

***

It didn't quite work out the way Alicia had imagined. She went to see Dorice. Her host, Dorice Gladbright, had invited three other ladies whom Alicia intended to invite herself to recount the story of her sailing trip. Of her sail. Too bad, she thought. That makes it four down and three to go. Oh, well, you can't win them all.

There was one other problem.

She soon learned that two of the girls—she preferred to think of them as girls, not ladies, regardless of age—have had some experience of sailing. She'd have to get her terminology right and go easy on exaggeration. Pity. She could have made it such a nice story. With storms and giant waves, and dolphins and maybe even sea monsters. She was hoping that all the girls would have been as ignorant of the open sea as she'd been until just recently. No such luck.

"Daaahling!"

"Daaahling!"

"Daaahling!"

"Daaahling!"

She was glad that was over.

Only two of the girls had hair straightened out. Why can't they keep up with the times, she wondered. As a matter of fact the short and curly looked good on them. Surely, it couldn't be the latest fashion. Not yet. She's only just got used to the long and straight. It took her six months to grow them that long. She wished whoever was deciding on the fashions would make up their mind.

The low table was set up in front of a settee and three deep armchairs. Beautiful china set for tea and an assortment of *petit fours* and colorful *amuse-gueule* were strategically placed along its length. No one would have to reach far to nibble. Dorice had done it before.

"Do have another one, daaahling," Dorice tempted. "We'll all go to my gym together," she smiled, a twinkle in her eye. "Tomorrow."

"And then do tell us about your sail…" Another lady encouraged. Was she the expert sailor?

A slight shiver tickled Alicia's back.

She couldn't delay any longer. She was desperately trying to remember which was port and which starboard, stern and bow, and wasn't there a bowsprit? And the main and genoa, or was it gennie… and jibs, and lines, stays and shrouds, only which are which… and warps, and… and of course the halyards—what on earth did they do?

She reached for another *amuse-gueule*. Or are they *amuse-bouche*? Oh, dear. Now I'm really confused, she sighed.

And… oh, my God, there were so many words that but a such a short time ago have been completely strange to me. Now? Now they are just confusing. And wasn't there keel somewhere? I looked for it everywhere. They talked about it but I've never seen it.

Just then her cell-phone chimed. She got it out of her handbag with trembling hands.

"Oh, my goodness, really, oh no… yes, yes, of course you can. Yes, at once, of course. Don't worry. Oh my goodness. Really? Oh, dear. Yes, yes, I too am sorry. I'll be right over."

She cut the connection and got to her feet.

"I'm most terribly sorry, I must leave you. Perhaps some other time? In my place? Soon?"

They all wanted to know what happened.

"It's Alec, my son. He's been hurt. Must run. Not serious but he needs me. You understand…"

They understood. They were all mothers.

Alicia ran out to her car. She took a deep breath. It's good to be a mother, she thought. One always has an excuse.

Alec put the cell phone down, puzzled. All he wanted to know was if he could be late for supper. Just a lousy half-hour. What on earth was mother on about? And why was she so sorry, he wondered? I would come sooner if she'd insisted.

Coming right over? Coming right over where? He wasn't even home. For crying out loud, that's why he'd called mom to begin with.

***

13
Machu Picchu

Alec had only read about the Inca Empire; he'd never visited Peru. But he knew from many pictures about the mystery of Machu Picchu. He'd seen a movie about it. Seen it three times. And now, here, he was in the forbidden fortress. But it was unlike any of the photos he'd seen. It was resplendent in all its glory. Not in ruins. It was as it had been. As he'd imagined it should be. And much, much bigger. And bustling and alive but in a very different way from any city Alec had ever visited.

He looked around.

The air was so pure that he could see minute details of intricate stonework from afar. Still farther, the surrounding pinnacles sported a sharp tonsure above a white ring of puffy clouds near the top. The somber crags looked like an army of ancient sentinels guarding access to the Forbidden City.

In spite of the thousands of people all around him, he marveled at the near silence—as though no one spoke here, only whispered. No cars, no railways, no planes, no blaring radios disturbed the elusive tranquility. Only the wind sang softly an air that invaded the narrow streets, carrying the intoxicating smell of the rain forest below him.

They'd landed on a platform about three floors higher than street level. From this relatively humble elevation they could oversee practically the whole plateau. There were some taller buildings, but few and far between. He could see the streets were laid out in an orderly fashion. Narrower than on

Earth, and mostly planted with trees, bushes and an incredible kaleidoscope of flowers. People walked footpaths carved in lawns, skirting larger trees, winding up and down, interrupted by cascading steps. Little arched bridges swung over bubbling brooks; swans posed for absentee photographers.

"You sure this isn't heaven?"

"Only if I'm an angel!" she laughed. Her laughter he actually heard. Not just felt. As for her answer, he wasn't sure it satisfied him.

"Those people like walking," he observed.

Suddenly, Alec became aware that he was still holding on to Sandra's hand. Before he had the chance to blush, he smiled and relaxed his grip. He only now realized that he had been holding on to her not out of fear, but because touching her felt good... It felt natural. It was hard to tell where his hand finished and hers began. Anyway, he was perfectly safe here. He belonged in this city, in these enchanted gardens of Babylon. Only the gardens weren't hanging. They were laid out before him, begging to be entered, explored, experienced.

An enormous sun, about four times the Earth's sun's apparent diameter, hung motionless above them. Aren't we too close, he wondered. And as the thought formed in his mind, a tattered cloud separated itself from a cloud lower down and drifted up and overhead to offer partial shade. I like this place, he thought. This is much better than on Earth. Much better.

"This is where you practice your skills," Sandra remarked.

He didn't quite know what she meant, but guessed that here you had to imagine whatever you wanted to come into your life. He suspected that things didn't happen much by themselves.

"Let's go down," said Sandra, and this time she took Alec's hand and led him down the steps. Not like leading a child, but more like two friends ready to explore a new mystery together. As one.

The broad stairs led them towards two intermediate levels, each as big as a tennis court. Only instead of lines defining the rules of the game, the floor sparkled with colorful mosaics, intricate patterns leading them towards the next flight that drew them in a seemingly predetermined direction.

Alec was spellbound. "Is it always so peaceful here?" he asked.

She smiled. "Look to your right." Just on the other side of the lower platform, there was a sheer drop of what must have been... well, a bottomless pit. A ravine so deep that his eyes could not reach its bottom. It was as though he were looking towards a dark horizon, only he was looking downwards.

"Down here, there are no limits to curb your desire for adventure. Not only the sky is the limit, but so is the very opposite..."

The words didn't make sense; the view did. Alec, grateful that Sandra was still holding on to his hand, drew back from the precipice.

"It is because you are willing to face the unknown that you've earned the right to be here. Courage is practically the only qualification."

Courage or not, her hand felt good in his.

They wandered along the wide path, greeting other people strolling, seemingly aimlessly, with a courteous nod. They smiled to each other, as though meeting old acquaintances. It was not personal knowledge that made them so familiar but rather the apparent sharing of the common purpose. All people who lived in this place had earned a right to be here. They must have done something right.

These must be the ancients, he murmured. Sandra smiled her approval.

"How did I know that?" he wondered.

"How do you know anything? One feels things. It is the only way one really knows anything." She smiled her approval.

"None of the people look a thousand years old..." he commented.

"Nobody ever does. But you could if you wanted to."

"What?"

"You are what you want to be. Some people here spend a few centuries as aged, almost senile doters. Of course, they are neither old nor senile. They assume this form to learn to cope with the infirmity of old age."

"Is that why some people on Earth cope so well although they are pushing a hundred years?"

"Hundred and more. On Earth we are lumbered with the limitations of physical laws. We respond to gravity, pollution, and mostly to the food chain. Here you can become young or old at a moment's notice."

"Don't we respond to the food chain here also?"

"Here you eat if you want to. If you don't, you don't."

Sandra let go his hand and reached up on her toes. She pulled an apple from a tree and offered it to him. "You can make one yourself, if you want to, but it's more fun to pick one, don't you think?"

The moment he took the apple, he became hungry. He'd felt no pangs before. This was a strange world. You responded to the stimulus, but you could also change the stimulus at will. One could learn a great deal about oneself that way.

"Precisely," Sandra agreed.

They walked hand in hand for some time. The buildings were all of stone, or what looked like stone, mostly off-white marble, or maybe onyx. Can you imagine? Whole buildings made of onyx? The structures were all arranged so as not to block anyone's view of the surrounding gardens. The windows seemed to be just openings in walls, allowing the clean balmy air of late springtime to breathe through the rooms. It must have taken great care to arrange all this. One had to take all others into consideration when planning one's abode. He assumed, of course, that these were the private quarters of people who lived here.

"Yes and no. These are the living quarters, but they are not limited to any particular person. Any empty house is at your disposal. When you're resting, of course."

"Don't people work here?"

"You don't remember much, do you!" Her face was aglow with mirth. "You worked harder than any man I saw. For centuries at a time!"

He wanted to say "who, me?" but held his breath. Learning, learning, learning, he repeated under his breath. He believed her that the memories were stored somewhere in his mind, but he didn't really want to face a thousand years of memories. Not if they were memories of hard labour.

"Where do people work?"

"This is a large planet. If you feel constrained, there are eleven other, lesser planets, and a total of forty-seven moons. At one time or another, they've all been visited by people seeking various challenges. You'll be surprised what imagination can create. And that includes your own."

"And this?"

"This is the holiday area. Of the billions of... of people inhabiting this system, only about a hundred-thousand ever rest at the same time."

"Workaholics?"

She laughed. "You should know. But seriously. People who spend any length of time here do so because they find joy in facing ever-new challenges. The range of the challenges is only limited by your own imagination. You can develop your skills in virtually any field."

"And we use those skills on Earth? Later, I mean?"

"What you do with them is, of course, up to you. But if you so choose, then you certainly carry with you a predisposition to certain talents down there, as we call it here."

"Like Mozart for composition?"

"Exactly."

If all this was here, ready and available, then why ever leave? What was there on Earth that was more attractive for anyone to choose the nether realms? All other worlds seemed redundant.

"Would you give up the Far Country?"

"Of course not! Ah, I see what you mean. There are many ways to skin a cat."

"I've never heard it put exactly that way, but yes. There are many different ways to grow. To become whole."

They reached a house on a slight hill and Sandra pulled him towards it. Somehow it seemed slightly familiar. It had curved arches for entry and windows. He could see that some of the ceilings were also arched, as in some cloisters on Earth he'd seen photos of. The place looked charming and inviting.

"I've been here before," he affirmed. "It has three bedrooms and a studio. Two of the bedrooms are always empty. We kept them for temporary visitors from Earth. They've been used only about a dozen times in all the years I've been here."

"A few times since you left." For the first time in a long while she emitted a girlish giggle. The giggle wasn't offensive in any way. In fact, he rather liked it.

"What is it? What's so funny?"

"You were the visitor on the last three occasions." This time she laughed out loud.

He didn't argue. He decided never to argue with Sandra again. "Can I come here on my own?" he asked.

"Without me?" She was definitely coy.

"Of course not! I mean from Earth under my own... ah, steam."

"I'm afraid not. I mean, not without a compelling purpose. You are here now for only one reason. The recall of your memories is a necessary stage before the next step."

***

"You've got to teach me, Alex. Teach me now. Really. It's urgent. Very urgent." She raised her voice slightly. "Alex, are you listening to me?"

Alicia was at the end of her tether. She not only didn't tell the girls any stories about her sailing trip, the stories she'd promised, but now the expert, the EXPERT asked her to give a lecture about the Caribbean.

"Alex!"

"Yes, darling. What is it?" He sounded sleepy.

"You haven't been listening, have you?"

"You said it was urgent, didn't you?" he replied triumphantly.

She gave him a dirty look and repeated her request. Then she told him why she needed to know.

"Why don't you just tell them that it was your first sail? Wouldn't that be easier?"

"I'd already promised. And I had one more sail in the Caribbean than most if not all of them. The others sailed mostly on Lac St. Louis, some on Thousand Islands, and none down south."

Lac St. Louis was a widening of River Saint Laurent that at its widest measured some miles across. Thousand Islands started around Kingston, at the eastern end of Lake Ontario.

"You promised what... no, you didn't. Surely. You didn't tell them that you'll lecture them about sailing the open seas?"

"Betty said they want to form a sailing club and proposed me as the president."

"To sail where? And what? Did you buy a boat I don't know about?"

"No, you did."

"It's not a bad idea, but I did nothing of the sort."

"Are you calling me a liar?"

"Darling!"

"Don't darling me. You won't even buy me a li'l boat." Her lips formed a perfect pout. For a mother of a thirteen-year-old, she certainly knew how to be coy. Actually coy and sexy.

Alex sighed, than sighed again, then put the newspaper down and started laughing. "That is exactly how you looked when you wanted me to buy you that stole. Did you know it wasn't even mink?

"I am not stupid, Alex. I am your wife."

"I can't argue with that."

As a matter of fact, at the time, Alex couldn't tell the artificial fur from the real one, except by the price. And by the joy Alicia had expressed, also at the time, she couldn't have either. He let that go.

Alex has been dreaming of owning a boat for years; ever since his Solent days. They'd spent many days dodging vessels coming in and out of Gosport, the military harbor just south of Portsmouth. Solent is the strait that separates the Isle of Wight from the mainland of England. His friend's sloop was just 25 feet, but she could tack on a pinhead. They had fun pretending that the sailboat had the right of way. Not all military vessels were amused when they tacked or jibed at the very last moment.

Aaah... those were the days...

He never imagined that Alicia would be keen on sailing. Not even after the Don experience. She gave him an impression of being a landlubber. Their sail on the Catalina did nothing to change his mind.

"You'd really like a boat?" he gave her a long look.

"I don't have to sail in... Of course I'd like a boat," she caught herself in midsentence.

"Of course..." Alex agreed. "Of course."

"I only wish the water was a bit warmer here..." she almost whimpered.

Alex had to agree that she'd look good on deck of a nice li'l boat. In her bikini, of course. He saw himself standing at the wheel; his chin thrust forward, his sights on the far horizon, his head adorned by a Commodore's cap.

"My name is Baldwin. Alexander Baldwin," he almost said aloud; shades of 007?

"Of course," he nodded. "Of course."

***

The Next Step again. Somehow it sounded rather forbidding. As though to gain it he had to give something up. But what? He didn't have that much as it was. It probably had nothing to do with any possessions. Probably with some concepts he would have to give up. Sometimes concepts are the hardest things to let go of.

"Some people never do. That is why they're walking in circles," Sandra whispered.

"Can't they free themselves even here?"

"Not all people come here. And if they do, they often just dream. It is the only way they can absorb new concepts."

"Just dream... Isn't that what I seem to be doing on Earth?"

"On Earth you are making up for the two children your mother miscarried since she gave you your earthly body. Mozart had achieved more, but Leonardo da Vinci and Winston Churchill had problems with reading at your age. Louis Pasteur and George Washington couldn't spell. You're not doing too badly."

"Then why do I feel so stupid?"

"That's one of the things you must overcome." Her tone was serious. "There is a great difference between humility and pig-headedness. You were never stupid, but you tend to be overwhelmed by the enormity of knowledge still facing you. That's a very different story." Then she looked into his eyes. "By the way, stupid means slow, and you are one of the fastest-growing boys I know. Even if you are just six feet tall."

Alec still looked uncertain.

"One man once said 'I know that I know nothing', Sandra added. "He was one of the wisest men on Earth. His name was Socrates."

Alec looked down. The ground was a lot farther away than it should have been. Six feet tall indeed.

Alec looked out through the window. Nothing appeared to have changed outside. As though time forgot to advance. Even the sun seemed to remain stationary overhead.

"How does time work here?" he asked.

"By Earth standards it is about ten times slower. But you can fill it with ten times as many things or activities."

He thought he knew what she meant. They must have been here for minutes, Earth time. It felt like hours. He supposed that in the Far Country time stopped almost completely. It felt like it. If he, there, could cover light-years in seconds, time must be obeying very different rules.

In spite of the stillness of time, he felt just a little tired; perhaps drowsy is a better word. Too many impressions all at once. He was grateful, but he needed time to make them all his own. He knew that, back on Earth, he was still a child. And as a child he had to contain the Universe that seemed really without end. A tall order.

A tall order for a boy who, down there, was a thirteen-and-a-half-year-old. Better than some, but not as good as Mozart, who at half his age, composed a symphony.

***

14
More Questions

M
other was looking down at him as he opened his eyes. "You've overslept, darling. Are you all right?"

For a moment he was confused. Then the memories hit him all at once. Not one after another, but like hearing all the notes of a symphony at once. He reeled and fell back onto his pillow.

He lay back and closed his eyes. Just for a moment. A minute or two...

And he felt a strange, smiling presence within his heart. He thought he knew who it was. What am I doing in my bed, he wondered. And that feeling of a Presence that was... that was mother. Only, surely, she'd only just come in. So what am I doing here?

He'd half-expected to wake up and find himself on a heavenly plateau, his hand linked with Sandra's, his eyes filled with sights he could hardly imagine. But here he was. He remained supine, in his bed, vaguely aware of his mother sitting on the edge, gently stroking his head. Then he gave in—he had no choice. He was back at home away from Home.

"I'm all right, Mother. I'm just fine." He never called mom, 'mother.' Something had happened. Luckily she didn't notice. "I'm OK, Mom, really."

Then she relaxed.

"You better just brush your teeth and wash your face and run downstairs. You're starting your exams today."

Exams! Cripes! He never, never forgot about his exams. In a single leap he was out of bed and into the bathroom. Mom will make my bed later. She always did on special occasions. And exams qualified.

The next three days he wrote the exams.

The three days passed like a whirlwind. From school he ran home, picked up the textbooks dealing with the next day's subjects, and ran through them in his own inimitable way. He read up on a subject and then he imagined the substance of the story. This worked fine on everything except math. With numbers he couldn't do that, but he didn't have to. Numbers were what he called 'pure logic'. They always added up, he had once quipped to the substitute teacher when Mr. Barrow, the math teacher, had a cold. The snubby sub thought he was, or perhaps wasn't, being funny. Well, he was right, one way or another. But Alec's humor wasn't appreciated. He was called to the blackboard and grilled for ten minutes. Finally the sub gave up. He couldn't catch Alec on any sums he was given. After that, Alec was known as Einstein, for a while; and that was before he found out who Einstein was.

Somehow none of the exams seemed difficult. He managed to finish each one ahead of the allotted time. Except for history, but that was only because he wrote too much. He had visited early settlers on two of his imaginary jaunts and knew a little more than was in the history book. But it didn't matter; he did answer all the questions, even if his writing suffered a little in legibility.

Then the exams were over.

On Saturday he played tennis with Pete. Each of them had done well in the exams and the match was more of a celebration of the end of the year than a life-and-death struggle. They both scored some marvelous points; both also put easy volleys into the net. They played just for fun. In fact, halfway through the 'match' they stopped keeping score.

The next day it was raining. Alec hated when it rained in summer, particularly once the holidays had started. The elements had the whole of spring and autumn for raining. To rain in summer was a personal insult to all the boys and girls who were finally free to play outside.

But, as he already knew, there was a reason for everything, at least in his own life. Even if it wasn't immediately visible.

Dad continued working; mother was busy with her painting club. There were four moms who rented a studio and hired a model they all painted. Or tried to paint—on canvas, not the model herself. Mother's attempts weren't funny—or, in a way, they were. Alec never looked too closely, because the lady they all painted was quite naked. I mean really nude—nothing on at all!   Mother told him once that gentlemen turn their heads when a lady is undressed. That included nude, he supposed. He always wondered how they could find out she was completely nude if they turned around. On the other hand, if they had already found out, why bother turning away? Surely it was already too late. Anyway, he always turned his head when mother was showing her paintings to dad. Dad didn't mind, it seemed. Women, and girls, were seldom logical. And this realization brought him, for the first time in a week, to Sandra.

Sandra was an exception.

There were questions. A number of them.

Why was he taken to the Home planet to start with? If Step Two was the Far Country, then where was the Home world? And if he'd already lived there for over a thousand years, what was the point of going there again? Not that he minded. He didn't mind going anywhere with Sandra. Anywhere at all. But why to a place he'd already been?

She'd said that the Home planet was a place where people practice their skills. Before coming down to Earth? Did they do this sort of thing on and on? What was really the point of it all? Now that he thought about it, what was the

point of life? There must have been a point because
everything happened on purpose, but what was the point? He
must ask her. Would she tell him, or was he supposed to find
out by himself? He'd seen a book on mom's shelves called
Wisdom of the West. It was by some guy named Bertrand
Russell. Actually, it must have been dad's book, because Mr.
Russell sounded English. Alec once looked at the pictures in
that book but never read any of it. It was about people who
were professional thinkers. Philosophers. That's all they did.
Just sat and thought. No action, no fun. Alec still preferred
action. He only thought to understand things. Maybe that's
why the other guys also thought. But not all the time, surely!
If he ever tried thinking for too long, he got a heavy head and
the vein in his forehead began pulsating. A bit more and he
would get a headache. Mom got headaches quite regularly
and took an array of pills for them. Maybe all she had to do
was to stop thinking and the headaches would go away.

Now imagining things was quite different. You didn't
think about things, you saw them. It was more like listening
than thinking. You thought about something and then you
listened and watched what developed. He'd learned that when
he was little. Much smaller than he was now. Oh, boy, was he
ever small!

But somehow the thinking and listening and seeing had
got all mixed up since he met Sandra. Sometimes you had to
do all three at once. It was all right for a while; but if he tried
it for any length of time, then he got tired. Maybe that is why
Sandra told him not to dream too much. To get on with his
life. Well, he was getting on very nicely, thank you, but this
was a rainy day. What is there to get on with when it rains?
He could read, of course, and there was TV and the Internet,
but he was on vacation. You do that stuff during the school
year.

But there were still those questions.

He felt that he ought to find out as many answers on his
own as he could. So, why did Sandra show him the Home

planet? Obviously he had to learn something before taking the Next Step. Whatever that was. And trusting Sandra, it would be as incredible as the First. Not counting the Home world.

Is this what growing up feels like? Being responsible for my own learning, for my own understanding? Maybe even my life. Not the food and roof-over-my-head aspect, but life in general. He was discovering that he had to take responsibility for his actions. Even thoughts. It was no good blaming others, as some parents did for their children failing their exams. Some boys were busy in the class hiding their chewing gum rather than listening. And Miss Brunt knew quite a lot, for a woman. So did Mr. Barrow and Miss Collins, of course. All the teachers knew a lot. Actually Sandra knew even more; and she, too, was a woman—on the Home planet, that is. As a matter of fact, he'd never met any man who knew more than Miss Brunt or Sandra. Not nearly as much. Maybe women, and even some girls, weren't dumb at all. Maybe they, the boys, were just jealous.

He made a mental note to discuss this issue with dad. Or better still, with Pete. Pete had a girlfriend he saw twice a week, as regularly as tennis. Only Alec never went to see her with him. She was Pete's private date. Alec had no idea what they did when they were together. No idea at all. Alec wouldn't know what to do with a girl for such a long time. Except for Sandra, of course. But Sandra was different.

***

Four moms getting together to paint was fun, but not as easy as it sounded. Not from the artistic point of view. Alicia, who until then painted only landscapes, and those limited mostly to her own garden supplemented by dozens of photographs, wasn't quite ready to face a naked body. Other than her husband's, of course.

Also, painting models with water paint got them all wet. What she meant was that with watercolor you have to blend paint in its wet state, or wait for the paint to dry. The effects of the two methods are quite different. And the models wouldn't wait.

She was thinking, quite seriously, of drugging the model with some sleeping tablets, to make her keep still for a longer time, but she wasn't sure if it were legal. Nor was she sure that the other moms, who ventured into the experiment with oil and even acrylic paint, did not seem to have the same problems.

Zaza was the worst. She could produce a painting in half-an-hour, and have people admire it. Actually she could also do very accurate figure drawings. Almost porno, but not quite. Her drawings were just too good. Much too good. She was that talented. No one ever called any of the Old Masters porno, did they?

And what, she mused, if the Alex were to agree to act as her model? Wouldn't that be fun? Alex stripping? Junior or Senior? Both? How about some other husbands? The next thing she began visualizing an Roman orgy.

"Down, girl, DOWN," she scolded herself. "You're not that frustrated."

In fact, physically, she was not frustrated at all. Artistically—perhaps…

And then it hit her.

What if she painted the last judgment? Michelangelo's done it? And Bosch in his Triptych? Or even Kandinsky's….

No. Kandinsky was more Zaza's style. Alicia preferred her people to look like people, not like something regurgitated by her cat. I don't have a cat but I could always get one, for Kandinsky… her mind was in a whirlwind.

"I wonder is he had a cat?"

Yes, Michelangelo was the best. Only she, Alicia Baldwin would introduce a twist. All people taking part in the Last Judgment would be innocent.

Innocent of any crime whatsoever!

It would be an explosion of joy unmatched in human history. Every single one of them, every human figure would be destined for heaven. Every single one of them...

Her eyes became dreamy.

"I would add each new model to the composition, and add an new one each week. Perhaps other moms would help me? They, too, would become immortal. Like Mrs. Michelangelo, or Mrs. Bosch, or even Zaza Kandinsky ..."

Then she smiled to herself. She long suspected that Mr. Michelangelo might have preferred men's company...

And then she grew pensive again.

Only where, she mused, where would I find a wall big enough. A wall stretching from earth all the way up to heaven?

***

So what is life? Does life have any purpose? Alec didn't really think so. Life was life. It was to be lived for its own sake. It was to be enjoyed to the fullest. Not at somebody's expense, of course, but, other than that, all the way. He certainly enjoyed his life. As best as he could judge, so did mom. Dad had some problems he tried to avoid, but most of the time he was in a good mood. Especially after a couple of beers, or a Scotch or two. Not that dad drank too much. Never. He couldn't. When he had what mom called one-too-many, he simply fell asleep. One-too-many for dad was a lot less than for most men. Alec thought that was because dad worked a lot. He was really tired when he got home. He put in a couple of twelve-hour days every week. On those days he just collapsed into his favourite chair even before supper. He would take a twenty-minute snooze and, more often than not, would be as good as new. Alec wondered why dad had to work so hard.

So life had no purpose other than to live it to the fullest.

That's more or less what Sandra had said. Live and let live. This involved tolerance of others. Helping them, he supposed. Some people said you should love one another. Alec thought that was going too far. He loved mom and dad, of course, but everyone? He certainly liked Pete, even Pete's parents, sort of, but... well, there were quite a few boys in the school he wouldn't waste his time on.

Of course, there was Sandra. How did he feel about Sandra? She was so much a part of himself he felt as though... he felt as though they really were two peas in a single pod. In the Far Country he could hardly tell her apart from himself. He heard her voice, but it was really like hearing himself talking, only with a girl's voice. Except it wasn't a voice at all. More like a feeling. Like ideas forming in his mind. Like understanding what music was saying. Funny, that.

So what was he supposed to learn before taking the Next Step? He remembered quite vividly the incredible endless precipice he'd leaned over on the way down from the platform on which they'd landed. Like a horizon, he'd thought, only downwards. Now that *was* scary. How low could one fall? But if there was no bottom to smash against, what was down there?

He was falling, seemingly falling for ages. The walls, solid up above, became diffused with grayish light. They looked soft, pliable, although he did not touch them. How long would the fall take?

The air was getting thicker. At the same time, the walls of the precipice receded, or became transparent, and he could see vast areas of quite primitive terrain. There were small but cruel mountains, their crests as sharp as needles. Between them he saw what looked like craters which became more common as he fell down. He felt he was receding not so much into a depth but in time. He was descending into its ancient history.

The rate of his descent seemed to slow. The landscape became more clearly defined, more colour-filled his field of vision. He became aware of heat penetrating through the now almost non-existent walls of the ravine. Then a roar filled his ears. He saw a volcano vomiting masses of ash and rock into the orange sky. That's right. Down there, or here, possibly as deep as any man has ever been, there was a sky. A curious sky. The clouds were dense, oppressive in their apparent thickness. They reflected the heat right back into the soil that continued to throw up whatever it didn't want. The surface of a lake nearby seemed to boil.

"How can anything survive in this land?" he wondered. "And what am I doing here?"

And then he stopped moving, although he didn't feel any ground below him. He felt suspended about six feet above the ground, a ground he wouldn't want to step on.

"What in the world am I doing here?" he asked again. "And where are my legs, and arms, and body?" His eyes traced the space where his body should have been. "Where am I, where is me???"

Something moved and caught his eye. He looked and was more confused than ever. A monster about ten times the size of an elephant was approaching him with slow, measured steps. The beast seemed quite unaware of his presence. It moved heavily, each foot covering no less than some five or six feet of the ground. The biggest feet he'd ever seen. Out of its jaw, which spanned from shoulder to shoulder, writhed snakes. Snakes with white balls on the end that looked like eyes. Some other snakes didn't have eyes but flat widening funnels at the end. As the monster lumbered forward, a sharp crevice opened between its front and rear paws. The beast's left rear paw spanned the two edges of the crack. It just walked on as though nothing had happened.

Alec, assuming he was still Alec, bodiless, didn't want to find out anymore and moved his attention towards some nearby hills. In less than a second he was hovering over slightly less coarse terrain. The elephant beast was far, far behind him. Here, there was some rudimentary ground cover that gave an impression of a grazing area. True enough, in a wide valley that opened beyond the first row of undulating hills, he saw a herd of very strange-looking animals. They looked like a grotesque assembly of parts collected from various animals now living on Earth, with a dozen or so quite absurd features that no self-respecting animal on any planet would want to be connected to. The eyes, for instance, stood out on long stalks, which waved to and fro, while even longer snouts ending with a broad mouth-like aperture munched the green-brown fodder that the ground offered. They looked like animals put together by some mad scientist who was experimenting. The herd ignored Alec's presence. Which made sense, because if Alec couldn't see himself, why would anything else be able to see him?

Alec moved his awareness right into the middle of the herd of grazing beasts. He was right. Not one of them moved their snouts or legs, and the eyes on their absurd stalks continued to wave, to and fro, as though nothing had happened.

He evidently was witnessing the archaic formation of the planet. He could accept that evolution had a way to go before she would arrange the diverse body parts into some semblance of order.

One could make horses, and zebras and anteaters, and platypuses and just about any animal on Earth from these prototypes. He wondered just how far back he'd moved.

The next moment he was back in his own room, a peculiar smell of saltpeter wafting from his body. He got up and ran outside. He didn't care about the rain. He was awfully glad to be home. His ordinary, earthly, real, solid home.

***

15
The Enigma Gets Worse

T hey left early. Alex Sr. drove their jalopy along the Lachine Canal, all the way to the St-Laurence Sailing Club. There was a time when a sports car, an open two-seater, was all he'd ever want to drive. Vroom, vroom, and all that. Those were the old days. Now the car could be old as long as it was comfortable. And open cars were not built for Canadian climate. No, sir, not for our winters. Unless you had two cars, of course, but even so getting down to sit practically on the floor was not something Alex would look forward to. Not anymore. Not since he became Alex Senior.

As they reached their destination, a big sign greeted them.

Yacht-Club Royal Saint-Laurent
The Royal St-Lawrence Yacht Club

This was Québec. Bilingual. If the opposition had their way, it would be unilingual—French only. For now it was French first and in bigger letters. *Comme il faut.* After all, the Québécois and Québécoises were in the majority. The minority were Canadians. As were some of the others, but they didn't brag about it.

Alex smiled. He remembered when only English had been spoken at the club. Then came French. Then French on the top of the sign, the letter of equal size. *L'Office québécois*

de la langue française, better known as the Language Police,
forced the club to enlarge the French letters, "or else". They
were not very nice people.

Alex had made arrangements with the Commodore of the
club to spend some time with Alice on the Commodore's
O'Day. A sloop, all of 32 feet OAL. That's overall length.
Actually the specs called for 32'2", with a 10'8" beam, not
much Alex thought, but with a draft of only 4'2", which was
as deep you wanted to be on a lake the size of St-Louis, or the
adjacent Lake of Two Mountains. Of course, a good Yanmar
engine didn't hurt either. Just in case. Real yachtsmen hated
using engines other then to get in and out of their berth.

They were here for Alicia's first lesson. She carried a list
of questions and a notebook. Alex would point things out to
her as she went through the list.

"Once you'll see it, you'll never forget it," Alex assured
his wife.

"You wanna bet?" she murmured, looking the other way.

The Commodore hasn't arrived yet. They strolled the
finger docks, looked at different yachts. Alicia was learning
even as they walked. Sometimes they'd look farther out.

"That's a spinnaker, out there on the horizon," he'd point
out.

"That balloon?"

"Spinnaker, darling, spinnaker."

She nodded. She knew a balloon when she saw one,
whatever they called it.

"Why are they scrubbing her bottom?" she asked. She'd
already learned to refer to a boat as 'she'. Alex had insisted
on that.

"That's hull, darling. The hull. To remove the barnacles.
They must have sailed in salt water, and the barnacles are
sucky things. They don't drop off in sweet water. So they
have to take the boat out on the hard, or dive to remove
them."

Recently barnacles had also been found in fresh water, probably brought in by touring yachts. But, there was no need to confuse her, he thought.

"On the hard what, ice?"

"No dear. On the hard means ashore. Out of the water."

"Why would they want to take the boat out of the water…?" she was thinking aloud.

Alex sighed. He's done a lot of sighing since Alicia decided to take up sailing. Even in theory.

"Oh, I see, you mean to clean her bottom?"

Alicia was leaning forward, bending slightly over when she'd asked that.

"Yes, dear. Her lovely curved bottom."

"The hull?"

He was beginning to like bottom better. It sounded sexy coming from her mouth.

Commodore Joshua Thémens, arrived at the stroke of noon. He caught up with them on the finger dock of his yacht, where they'd agreed to meet.

"Ah, so you've found her, I see."

The men shook hands with Alicia getting a kiss on both cheeks.

"You're just in time," he added, taking Alicia by the arm and leading her towards the clubhouse. "They serve the best Martinis in Town, my dear. Absolutely the best, *n'est-ce pas*?

The Commodore was of English mother and French father, and was perfectly bilingual; ideal for the job of the Commodore. That way he didn't offend anybody. Or both, as the case might be. He probably wouldn't anyway. He oozed French charm of Maurice Chevalier.

After the third four-ounce Martini he called for menus. "Better have a snack before we cast off," he mused, his word on the verge of becoming slurred.

"The wine list, *garçon*," he added when the menus were brought.

Alex was beginning to wonder about sailing after three four-ounce Martinis followed by wine. Still, the Commodore was the boss.

"Please, call me Josh," the Commodore asked, trying to cajole the last drop of his third Martini. Joshua was a true old salt.

He was also a very good-looking man. Tall, dark, with just a smattering of grey adding distinction to his noble profile. He also looked good in a Commodore uniform. Well, a club jacket and white trousers, anyway.

Alicia was beginning to enjoy sailing. She was beginning to enjoy sailing a lot. She quite liked the Commodore, also.

***

So what is the purpose of life? Surely, not to fall into the abyss of time. For that is what his experience yesterday must have been. And Alec hadn't gone there on purpose. He hadn't created the experience with his imagination. Nor had he asked to be detached from his body and hung over a herd of wild misbegotten monsters.

The next moment he felt ashamed at his cruelty. Poor monsters, he thought. I wonder how long it took the mad scientist to make head and tail of them. Then he laughed under his breath. Making out head or tail of those beasts wasn't as easy as you might think. It's as though the scientist couldn't make up his mind which end was which. Nor could Alex.

Who designed those animals? Were animals designed? They couldn't just happen. Nothing just happened… a purpose to all things, and all that. But surely, anyone with any brains at all could do better. Unless… unless they'd never seen a grazing animal. Unless there really was no model on which to base your design. And that huge moving mountain of flesh, that elephant thing. Why so huge? Was it necessary for their survival? What did they eat, anyway? Alex hoped it wasn't the double-ended cattle, or whatever they were.

What a strange world he'd visited.

Why wasn't he more scared? Was it the absence of a body? His own body. Is it your body that makes you scared? Perhaps when you don't have a body, you don't have anything to be afraid for. That sounded right. No body, no pain. He supposed—no death. So life had nothing to do with body?

That didn't make sense, either. There must have been something which held his consciousness. It may have been invisible, but it must have been there. Otherwise he would be, sort of, spread all over the place. And his attention was definitely focused from definite coordinates. Coordinates. That sounded right. That was a word dad had used when talking about their sailing trips. In the vastness of the ocean, the coordinates defined where you were. So it must be with consciousness. Your body, or something like a body, defined your coordinates in relation to the world. Maybe to the Universe.

Whatever life was, it was fascinating!

Vacuum cleaners! That's what they were.

The great, big, monstrous behemoths with six-foot feet and jaws to match were the vacuum cleaners. That's what must be happening. The herd kept the bushy grass from running away with itself. And the big monsters must eat the excess of the herd animals. When oversized, the monsters would fall into the ever-forming crevices. They would burn up and be thrown up as fertilizing ash. That was the food chain. There must have been thousands of other biological experiments, but this trio was meant to show him the cycle of nature. No animosity, no hatred, just a cycle to keep things clean. Vacuum cleaners.

But how can animals kill each other without anger, without ill will? Obviously without remorse. Why were humans not allowed to kill, while other animals could? Unless they encroached on human interests, of course. Then they were exterminated. Usually also without remorse. Some people actually liked killing. They derived pleasure from it. Alec could not quite understand it. He would fight for his life if attacked, kill if that's what it took, but to derive pleasure from it? That would be sinking lower than the behemoth in the abyss of the Home planet. At least they were just doing their job. Mind you, they were probably too dumb to enjoy or not enjoy anything at all.

Animals must be programmed; they must carry some software, like his computer, which made them behave in a certain way. Yet if humans were also animals, then in what way did their program differ from other species? Did it differ?

Were we any different from other animals?

So the world was designed to keep itself clean. Was this the purpose of life? A sort of glorified hygiene? 'Thou shalt keep the Earth clean and tidy' principle? That didn't sound right. But if humans could detach themselves, or be detached from their bodies as he had done, then what was the purpose of our bodies? But he'd established that already. To determine coordinates. But why should that be so important? Perhaps having one's consciousness spread evenly over the whole Universe was just as good...

In fact, isn't this what God does? Be everywhere, at all times, forever? Just be?

But what if He wanted to have a *particular* experience. He couldn't do it without a body to give him coordinates in relation to the rest of the Universe. He would have to *assume* a body that was apart from other bodies. Then the experience would not be universal, only particular.

Maybe being God wasn't so much fun, after all. To be spread all over the place without identifying with anything in particular would be no fun at all. Unless it had something to do with the pods. Unless he and Sandra were in one pod, and Sandra and other Princes and Princesses were in another, and the Kings and Queens... Unless God got His experiences through all these coordinates, the world over. And he, Alec, and mom and dad, and all the people gave God those particular experiences and a free ride in the process.

Is that what life was all about? Providing an abundance of experiences for God?

***

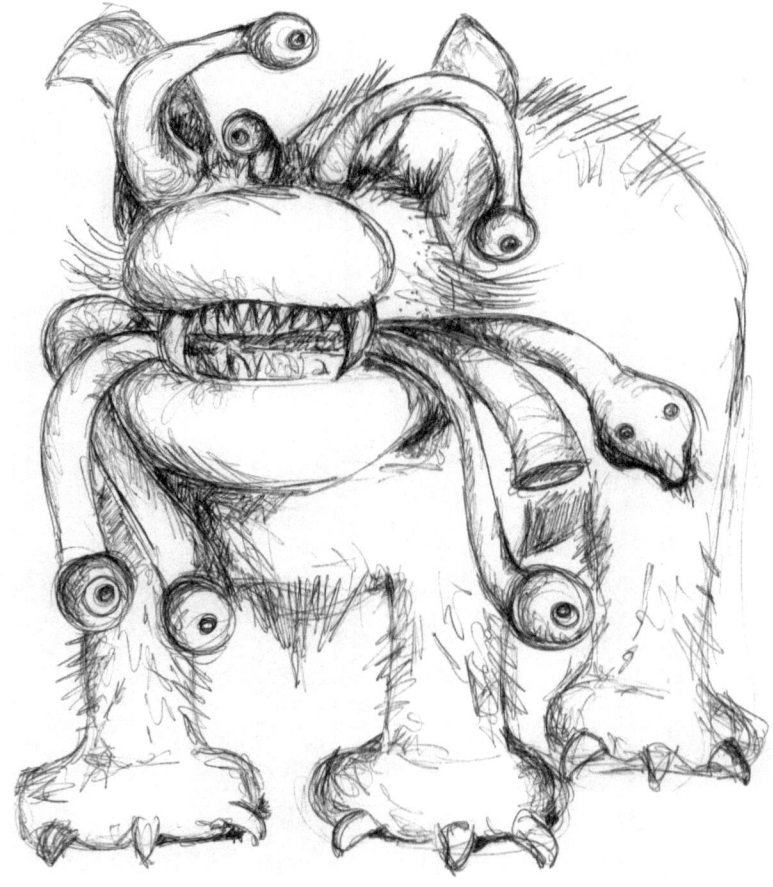

16
The Abyss Revisited

It was raining again. Sunday tennis was again washed out; mom and dad went to the cinema to see a film that Alec was told was a real tearjerker. Alec didn't like tearjerkers. Not because he didn't like romantic stories, but because he was too embarrassed to be seen crying. His mom loved them. Even in front of the TV, on a good day, she could go through a box of tissues.

Well, almost a box. That, and both sleeves.

When Alec felt tears welling up, he always found a pretext to go to the bathroom, or remembered something he had to do. Some people just didn't understand that boys, or men for that matter, don't cry. Not in public, anyway. Not even in front of mom and dad.

Only once he couldn't hold back his tears when he thought that he'd never see Sandra again. It was late last week. It was the first time they were together on the Home planet when this wondrous world was asleep under a cloak of darkness. The sky was, well, you know, it was out of this world. The stars were all different colors, some steady as cold diamonds, others winking at him, as though sharing in some secret joke. They were strolling arm in arm—there was no one else around—just enjoying the night air filled with the scent of tropical flowers. Sandra looked particularly beautiful that night.

"You must learn to do this on your own, Alec," she said, her eyes shining with an unusual light.

For a moment he was sure that this was Sandra's way of saying a final goodbye. It was then that he couldn't hold back his tears. She pretended not to notice and said immediately that she meant that he'd have to learn to light all the stars and fill the night with the aroma of flowers. By the time he realized what she meant, it was too late. Two great, painful tears were rolling down his cheeks. By then, also, he was so happy that he didn't even bother to wipe them off.

But that was all behind him. She would never, never see his tears again. Never.

Anyway, now with summer vacation coming up, there were so many things he *had* to do. There was not just tennis, but swimming, trips to museums, galleries, fishing, hiking, planning for the big sailing vacation... and all sorts of other things.

Home alone, he was looking for one of those things to do.

When he became aware of what was happening, he was already in a free-fall into the bottomless pit. That's what he called the Home planet canyon. Or whatever it was. One minute he was sitting in dad's favorite armchair, his eyes wide open; the next he was in free-fall. Yes, it was scary. Even the second time around.

Strolling the gardens with Sandra, he'd learned that on the Home planet one could visit any period in history: human, pre-human or, and this he didn't quite believe, *post*-human history. Not that he'd lost his trust in Sandra, but the Home planet was a training college relying on imagination, and he couldn't quite imagine going forward in time. After all, the canyon went in one direction only. It descended forever... And above was the Far Country. At least, that's what he knew so far. So how could one go forward in time?

By the time he realized what was happening to him, he was already slowing down. The landscape was even more forbidding than on the previous occasion a week before. As far as he could see, volcanic cones of all sizes were separated only by green slime. The disgusting soup was bubbling with the most foul stench of any witch's cauldron he could imagine. He didn't relish going out into this environment. Not for all the tea in...

The next instant he was suspended no more than a foot above the bursting boils. Here the smell was even more overpowering. He knew that if he had had a stomach, he would have thrown up.

"What on earth's happening to me? I'm in hell!" he screamed.

Alec mastered all his will and, to his utter surprise, he found himself about ten feet higher up. Not that the air here was any better, but the sight was just a bit less revolting. There was a slight detachment from the reality below. He recovered somewhat from his attack of panic. If he were to be sentenced to hell, Sandra would have told him. Nevertheless, if there really was a hell, then they wouldn't have to look any further. This would do just fine.

What in heaven's name am I doing here, he asked himself. Another lesson?

Of what?

And how come I can smell this green vomit if I don't have a nose?

A larger bubble, almost directly below him, expanded suddenly and exploded, spewing its slime almost as high as he was. This time it was a lot easier. He raised himself another ten feet or so. "You have to learn the laws of each reality," Sandra had said. He hardly thought this reality had many laws. He couldn't stop wondering what he was doing here. What can one learn, hovering over a field of green slime with volcanoes regurgitating their supper all around him?

A question zipped across his mind: was this the beginning of life?

Something inside him nodded. Of biological life, he corrected himself. Life itself had little to do with it. This was the original laboratory in which the self-reproducing unit of biological life started. The gene, the self-reproducing gene.

How do I know that? What is a gene, anyway?

And then he remembered something else Sandra had said. It hadn't made any sense at the time, but now it seemed to. "In the Abyss, you can travel in both directions." Apparently he just had. Simultaneously. He'd fallen down the same crevice, but somehow he'd ended up further back in the planet's history. And at the same time, he'd recalled all the details of a lecture about genes he was going to hear when he was eighteen. Both backwards and forwards in time, in the same instant. And the memory of the future lecture was perfectly clear. The only purpose of a gene is to procreate itself. It is the essence of biological life. It is the original building block. The purpose of any advanced biological form is to make the gene mobile and thus further assure its survival.

Pretty selfish, Alec thought. But again, isn't all biological life pretty selfish? He heard about it in school.

And then another enigma presented itself. If this is the beginning of life, that means that man hasn't evolved yet. Then, once again, what am I doing here???

In fact... Who am I?

"Who am I?" his awareness repeated. I have no body, none that I can see or sense, yet I can see and sense all that's around me. I hear the bubbling slime, I smell the stench, I am aware of the heat rising from below...

Who am I?

Something exploded. Again.

This time the noise was so ear-splitting that he was glad that he had no ears. A sonic boom mixed with a swoosh, a splash, and a reverberation that sent tsunamis in all directions. A large chunk of the nearest cone was splattered all over the vicinity. This same instant Alec realized that he was observing all this from a mile up. He must have reacted to the cataclysm the instant it happened. What had just happened? An eruption? A meteor, maybe? He looked up. The clouds were closing quickly, filling in the hole that had just been ripped through them. From the ground a plume of liquid fire shot up into the air. Probably tens of kilometers high. A beautiful and dangerous sight. At least I'm far enough away. I don't think I would survive that, he thought. Come to think of it, am I even breathing? He could smell and even at this height the smell didn't resemble any air he had ever breathed, even when he had lungs.

Can life be born in such surroundings? Life as we know it on Earth today? Can this be our biological kindergarten? The beauty of flowers, the softness of a kitten's fur... the clear blue of the summer's sky... It all comes from this slimy hell?

How can green slime be the progenitor of a human being? Of our intelligence?

None of this made sense.

He'd been brought here by whatever forces transformed this witches' brew into the world above. He obviously had some connection with both. The selfish gene and the bodiless awareness. But what was the connection? Was he, like all people, the missing link? Are we the pinnacle of evolution so far? The best? Or are people just a link that joins the animate with the inanimate? But stones and rocks and all minerals were inanimate.

It had to be something else.

This was the Next Step. He knew it instinctively. The answer lay right here before him, if he could only see it. For a moment he felt like trying to move himself forward in time. Surely, by then he would have found the answers to these questions. On the other hand, if he knew the answers, then he wouldn't be here looking for them. No. It all had to do with the Next Step. And only Sandra knew about that. And Sandra was nowhere to be seen.

***

The next step for Alicia was to take the boat solo. It was still chilly but warm enough for a quick sail. Alex Senior thought

it was like with flying. Sooner or later you had to prove to
yourself that you could do it. No matter what. Alex knew that
if he suggested to his wife a solo sail she'd never do it. He
had to devise a way to make her take the helm into her own
hands, so to speak.

But it was not to be.

He had it all figured out how he'd pretend to twist his
ankle and thus have to stay below, while Alicia would be
forced to cope as best she could on her own. He was ready to
suggest the trip to Lake St-Louis where he could easily rent a
boat for a few hours, when he'd learned that he had to take
another commission, this time in Saskatchewan, in central
Canada. Apparently, they faced annual flooding. They wanted
him to consult on permanent measures to alleviate the
problem. He left early in the morning, for what looked like
two or three days. It turned out to be almost a whole week.

Alicia didn't seem to mind. She and her group of artists
had hired another model to pose for them. She was wondering
what it would be like to strip naked in front of other people.
She went upstairs and stood in front of a mirror. For a while
she contemplated the dilemma and then, slowly, not taking
her eyes from the mirror, she began to take of her clothes.

She got as far as her slip when music reached her from
Alec's room. It was the latest bestseller tune that only the
youngest generations could dance to. Their dancing consisted
of twists and hops and jerks such as no sane person could
possibly call dancing. She thought they called it break dance.
She was sure that sooner or later she'd break a dozen bones if
she'd ever tried it.

Yet the music, if one could call it music, persisted with
hypnotic consistency of jungle drums.

The image she regarded in the mirror seemed to have a
life of its own. As she took off her slip, standing there in bra
and panties only, she unwittingly began moving her hips to
the powerful and unrelenting sound of the percussion. She
continued to regard herself in the full-length mirror. She

completely forgot about the model in her painting club, and began to wonder, instead, what would a stripper feel like if fifty of more pairs of men's eyes regarded her over their glasses of beer.

For some reason, her hips began to swing even more, then the rest of her body…

She stopped abruptly.

"What on earth are you doing, Alicia," she asked her own image. What she saw in the mirror was a broad grin, flushed cheeks and a figure that her husband called, "to die for".

Regretfully, she picked her slip and bra from the floor, and put them on again. She preferred not to look in the mirror again. There was a person there that she hardly knew.

And yet…

Slowly, almost reluctantly, she got dressed. I'm a mother or a teenage boy, she told herself. I must act my age.

And yet…

She shook her head. Thinking of her son she smiled. Last week he'd asked her if her father would still marry her if he knew how to cook.

"What on earth makes you ask such a question?" she was amazed.

"Well," Alec confessed, "Dad is completely useless in the kitchen. If he could cook he could be gay and cook his own meals."

"But your father is gay. He's always full of humor, darling. Why would you ask such a thing?"

"Gay, Mother, gay as in homisexy."

He called her 'mother' more often lately. She wondered what had happened to 'mom'.

"You don't mean homosexual, do you?"

"That's the word! Don't men marry women because they can't cook?"

She was determined to force her husband to have a birds and bees talk with Alec. She was told that they took care of things like that in school, these days. Evidently, there were gaps in Alec Junior's enlightenment.

"No, darling, they don't marry because they can't cook. There are other reasons."

Suddenly Alec's face turned bright red. She thought that he'd just put two and two together. All by himself.

Bright red. A little like her face was, just minutes ago.

Alex Sr. called later that same day. He sounded tired.

"You won't believe it, darling. For the last twenty-something years at the very beginning of spring, they wait till the water starts rising. Then, in a great hurry, they start piling-up bags of sand around their houses. The bags are never enough. Water seems an inch or two higher each year. Next year they add an inch or two. The water goes over again. Each time they claim compensation from the Provincial Government, as insurance companies have long refused to cover them. What do you think of that, darling?

There was a moment's silence.

"The water has since receded, and they want me to stop the water going over the bags next year, would you believe it?"

Alicia didn't know what to say.

"Alicia, are you there?"

She cleared her throat.

"Darling, did you ever dance a thing called break dancing?"

This time there was silence at the other end.

"Goodnight, sweetheart," he said after a little while.

"Good night, darling…" she replied, her voice just a little bit dreamy.

Somehow she forgot to ask Alex if he could cook. It didn't seem that important. Frankly, she didn't care. She didn't care at all.

***

17
Lake Champlain

Alec's father had bought a boat. No, it wasn't a forty-two-foot Katrina, or whatever the rich Texan's boat was called; but it was a twenty-seven-foot O'Day, and it was definitely a proper yacht. She had a four-foot keel, a smooth bottom, a large rudder, and a cabin in which five people could sleep. Two-and-a-half cabins, to be exact. A vee-berth at the bow that dad called the fo'c'sle, which he explained was English for *forecastle*. But dad was born in England, and every English name was almost holy.

Dad said the yacht was small, but to Alec it was by far the largest boat he had ever sailed. And he did sail quite a lot. Practically every holiday since he was five or six. First with his parents, then the school had organized some sailing holidays. Dad had always had a weakness for water, and Alec strongly suspected that the O'Day was at least a partial fulfillment of his dream. So to Alec the boat wasn't small at all. The mainsail, or the main'sl, as dad preferred to pronounce it, alone was as tall as his house. And the jib, the genoa, was wrapped around the forestay. It was called a furler, because you could just pull a string (a sheet, dad corrected), and it furled itself around that tube up in front. I mean at the bow.

In spite of Alec's fair sailing experience, there were many words on board he had never heard before.

Dad bought the boat because, he said, they needed a country cottage. And since he couldn't afford a cottage on a lake he really liked, he thought a boat was a good alternative.

Their very first sail was going to be all the way to Valcour Island, the site of one of the biggest naval battles of the Revolutionary War. Alec read up all about it before they left.

The trouble started, he learned, in the spring of 1775 when Ethan Allen and Benedict Arnold led their colonial boys across Lake Champlain from Vermont and captured Fort Ticonderoga, held by the British Garrison. There was no way the Brits could ignore such a slight. Things went from bad to worse, until in October of 1776 Benedict Arnold's fleet, led by his flagship *Congress*, and accompanied by galleys, cutter-galley, topsail schooners, a sloop and gondolas, was overtaken by the British Fleet, resulting in the Battle of Valcour. The British fleet was led by the Ship-sloop *Inflexible*, supported by radeau (some sort of raft), topsail schooners, a gondola and some twenty smaller vessels. No mean confrontation. Arnold's fleet waited for the Brits to arrive from the North. On October 11th, the Royalists, riding a north wind, spotted the colonial fleet anchored in the lee of Valcour Island. The battle started in late morning. The Brits turned north and had to beat to windward to get within cannon range. After a few days the British eventually won, but that didn't really matter to Alec. He was ready the first morning on the deck of his flagship, the *Congress*, to fight the British fleet again.

At sunrise, he fired all cannons across the enemy's broadsides. The battle continued until the smell of fresh morning coffee dispelled the morning mists. The other yachts at anchor in Spoon Bay retreated into their original shapes; the brisk wind subsided, the six-foot waves that had been hammering Alec's flagship resolved into a glistening mirror. The battle was over, but not before Alec had sunk at least three topsail schooners. Luckily the northern wind turned 180^0 to blow from the south, and Valcour Island offered a beautiful protection for a quiet breakfast.

There was no end of fun.

Alec regretted that there were only three weeks left of his summer vacation. After that they could still sail, but only on weekends; and on weekends there were many more people. It's not that Alec didn't like people, but they did nothing to contribute to his fantasies. And the yacht offered a needed rest from the abysmal experiences of his Home planet. Anyway, Sandra didn't push him. They were meeting about once a week, but only in his night-dreams. She was always the same, the same age as he, as beautiful as ever. And she did repeat that his first duty was just "to live." Now, on the boat, he could "just live" with a vengeance!

Sailing as such was only part of it. He had to learn the skills of rigging a larger vessel, of tacking and yawing with sails twice the area he'd ever handled before, as well as the skills of navigation. And all that only after he had learned to wash down the whole deck with a plastic bucket and scrub it with a long-handed brush. On completion, dad would make an inspection and declare the yacht shipshape. Or Bristol, as he called it. Alec thought the boat hadn't changed shape or colour regardless of the scrubbing, but dad had it his way. Dad carried more nautical words in his head than Webster's Dictionary, and then some...

But the rest was short-lived. His parents had gone ashore in their inflatable dinghy, for supper. Alec's stomach was a bit upset, probably the aftermath of his first real sail, so he chose to stay on board and look after the yacht. Just as well. To go ashore, his parents had to motor around the North end of the island and cross over to the Snug Harbor Marina at Olde Valcour. That's right Olde with an 'e'. It was a good fifteen-minute spin at six knots, each way. The moment his parents left the boat, he began to feel queasier. He assumed it was his stomach. He sat down on the berth but not in time to stop himself from falling. He tried to brace himself against the landing, but he kept falling and falling and falling.

"Not again," he whispered, while he still had lips to whisper with. And then there was only darkness.

**

"For a moment there, I thought we wouldn't make it," Alicia said, hoping that pallor of her skin wouldn't show through her suntan.

It was her fourth outing, and she was still scared out of her wits each time a gust of wind would clear one of the islands, and the O'Day would lean more than ten degrees off the perpendicular. After the stability of the Catalina, which sported almost fourteen-foot beam, to her the O'Day felt like a canoe abandoned in the middle of an ocean.

Alex Senior was learning to ignore her little qualms. Most sailors feel queasy before they learn that when the boat heels, she spills wind from her sails, and thus rights herself automatically.

At least the O'Day did—a lovely little boat. A yacht, he kept reminding himself. At long last I own my own yacht. It didn't quite match Commodore Thémens's boat, but it was his own. He was the skipper.

Actually, officially Alicia, the President of the Aspiring Caribbean Cruisers' Club, was the Captain, but only when she wasn't hiding below deck.

Yes, she had delivered a lecture. She'd filled it with lots of humor and got away with it. And she threw in sufficient number of naval technical terms to make herself sufficiently incomprehensible to most attendees as to be convincing. The ladies were impressed.

Actually, Alicia's real or imagined pallor was not due to abject fear for her life. Today was the first time that she took the boat out from the marina, sailed her all the way to Valcour Island, took her around the island, and dropped anchor on the lee side of Spoon Bay, with good protection from the prevailing winds from west by northwest. And she accomplished all this almost singlehanded with appropriate amount of huffing and puffing and wiping the sweat of her forehead.

Hence the celebration.

Normally they ate on board. But Alex, Alex Senior that is, thought that she well deserved to stay out of the galley, and be treated like a skipper should. With a dinner and a bottle of Champagne.

Their little dingy took them ashore to the best restaurant in a marina south of Plattsburg. Alec phoned ahead to time to get a table overlooking Valcour Island. Once seated, Alex didn't wait long.

"Champagne," he said, gazing sidewise at Alicia.

Her eyes perked up.

They were seated with a beautiful view of the Valcour Island, with sunrays just touching the very tops of the trees.

"Dom Pérignon, 2000, Brut," Alex spelled out, as if he was having it daily for breakfast with orange juice.

Actually he hated Mimosa, and didn't think much of Champagne. As for Mimosa, he thought it was a waste of good fruit juice. He'd rather have a good red wine, later on in the day, but this was Alicia's day, and he's been married long enough to know what women liked, and Alicia was very much a woman.

Around ten, with moon just clearing the trees, Alex asked for the check. He paid with a credit card. They were still sipping coffee. He was in a splendid mood. In spite of Alicia's apparent demands, he was taking a big risk buying a boat, before he was sure that his wife would really take to it. Now he was sure. He could see with satisfaction that when she gave commands to drop anchor she kept her eye on the depth-finder. And only seconds after she told her son to drop sails. For some reason she'd done it all without firing the engine. It was as good a mooring as he'd ever seen.

"Isn't it time we got back to *Alicia*?" he asked, now regarding his wife with additional admiration.

"I'm right here darling, and it was a wonderful dinner," she replied.

"And now back to *Alicia*?" he repeated.

She gave his a slightly puzzled look.

"Darling, don't you remember? You share your name with our boat, *Alicia*. Do you mind?"

Two tears of joy forced themselves into her eyes. She did her best to blink them away. There were just too many emotional events taking place today. Her 'solo' sail, then the docking, then the unexpected dinner, then the Dom Pérignon... It was all too much. It was all just too much!

"No, darling, I don't mind at all," she replied, "and I didn't forget."

And she couldn't hold the joy out of her voice. She also got up, walked around the table, and planted a great big kiss right there, in public, on Alex's lips.

And then they left without a word.

***

For a long time Alec remained motionless, waiting for something to happen. Finally, after what seemed like an eternity, he prodded the space around him. There was nothing. No life, no volcanoes, no rocks. Nothing. He reached farther out. If this was the Far Country, then he'd traveled in the wrong direction. In the Far Country there were countless stars. Here, there was only a yawning void.

Even the darkness wasn't intense. Not like the black velvet of the Far Country. It was not the presence of black; it was the absence of *any* colour.

The loneliness became palpable. It was pressing on him from all sides. It was stark and empty and without thoughts or feelings or... without any signs of life. He screamed and no sound emerged from his innards. He had no innards. He didn't really exist, either. He was as much a part of the darkness as the darkness itself. No amount of probing revealed anything. No sound, no matter, no energy. Nothing. Whatever existed, existed only in his mind. And his mind swept about and found nothing. All there was... was darkness. And emptiness. Emptiness except for himself. He was everywhere yet nowhere. Because there was no everywhere.

Soon things started to emerge in his mind. Thoughts, ideas, places. He remained in the non-space for what seemed like eons, and he began to fill the endless void with innumerable possibilities. Countless, wondrous possibilities. With ideas that heretofore had their being only within himself. Things from within his deeper mind.

It now was a void that was no longer void. Countless invisible sparks traversed immeasurable substance of time. Ideas? Concepts? The sparks multiplied, exploded into stars, invisible stars, seen only in his mind's eye. They, too, were swept aside by oceans of his swirling thoughts. The next instant they also disappeared, only to be reborn, expand, and once again dissipate throughout the original void. A void that was now no longer gray but vibrant with innumerable colours.

"Light is knowledge," he heard deep within himself.

Wherever he now looked, the void was filled with his presence. His thoughts were not manifested as yet, but they had the potential to become anything, almost everything. They had no form, no substance. They were pure ideas. Unpolluted by compromise. They were perfect. Perfect in every way.

And he dreamed for a few more eons. Yet he still felt lonely. Perhaps more so than ever before.

Before there had been just emptiness. Now it was filled with infinite potential. It could be converted into vibrant forms, into concrete ideas, into self-reproducing ideas. How could he do it?

It seemed to him that he'd done all that he could. After all, he'd done everything. He felt he had spread himself as far as he could. The presence of his ideas, of his concepts, of his desires was everywhere around him now. And he realized that he had to find a way to separate the ideas from himself. He had to give them a reality of their own. He wanted to look at himself in ideas outside himself. He knew that that was impossible, for he knew there was nothing outside himself, but he wanted to pretend. To play a little game. Just so that he could share his ideas with something which had its own power to generate more ideas. A sort of self-generating, and re-generating being. Instinctively, he knew that the only way he could do that was to give up parts of himself into his creations. The two, and the endless number of his parts, would forever remain indivisible. But it would be such a wonderful game. And he... he would no longer be lonely.

In that precise moment, for the first time, he raised his heavy eyelids. And as he opened his eyes, the first ray of light formed and pierced the darkness. And the next instant there was light all around him.

Alec woke up on the starboard berth in the cozy cabin of his boat. He was covered in sweat, shaking, and filled with utter, complete, unrestrained joy.

He had never felt so grateful for being alive.

***

18
Alicia

"**P**ermission to come aboard?" asked his father.

"You should have come with us, darling. The food was just marvelous. Just marvelous," mother interrupted before Alec could answer. Her long legs descended from the cockpit into the cabin backwards.

His mother was wearing shorts. Short shorts. If it were anyone but Alec, he would have probably remarked on their beautiful shape. If not aloud, then at least to himself. Alec did neither. He looked at his watch. It was ten-thirty. He'd spent countless eons in the abysmal darkness before the Universe came into being in just under three hours. Was it Einstein who said that time was relative? Or was it aunt Bertha? Before she passed away, of course. She liked making profound statements.

"I'm glad you enjoyed it, mom," he answered. She had completely forgotten that his stomach had not been disposed to take much food, regardless of quality. Anyway, he now knew why he'd had to stay behind. The time had been ripe for his final descent. Somehow he knew it was final. He could hardly go back to a time before time was even invented. And where he'd been, there was no time. No time at all.

There was nothing else there, either.

"*Alicia*'s shipshape?" father asked again.

Alicia, Alec knew, although it took some time to get used to, was not only his mother's name but also the name of the boat. O'Day was the manufacturer's name. Not her proper name. Alec remembered when dad had first brought him and mom to the marina and mother had seen her own name painted in large letters across the transom. She'd jumped up and down, ending in father's arms. He had looked as pleased as punch. Another of dad's English expressions.

Shipshape simply meant that everything was in order. That she, the boat that is, was ready to sail. Not that they ever sailed anywhere at night, although it would be fun to try. For Alec anything new was worth trying. Anything at all. Only they would first have to fix the navigation lights. They worked at the bow, but the mast light seemed disconnected. Dad would fix it, no doubt. He was good at that sort of thing. Just as mom was good at other things. Like making sure they had enough food and drink for three or four days' sail. Somehow she knew how hungry they would all be before they cast off. Clever that, Alec thought.

The next day they sailed to Malletts Bay. They had to negotiate a narrow entry, only to face what looked like a miniature inland sea. This was the Outer Bay, and it was just the beginning. Dad steered them through another strait into Malletts Bay proper. The western breeze of about thirteen knots kept them sailing at a decent pace until they turned into the lee of the Northern coves. Here the wind became so gentle that they didn't have to switch on the engine to cast anchor. They decided to spend the night in a tiny cove named after Gail. Gail's Cove was recognized as one of the most beautiful spots on the lake. The three- to four-story rocks descended right down and continued under the water. At the entry to the cove, the rock had been undercut by years of erosion, until the overhang created an arch over the water. The shore that rose away and up from the cove was thickly forested, with deciduous as well as coniferous trees. Today it was a little private haven. Very private. Tomorrow it would be full of people, but today was Thursday. Dad wanted to show them some places before the weekend armadas converted the secluded havens into parking lots. For dad, the purpose of having a boat was to get away from people, not to spend your time in each other's shadows.

After dropping sail and furling up the genie, they dropped anchor, about forty yards off shore. Dad tested it for holding while Alec changed into his swimming trunks. He and dad swam to the shore while mom, after only a quick dip, decided to rustle up some sandwiches. Dad offered help, but mom thought that taking Alec ashore would better serve them both. Alec didn't have to be asked twice. He jumped into the water from the stern and was climbing the rocks before dad descended the ladder into the tepid bath. It was the warmest water ever noted on Lake Champlain. Dad claimed total credit for this statistic. Who knows? Alec didn't really mind who took the credit, as long as he was on the receiving end.

On the way back from a half-hour hike, Alec jumped into the water from one of the overhanging rocks. Since the experience on the Home planet, he liked the idea of jumping into anything that exhibited some semblance of a bottom. He would never volunteer to jump into the chasm again. He suspected he wouldn't have to. Here, as his feet hit the water, he let himself sink down till he touched bottom, some twenty feet below. He almost miscalculated the capacity of his lungs. The next time he would spread his arms to slow his descent.

He was glad there would be a next time.

After the first night on board, his parents decided to sleep in the main cabin, while he was given the V berth in the fo'c'sle to himself. He had his own hatch through which he could look at the stars and let his imagination fly unrestrained.

He lay there looking at the Milky Way. For a brief moment a cloud covered his field of vision. This brought him to the Void, where no stars, no light of any sort was discernible. He strongly suspected that he had witnessed the world before it was created. He had seen, in turn, how the world worked, how life, or at least biological life, began, and finally how It All began. He'd seen it but suspected that the real secret of the lessons lay elsewhere. As the stars framed by the square hatch reappeared again, he thought that it had to do not with what he saw, but with the vantage point from which he was observing his lessons.

Assuming they had been lessons.

If he was right, then the main lesson lay in making him aware that he had witnessed the world without having any awareness of his physical or even imaginary body. By some trick or guise, all his senses were in perfect working order, while the organs that controlled these senses were absent. Perhaps the organs don't control my senses at all, he thought. Funny that! He knew that dreams could take all sorts of liberties, but he was also convinced that everything happened for a reason. If he was shown something in a certain way, there was a reason for it. And it was his job— his dad would call it duty—to discover what it was.

He thought he had it, but... it would have to wait. He was getting very sleepy. All this fresh air, the water, the wind, the...

...he jumped from a rock a thousand feet high. He flew, not straight down but, as he spread his arms, descending in a gentle swoop towards the water. As he reached it, he continued uninterrupted into its cool embrace and explored the underwater caves, nooks and crevices. He didn't have to move his arms or legs except to change direction. He was surprised to find the bottom of the lake full of variously shaped corals. Winding between their intricate arms, he admired an abundance of colorful tropical fish. There was no end of them. It was as though all the fish from the entire lake had come to Gail's Cove to show off their regalia—to him alone.

Sailing is great, he thought as he finally emerged from the festive depths. But this is even better. He had never seen such colors arranged in such complex and diverse forms before. Except, maybe, the mosaic patterns on the Home planet. Hard to tell. This is just great, he repeated as he turned on his other side.

The next day he changed his mind.

***

The seniors needed a rest. Alex took his wife home to get a really good night's sleep. Also, Alicia had to pay a visit to her painting friends. At least, that's how Alex thought of them. Paining was all they ever talked about. They promised Junior to be back early the next day.

Alex Sr. was sipping his Black Label with obvious pleasure. They were going out this evening, his wife's somewhat dotting—as in fatuous or silly—friends, and he felt he had to fortify his patience before they left. Alicia was still performing final touches in, what she liked to call, her boudoir. It always took longer than he imagined.

He didn't really mind Alicia's painting friends, if it weren't for the fact that they imagined each of their creations to be an immortal work of art. And some of them really did have talent, if not fully developed as yet. But, well, he was an engineer. His animals needed to have fronts and backs, or more precisely heads and tails. Except for apes, of course, which could look like humans.

Or was it the other way round?

The last time he'd tried to make this very point was when they went together to the studio. He had to keep his left hand in the pocket for an hour. He hadn't been told the oil on the canvas was still wet, and was too embarrassed to admit his ignorance in "public". In front of the ladies, that is. By the time they got home, the paint had set. It took him hours to wash it off, later, with turpentine.

By now he could smile at the memory, but at the time he was livid.

He sat back in his favourite armchair, reminiscing about that evening on board the *Alicia*, when Alicia had asked him a most peculiar question. They've been married for nearly fifteen years, and she still managed to set him back on his heals.

"Darling…?" Her voice was sleepy; perhaps dreamy was a better word.

In fact a week had passed since the Champagne feast, but he still recalled that evening as though it were yesterday. On that night they shared the v-berth in the fo'c'sle, leaving Alec the whole cabin and the quarter-berth to do with as he pleased. At least, if need be, the fo'c'sle had a door they could close.

"Yes, dear, what is it?" His own voice had been slightly slurred. In fact after all the Champagne, he'd already dozed off.

"Are you sure you can't cook?" she'd asked.

"Why are you asking?"

"Just wondering…"

"Well, I'd once put the cattle on. I waited for hours and hours and the water just wouldn't boil…" he confessed.

"Did you switch on the burner?"

"Ooh…"

"I love you."

"Me too."

He took another sip, this time a bigger one of his Scotch. Then he closed his eyes, trying to visualize Alicia's face

"Here's to you, Blue Eyes," he muttered and finished the rest of his drink in one gulp. Alicia's eyes were never so blue, he mused, as when aboard a boat in the middle of a sunny day. He wished he didn't have to go to see her friends tonight. It was fun just sitting back, reminiscing.

I wonder if that's why I love sailing so much, he mused. Those eyes… I wonder… And he got up to refill his glass.

***

19
The Gale

This time he really was going to drown. Water was coming in through his mouth, nose, even ears. He could not even catch a single breath. Goodbye, mom, dad. Goodbye, world. Goodbye...

SANDRA!

Alec hit his head on the bulkhead as he sat up. He wasn't sure if it was the noise of the water coming in through the open hatch that woke him up. He pulled the hatch shut even as the next wave splashed over the bow. After the previous night, Alec's father decided that the main cabin would be more comfortable for Alicia and himself. Alec inherited the v-berth in the fo'c'sle. He didn't mind at all. He could look straight up at the stars through the hatch in the ceiling.

"Dad?"

No response.

"DAD!!!"

The door to the main cabin was open and dangling on its hinges. His father was trying to sit up on the starboard berth. His eyes were still closed, though he seemed to be making a colossal effort to open them.

"It's still dark, son. What is it?"

It wasn't dark. It was the beginning of daybreak.

"There's water coming into my v-berth."

"What?"

Alex Baldwin Sr. was instantly wide awake. The boat was performing an irregular dance of a jerky fandango, swirling and jostling like a cork in a bathtub. His dad was not amused.

"The bloody wind changed. I wish they would give us a half-decent forecast."

During the night the westerly wind had swung towards the south, exposing them to the whole bay. Not a large bay, but large enough for a build-up of a three-foot wave. As the stern of the boat swung away from the wind, the bow took all the punishment, covering Alec's hatch in spray. They were in no danger, or so it seemed, until dad looked up the companionway and saw sheer rock no more than ten feet away.

In one smooth motion he leaned down to switch on the batteries, then reached over, stretching himself flat across the cockpit, to pull out the chock and start the engine. There was no time to check for possible gasoline vapors, which if present could turn their boat into a ball of fire. Or so they said.

The regular purr of the engine gave dad a moment's respite.

"What is it, darling?" mom asked, carefully opening one eye. "Can't you keep it down?" Then she sensed that something was definitely amiss, as Sherlock would say. "What is it?" she repeated, this time with both eyes open.

By now dad and Alec were in the cockpit. Alec knew exactly what to do. They'd discussed just such a danger two days ago, still on the way to Valcour Island. Alec punched in the gear and eased the yacht gently forward, while dad made his wavy way towards the bow to lift anchor. As he raised the Danforth from the sandy bottom, Alec advanced them a bit more forward. They were now clear out of danger, and into an even wilder sea.

Dad came back and took over the tiller.

What had happened was quite simple. When they had dropped anchor, they were, according to the depth-finder, in twenty-two feet of water. This called for about one-hundred-ten feet of nylon rode, plus the chain, to give them a scope of at least five-to-one. As the boat drifted away from the anchor, towards the East, they ended up about forty yards from shore, in sheltered water. Perfectly safe.

The wind was supposed to veer south by mid-morning. They had plenty of time to raise anchor and head into the sea, for a beautiful broad reach sail back towards Valcour Island. But the forecast had proved inaccurate. As the wind changed, presumably around five a.m., their stern swung round to back onto the North shore of Gail's Cove. The forty-yard leeway shrank to a mere ten feet. Had they dragged the anchor, poor *Alicia* would have gotten her rear end splattered all over the rocks.

"It's awfully hard to sail a boat with its rear end missing, darling," dad concluded as Alicia—the mother, not the boat—stopped looking nervous. "We're all right now, thanks to our Number One. If it weren't for you, son, we would have an awfully long swim home!"

Alec knew that, but he would never admit that he'd called Sandra for help. He was sure his dream would have gone on for some time, and dragging an anchor on a mere 5:1 scope was all too common. With the wind from the south, they would have had to increase the scope to at least a 7:1 ratio, and even then they would not have been comfortable.

"I suppose this means no breakfast?" he asked instead.

"Oh, I am sorry, darling. Of course I'll get you something. You deserve it. You've saved our lives. All our lives!"

Mother liked to jump from one extreme to another. Later, as it turned out, she proved to be pretty close to the truth.

There would be no hot breakfast today, not even coffee. But within a few minutes mom pressed a sandwich into his hand, holding on to the grab-rails in the choppy sea. Apparently, the forecast was worse than even dad imagined. The wind was mounting, and on top of that there were sudden gusts; anyone who chose to remain in the cockpit was covered with a fine spray. Thank heavens it was warm. In autumn such conditions wouldn't have been funny. Not that they were so hilarious even now.

By the time *Alicia* cleared the second cove, dad pointed the bow westward, but not before they hoisted the main, albeit reefed down, and let out about 50% of the genie, while still facing into the wind. Finally he cut the engine. The relative silence was a delight to the ear. The waves, the swishing of the wind, even the bobbing up and down without any rhyme or rhythm wasn't bad.

But their problems had only just begun.

As they reached the Outer Bay, much broader than the Malletts Bay they had just left, the wind seemed to double in force. The forecast was 10-15 knots, not bad for a boat *Alicia*'s size. Much more was not that comfortable. The wind was supposed to rise up to 15-25 knots by late afternoon, but by then they expected to be snugly tucked away in one of the many Valcour's bays that offered excellent protection from the south. Obviously the forecast was off by about four to five hours.

After hoisting the sails, dad again took over the helm. Not that the tiller needed physical strength to control it, at least not yet, but he felt responsible for his family. There was nothing Alec could do to make himself useful. He sat with his back to the bow on the starboard that was the lee side, the driest place in the cockpit. His mind wandered to Sandra's words: "Your job is just to live..." or something like that. Although right now he was not actually doing anything, he felt very much alive. At any moment dad could call for his help. He was ready, willing, and hopefully able to face anything. He always was. This was the joy of living. To face the unknown.

They were approaching the narrow entry that separated the Outer bay from the lake proper. Dad must have remembered that once they cleared the Outer Bay, they would face the full wrath of the southern wind, which could build up the waves along the entire length of the lake. The crossing from the Malletts to Valcour was said to be the most choppy on the lake. Not something he would choose to do, given an alternative under the present conditions. But the south shore of the Outer Bay was flat. No hills to afford any shelter from the southern wind.

Dad went below, handing the tiller to his son. In spite of the wind, Alec could just hear the radio that dad had switched on to get the latest forecast. Not that it cheered them up. Quite the opposite.

"There is a gale warning for central and northern Vermont and New York states. Winds up to 25 knots are expected with gusts up to 35. This is a gale warning for..."

Dad cut the radio. Alec supposed they should be grateful. He knew that gales on the lake didn't last too long, too many mountains around; but on the open sea, a gale force wind can range from 25 to 75 miles an hour. That's a lot more than their little ship could take, under the best conditions, and their hull had been built some twenty years ago.

"That's living, Sandra," he whispered under his breath. How come I only think of Sandra when I'm a bit, well, a bit lost? For some unexplained reason he felt that she didn't mind. After all, she had told him to live his life to the fullest. Right now the fullest was getting pretty wet.

"Take her into the wind, son," dad commanded.

You don't argue with the captain. Never. Not even to find out why.

"Take her in, easy now, hold her pointing due south," dad added.

Alicia creaked as Alec carried out dad's order.

"Now hold her steady..."

Dad was already at the mast, lowering the main another notch. They would be double-reefed for the rest of the trip. Then he hoisted the main sheet tight again and staggered back into the cockpit.

Or almost.

At the very last moment he was thrown against the life line, almost lost his balance, righted himself, and with the next heave he fell crashing on top of Alec. A deep-throated groan gave Alec the jitters. His dad seemed to be in agony. His right arm was bent backwards, not the way arms are supposed to bend. Alec, his father still half splattered on top of one of his own legs, swung his free leg over the tiller, to free his arms. Then, biting his lip and thankful for the first-aid course he'd taken, he jerked his father's arm back into position. His dad did not take time to thank him. He fainted instead. The setting of a dislocated elbow is much more painful than the dislocation itself.

"Mom!"

Mom was right there, frozen in total immobility.

"Mom, get dad off me!" he screamed over the wind. "NOW!" he added when mother still didn't move.

This worked. Mother's lithe body had a lot more strength than was apparent. She half lifted and half dragged dad's limp body down onto the floor of the cockpit and into a half-sitting position. By now dad was coming to, his eyes trying to make sense of what was going on. Then the pain in the arm hit him, and he did all he could not to pass out once again.

By now mother had her shirt off and was making a makeshift sling for dad's arms. Once mom got going, she was the best. She then propped him up so as to protect his right arm.

"Thank you, daaaah..." The 'darling' came out as a whimper.

Alec steered the boat back to face the outlet from the Outer Bay. He made the narrow passage through dead center. Luckily there were no other boats competing for the space. And then the full force of the wind hit them.

Holding on to the tiller with one hand, Alec reached forward and let out the main sheet another two feet. The boat righted herself by about five degrees. Then he did the same with the jib. Another degree or two. Now he had to steer the boat as best he could till they got into the lee of Valcour Island, some two hours away. Two hours in these conditions would feel more like six. The sloop pranced on her stern, tried to veer into the wind, then danced away as though giving up. Alicia was looking after dad who, it transpired, had also cut his knee and lost some skin from his other hand. Dad would be useless for the return trip.

"How the devil am I going to throw the anchor?" Alec wondered. "I could hardly lift it the last time I tried..."

He decided to keep the thought to himself. If Sandra wanted him to live, here and now, then he had a lot of living to do right now before facing that problem. "One thing at a time..." he told himself. "One thing at a time."

Every few minutes Alec had to change hands just to hold the tiller on a good heading. Not just the sails, but the hull itself caught the wind, pushing the sloop diagonally across the waves, which in the middle of the crossing mounted to four, maybe five feet. That's one foot over the gunwale. Alec had no choice but to release the sails still further, slowing down progress but righting the boat. The sloop only carried a four-foot draft and the keel was a mere five feet long. Not much to balance the forces the hull was taking from the gale-force wind.

"Easy, boy," he whispered, his face covered with spray. "You faced harder conditions on the moons of Jupiter..."

A vague memory of one of his jaunts crossed his mind. There, too, his lieutenants had been lying at his feet even as dad was now. He clenched his teeth and jutted his chin towards his destination. Where no man has gone before...

He lost all sensation of time. The rocking-twisting motion of the boat would have given him seasickness, had he been below. Here, facing the elements, constant spray blinding his eyes, he had no time to be sick. He was at the helm. Alec Baldwin Jr., the Sea Captain.

By ten o'clock they'd made it to the lee of Valcour Island, where the waves were a mere foot high. Outside the lee all hell was breaking loose. The white crests seemed bent on overtaking each other; the wind was swirling in irregular gusts, as though to discourage the intrepid sailors from braving their fortunes. There was no need. They hadn't seen a single boat on the way back from the Malletts. Not one. No one was crazy enough to venture into the angry sea.

Exhausted from the two-hour battle, Alec switched on the engine and dropped the main. His father's head appeared from below. Mother had taken him there to keep him dry. Alec hadn't even noticed when. Now, with the boat behaving like a boat should rather than a tin can bobbing in a pool full of rowdy children, dad could hold his balance pretty well. He sat, somewhat heavily, next to Alec.

"You need some help, son?"

No. Dad wasn't himself yet. Alec would have to steer the boat, tie the main, furl the jib and drop the anchor. Apart from that he was free just to sit around.

"Thanks, dad," Alec actually managed a smile. "How's your arm?"

"Arm?" Alex Senior looked down at his arm as if it belonged to somebody else. "That old thing? Ha, ha, it's quite useless, I'm afraid, son. At least I think so. Can't move it at all."

"Can you take the tiller?"

"Sure can." Dad reached out with his good arm and grabbed the tiller. "You do what you have to, son. I'll be fine right here."

Alec did what he had to do.

To give himself more time, he reduced gas to idling. Then he steadily walked to the bow. And, yes, he did lift the anchor himself, and did let out the requisite length of scope, and did tie the other end to a cleat. Then he went about putting things in order. He switched off the engine, cut the main switch to disable the depth sounder and the speedometer. He then pulled the cover, just partially, over the main to let it dry once the rain stopped, and arranged all the sheets so as not to trip over them lying loosely all over the place. He was grateful he didn't have to pay out the fenders, as he would have, had they been mooring at a finger dock. All in all, it took him about a half-hour, and by the time he had finished, the boat was shipshape and Alec was covered in sweat.

"Bet you're wetter on the inside than the outside," his dad quipped, his eyes unable to hide the admiration for his son.

Had dad accomplished all this, he would have given himself a healthy shot of Scotch. Alec, smiling at his own thoughts, did the next best thing he could think of. He jumped overboard. The water was exactly what the doctor ordered. The first shock washed all the sweat away. He dove again and again through the water, working his stiff arms and legs. Recharging himself. Eventually he just floated on his back. His arms and legs felt massaged by the gentlest hands that ever touched him. Actually, he'd never had a real massage. But, now that he thought about it, he decided to have one the moment he grew up. He wondered why boys didn't have massages. Mr. Grimm, the gym/tennis pro, once gave him a massage before an important match. He remembered enjoying it.

The wind was dying down. Or so it seemed. The open waters were still covered with crests, but they didn't seem to be roaring with vengeance. They seemed to skim the surface of the water, as though chasing each other just for fun. Anyway, in the lee of the Island they were in quiet waters. Hardly a ripple close to shore. And… they had the whole bay to themselves!

"How about some breakfast, mom?" he asked before he even dried himself.

Mom didn't hear his plea for breakfast. She was preoccupied with dad, still feeding him all the painkillers she carried in her bag. Knowing mom, dad wouldn't feel much for quite a while. Luckily dad did not get his scotch. Not even a snifter. He tumbled jerkily down and stretched himself on the cabin berth. A minute later he was asleep. Just as well, Alec thought. Sleep is a good healer.

She climbed down to sit opposite dad, looking at him as though he were about to die. Then she leaned back, drew her legs under her chin and also dozed off. Alec didn't really mind. He could make himself a sandwich.

***

20
You Called?

"You called?"
Alec heard the same question for the second time. He hadn't heard Sandra's voice for a while. Or at least it seemed so. Then he laughed. He remembered calling her name when he was, or imagined he was, drowning in Gail's Cove. Just before the real problems started.

"Time doesn't matter to you much, does it?" he almost giggled, and quickly stopped short when he remembered that men don't giggle.

Alec removed his bed-sheets from the fo'c'sle and laid them out over the boom to dry. Then he stretched out on the v-berth foam-rubber mattress with the hatch wide open. He was tired. He had absolutely no idea what he had accomplished today. He'd fought the elements in so many of his dreams, his imaginary jaunts, that he wouldn't dream, sorry, wouldn't *think* of taking credit for any of this morning's accomplishments.

"You looked rather busy," Sandra said contritely.

He'd never heard anyone who had so many vocal—or really tonal—intonations as Sandra. She could laugh, giggle, express sorrow, admiration, concentration, and even frivolity, all without saying a word. It was the tone that gave all her moods or intentions their value. Alec loved that.

"Well, sort of...." Alec admitted.

"You've done rather well," she said.

"Thanks." Alec couldn't take applause on the tennis court, either. And there were never any accolades in his inner travels. He just did them.

"You saved their lives, just like you did mine."

"Yours?"

"In the dungeon," she affirmed gravely.

Well, that was different. He had saved her life down there. But this was just a sail. Anyone could have done it. Yet, despite himself, he felt a very distinct pleasure from Sandra's words, or from the way she said them. She always knew exactly what to say. Even if others didn't.

"They will. Once they realize it," Sandra assured.

Alec felt ashamed. He knew that they were both talking about his mom and dad. He also knew that dad was under sedation, and mom was scared stiff. He also knew that they would thank him for his efforts once they'd recovered from their present condition. It was different for him. It's always different for whoever's at the wheel. Or the tiller, in this case. When you have to make all the decisions, you don't have time to worry. You really don't.

He felt another caress from Sandra. No words, just a caress. A sort of warmth spreading all over his body. How did she do that, he wondered. She could make you feel good even when you were tired, or lonely, or sad, or just about anything. Maybe she really is always with me. All the time. I mean I know she is, but it doesn't always feel like it. Maybe she was also holding onto the tiller when my arm was hurting from the effort. Maybe...

"It was all you, Alec. I never interfere when not invited," she insisted.

She would never interfere. He knew that. But she was there to give him confidence. Even when he didn't actually think of her presence. He knew that, too.

"What do other people do?" he asked.

"How do they find challenges?"

"Well, yes. I mean you can't always sail through gales, and you said that I should just live. I mean—not dream all the time."

"There are as many challenges as you care to look for. You're right that all people can't sail the seven seas, but challenges can be found in every walk of life."

"Like tennis?"

"If you like. But I was thinking more of a surgeon attempting to save someone's life, an architect designing the best, the most beautiful building in the world, a scientist splitting the atom and resolving its inner structure... there is no end to extremely challenging opportunities for those who look for them."

Alec thought about that. She sounded right. She always did. If you really dug in, just about everything was fascinating. You really had to dig in, though. You couldn't just skim the surface. Then his mind turned to a matter that had been bothering him for some time.

"Remember telling me, on that first occasion, that the Home Planet is two galaxies away? How come we don't have one in our own Milky Way?"

"Perhaps we will, one day," she smiled again.

"When?"

"When people are ready."

So we're too young for such a... such a place.

"So how come you took me?"

"You really like asking questions, don't you?" Alec still seemed frustrated. As he would not be so easily dissuaded, she continued. "The Home Planet doesn't just happen. It is the sum total, the product of racial effort. Often of many races from as many different planets."

"You mean there are other Home Planets?"

"Of course. That's why I always call it *our* Home Planet. Remember?"

He did. He remembered every single word she had ever told him. Every single word.

"So there are many races?"

"As many as there are stars in the sky."

"WHAT!"

"Shhh..."

"Sorry. But that's an awful lot of people." Then, after a moment's silence another thought struck him. "Do they all have legs and arms, you know, do they look like us, or are they all sorts of monsters?"

"People are not defined by the number of extremities, heads or digits on their hands. Those change with the requirements of the environment. Like being short or tall, or black or pink or yellow, or any other local characteristic."

"Then how come I did not see any two-headed monst... I mean people, on the Home planet?" he asked triumphantly.

"You saw what you wanted to see. That's what Home Planet is all about. As for the people there, they are all united by the same interest. They looked like you because they share your purpose."

"You mean they look different on their own planets?"

"Home planet *is* their own planet." Then she relented. "I know what you mean. Yes, on the planet on which they have their physical being they look very different. But don't forget that on the Home planet you looked quite different to them."

"Is that why you looked... about eighteen years old?" he asked, and for some unknown reason he blushed.

"Yes, exactly like that." She didn't seem to notice.

***

They couldn't hold back any longer. She only had a few days in Montreal to get things done. By Friday they would be back on *Alicia*, on Lake Champlain. Now that there was seven of them, and five already had eight and ten canvasses each, it was time. If there were any more, there wouldn't be enough room to exhibit them.

"The guy on Sherbrook Street said he'd let us have a joint exhibition for two weeks. But... as we are apparently unknowns, we'd have to pay for the space," Joan announced, not looking very happy.

"Would he also take a cut from our sales?"

"What sales?" Pat whispered. She was painting just for the fun of it. "Not like Zaza," she mused, but didn't say it. She had her suspicions though.

"Forty percent. That's about the going rate in the city," Joan affirmed. "It's up to us. We can just continue painting and look for our own opportunities."

"But if we did exhibit, it would look good in our curriculum vitae," Alicia added.

"In our what?" This was Zaza.

"Our bio, you know…"

"I am not stupid, Alicia. I know what a bio is. I just don't speak French."

Alicia didn't say anything. Zaza's linguistic skills did not match her obvious talents with the brush. She was really good if on the very edge of eroticism. After all, so did some of the great masters of the past. Zaza was also an ardent federalist, a rarity in Quebec. For her 'French' was a dirty word, but her husband had been transferred here from the head office in Ontario. He was still climbing the corporate ladder. She had enough money of her own to stay in Toronto but she enjoyed what she called: "fringe benefits", by accompanying her husband to Montreal.

"There would be a limit to seven paintings each, four by four maximum size. M. Cellini has fifty spaces."

Monsieur Cellini's gallery was on Sherbrook's "golden mile", most frequented by well-to-do tourists. Sherbrook Street was posh. It was as good as it got.

"But I only have three paintings…" Maria moaned, "Do I have to pay the full amount?"

"I'm sure we can find an equitable arrangement between ourselves as far at the cost is concerned. We can divide the total by fifty, and multiply by the number of paintings each one of us wants to exhibit," Zaza, who needed extra space, offered.

No one commented.

"That's only forty-nine. Can I have the last one? I asked first?" she added, a twinkle in her eyes.

There have been days when Zaza had as much paint on her face as she had on some of her canvases. But she was also blessed with a sense of humor.

"You can have sixty-nine for all I care, as long as you pay for it," Maria blurted before she understood what they were talking about. It seemed that she was jealous not only of Zaza's money but also her very young husband.

Zaza looked at Maria with wide-open eyes. "What's with you?" she seemed to ask. "I only meant...?"

"If I want sixty-nine I don't have to pay for it like..." Maria almost said "like you" before she bit her lip. Maria knew that after Zaza's first husband had died in a car accident, and a year later Zaza married a man half her age, or so they said. She was also her late husband's sole life insurance beneficiary. As for Maria's husband it was well known but never mentioned that he was much, much older than Maria.

"Girls! GIRLS! We're all friends here, remember?"

This was Alicia. She was not the oldest but seemed to have the most common sense. "If anyone is short of space she's welcome to one of mine, for free, of course.

This got the fever down a few degrees although Zaza and Maria exchanged a few more dirty looks.

"So do we go for joint exhibition?"

The heads were nodding almost in unison. So that was that. The date was fixed for Early September. Assuming there would be a vacancy, of course. There was no point having one while people were on holidays. Nor much later, when it got cold and wet. Alicia and Joan were to make it happen.

It seemed that Maria's comments might have been precipitated by one of Zaza's oils as well as other nuances.

All the great masters of the past had pained nudes; in fact that was what inspired the women to hire nude models. However, it just so happened that one of Zaza's oils was pretty implicit if not quite explicit, but most certainly suggestive, of "sixty-nine", and Alicia had no idea where to hide it. Perhaps there could have a little accident?

Still, Zaza's husband apparently liked it. Alice suspected that the subject of Zaza's painting had also been precipitated by her sense of humor. She liked shocking people.

Perhaps he could buy it from his wife before the show? There was no harm in hoping. She had to. Alice made a mental note to ask Zaza when was her husband's birthday. Perhaps the girls might all chip together and buy it for him? Alicia wanted her son to see it, the exhibition—not the painting. Not now that Alec was already putting two and two together. That was enough math for now.

As Alicia walked out, Zaza met her outside. She seemed to hedge as though looking for the right words.

"You know what I mean, don't you Alice?"

Alice had no idea. She said as much.

"Well," Zaza began, wiping off a tear forming in her eyes. "It's John."

Alice knew John to be Zaza's young husband.

"Yes…?" she encouraged.

"John is loosing interest…" She blurted right out.

The difference in age, Alice suspected. John was young, virile and successful. And then it dawned on her. Zaza was using her paintings to stir desire in John. Only then she realized that all of Zaza's nudes carried a resemblance to her own face; perhaps her figure too, she mused.

She reached out for Zaza and held her in a friendly embrace. "You had ten good years," she said. "Some of us don't even get that," she said, suggesting that it was her problem also.

"Really?" Zaza looked up.

"Of course, dear. Of course. Don't worry. You have your painting and you have us—your friends. That is more than most."

Zaza seemed to perk up. Her usual seemingly carefree smile returned to her face. In fact she and Alice shared a very similar smile. Perhaps an expression of a grateful heart?

"Thank you, Alicia. You're a real friend," she said, and made for her car.

That same night Alicia made sure that she was only kidding about sharing Zaza's problem. She was proven right. And frankly she had no idea what she might do if Alex were to lose interest in her. Would life be still worth living, she mused? Or would she start painting nudes with her own face?

***

For a while Alec lay there, lazily watching the clouds drifting through the square opening above his head. He listened to the gentle lapping of waves against the hull. The clouds had begun to separate, to break apart. And now even the wind was dying down. Not down to doldrums, but to a more manageable ten or fifteen knots. Alec's lesson was over.

And then he remembered the battle he'd 'fought', side by side, with Benedict Arnold. It struck him that too many of his imaginary jaunts had to do with killing. He would never dream of really killing anyone. Not really. So how come...

"Of course you wouldn't kill anyone. No one ever does. But this is more complicated. In your imaginary battles you don't have any qualms about firing your cannons at the enemy, because you know you're just pretending. That reality is relative. It is just as real in the imaginary world as it would be in the physical world. But the laws of the imaginary worlds are different. You might remove someone's existence from your reality and, within *your* reality, they would no longer exist. But this would not really terminate their being. They would continue in their own reality as though nothing had happened. It is a little like an actor dying on the stage. He no longer exists in that particular play; but the next day, a new audience can see him die again."

"You mean no one ever dies?"

"In some respects, we all die. We die to our concepts of yesterday, we are born, daily, to new ideas, new concepts, new challenges."

"Is this true of the physical world also?"

"The physical world has completely different rules."

She paused as though to gather her thoughts. Alec felt a peculiar feeling of being moved from place to place, or rather from time to time. The square opening over his head lost its geometric definition; it wavered like the air over a hot pavement...

"You'll learn in a few years that your physical body doesn't really exist. Every atom, even the subatomic particles, wink in and out of existence in fractions of a second. You are continuously being created and dissolved. You live on the very brink of physical reality. It is this uncertainty, if you like, that enables you to make trips in the inner worlds."

Somehow Alec understood what she was saying. In fact, it sounded familiar to him. As though he knew it but had forgotten it for some reason.

...and then everything came back to normal. There was so much Alec wanted to discuss with her. There was his descent into the mad scientist's domain. Later into the witches' green, foul-smelling cauldron, and finally into the No-Man's-Land. This last he wouldn't know even what questions to ask. It had to mature within him. Or perhaps he had to grow into the reality he'd witnessed.

Suddenly he felt incredibly privileged.

"Gosh, I'm lucky. I'm the luckiest guy in the whole world!"

And once again he felt bathed, all over, in a wondrous smile. Or it could have been the first rays of sun winning the battle with the receding gale. He didn't care. It felt great.

***

21
Coffee

For the first time in his life, Alec felt his bones. It wasn't like after tennis. After a good match he felt his muscles. This was different. Sure, some of his youthful muscles felt a bit sore, but it was the bones that he felt most. It was like being wrung through an old-fashioned mangle. Like Miss Brunt, the geography teacher, must have been, he remembered. It wasn't pleasant at all.

Poor Miss Brunt, he thought.

Yet the smell of coffee, something he'd just started to enjoy, reached him from the galley and was stronger than his desire to remain prone. Nothing, nothing can compare to a coffee after a three-hour sail across a stormy sea, while sitting in a quiet bay, sunning one's tired bones.

"I thought you were still asleep," dad said as Alec peeked in from the fo'c'sle. Alex Senior was propped up on two pillows against the toilet bulkhead. He looked a lot better.

Alec glanced at his watch. His parents had been resting for almost three hours, but he'd hardly napped. The rest of the time he was reliving the gale with his usual heroic overtones. Only his chat with Sandra gave him some detachment.

"Give me a second, Mom." And before his mother had a chance to answer, he pulled himself up through the square hatch in the ceiling onto the deck and dove overboard.

Just the thing for his tired bones. The cool and warm water was simultaneously bracing and invigorating. The tension seemed to dissipate into the water around him like ice in water. The coffee would taste so much better now.

"By Jove, it's good to be young!" Alex Senior sighed, his eyes following his son through the starboard porthole. He raised himself from his cushioned perch when he heard the splash.

"Whatever do you mean?" Alicia wanted to know.

When Alec climbed the ladder, the smell of coffee was accompanied by the inviting aroma of eggs and bacon. Mom could do miracles in their small galley. Just two rings. One for coffee, the other for the eggs. What more could one possibly hope for?

The table had been laid out. Usually dad sat on the port side, with mom and Alec facing him from the starboard. Now, while Alec was swimming, dad moved to the other side to join his wife on the starboard bunk and leave the 'captain's place' for Alec.

After Alec dried himself in the cockpit and came down the companionway steps, dad whistled him in. Like a real captain. His mother stood up and saluted. Alec stood at the head of the table and said, "At ease, men!"

"Here's to Captain Alec Baldwin, Junior," his dad said as he raised his coffee with his good hand in a salute. "May he brave the seven seas as he'd braved the gale."

"May he live long and prosper!" Alicia added, holding her hand up in Mr. Spock's salute. With her other hand she also raised her coffee cup.

And they all laughed. The first relaxed laughter since last night. It was high time to forget the horror of the sail. The horror, but not Alec's accomplishments.

Their impromptu celebration went on for a while. Alec was feasted, feted, and after breakfast squeezed by his mother to within an inch of his life.

"What on earth would we ever have done without you?" she asked more than once, while dad looked on him with real, unabashed pride in his eyes. "That's my boy!" He repeated too frequently, as if daring anyone to contradict his words. "That's my boy!"

Alec tried to explain that he only did what he had to do. He told them that a dozen times, but it seemed to make no difference. His parents were determined to treat him as a hero and that was that. Trying to change the subject, Alec asked what they should do with their afternoon. Happy to get off the boat for a while, they decided to go for a walk on one of Valcour Island's nature trails.

It was fun to be on land again. Even after only two nights on board, those first few minutes felt different. Then the landlubbers got their legs back. And his father's arm was much better. He couldn't use it yet, of course, but walking and generally moving around didn't hurt. Much.

Since the footpaths were narrow, they walked in single file—Alec ahead, mom close behind him and dad bringing up the rear. Alec's mind, however, wondered off in a different direction every hundred yards or so. Hearing the footsteps behind him, Alec was suddenly the scout leading the revolutionary band towards the British garrison. He scanned the bushes for any sign of the enemy. Looking anywhere but the path in front of him, he soon tripped over a root sticking up from the ground. His reality changed instantly. Having been bitten by a snake (the root, actually), he doubled his pace to get to the field hospital. He knew he would make it, but time was of the essence.

"Alec, take it easy!" He heard mom's plea. "We can't keep up with you."

He slowed up immediately. The wounded needed a rest. He sat on a stone and waited until the convoy caught up with him. He knew he would have to treat the gun-wounds with makeshift supplies. No matter. That's what army medics were for.

"C'mon, son," dad stood before him, the pride in his eyes still visible. "We'll rest when we get back."

They got back in less than two hours. There was plenty of daylight left. Alicia and Alec swam to the shore while dad did some reading. Later they all relaxed with a glass of juice by their side. Dad was given his first and only Scotch. A small one.

Alec was not pleased with himself. Sandra had told him just to live, and his mind kept drifting off in all directions. He just couldn't help it. Or could he? Don't we all define the worlds we live in? She'd said something like that. She'd said so many important things. Like this business of what defines people. He still wasn't satisfied. How can so many different beings all be people? Some men and women, even on Earth, behaved more like animals than people. Who knows what might happen on other planets? Billions and billions of them on planets circling billions and billions of stars. It was as though intelligence had spread itself too thin...

And anyway, aren't we what we eat?

And then he felt the familiar smile.

"Animals are what they eat. People are not defined by what they put inside themselves but by what emanates from them. From innocent little thoughts, to whole Universes..."

"Sandra?"

But she was gone. A smile, a word and that was it. Not even a goodbye. Of course, if she's always with me, she can hardly say goodbye. He smiled to himself and sensed concentric circles of contentment emanating from within. The waves expanded into wider and wider circles, skimmed over the water, then rose up in the air and mixed with the sun's rays. Together they bathed the trees and bushes and flowers and anyone who cared to bask in a moment of joy.

The sort-of-nap he'd taken in the fo'c'sle had helped but hadn't really been enough. He needed real rest badly. His body took care of itself, but his youthful yet wrought nerves needed switching off for a while. A gale takes a lot out of anybody, more from him who is at the bridge. Finally, for the first time since early dawn, Alec fell into a deep, dreamless sleep. His last thought was that he always got what he needed. We all get what we need... How come people didn't know that?

And he was gone.

***

22
The Last Sail of Summer

S ailing season does not end with our definition of summer. The best sailing goes well into September, often into the beginning of October. Even so, six more tennis matches, as many days sailing, and the season of the three/four-day sails would be over. Dad couldn't take any more time off from work, and Alec was returning to school.

This year would be his penultimate year in school. He was born in a month that entitled him to join a class ahead of his age group. On top of that, he'd skipped a grade in elementary. So, all in all, Alec was two years younger than most of his class. But soon, like everybody else, and despite being only thirteen, he would have to decide what to do with the rest of his life.

His problem was not what to do; it was what not to do. Offhand, he couldn't think of anything that did not interest him: Nature, as in geography, biology, physiology, physics and even chemistry on the one hand; and history, and literature, and all aspects of fine arts on the other. When mom took him to a symphonic concert, he wanted to learn to play all the instruments. After a trip to a museum, he became determined to learn painting, and sculpture, and etching, and just about everything else to do with art.

What am I going to do? He wondered. What am I supposed to sacrifice?

Sandra would know. The problem with Sandra was that when he was really busy—whether working, studying or just playing tennis or sailing—Sandra was nowhere to be seen. Or heard, for that matter. She was right, again, when she'd said that she never imposed her presence.

He wanted to ask Pete, but, other than playing tennis, Pete was always busy with his girlfriend. He ran to her like a trained poodle.

Alec began to regret that his inner worlds had taken the place of developing friendships with other boys and... yes, and girls. He had no desire whatever to become a trained poodle, but having someone his own age to talk to would be nice. He didn't mean Sandra, of course. He meant someone he could see and touch. With whom...

With whom he could just live...

Why was it that his Sandra was always right?

The summer had been marvelous. The best Alec could remember. To be honest, he thought that about every summer. He wondered sometimes what would happen if they lived in the South. In a climate of continuous summer. No one could do any work. No one could go to school or do anything really useful. What did people in the South really do? He found it hard to believe that when immersed in balmy weather one could concentrate on work. It just wouldn't be proper. You could study fish and nature, but not really from books. You had to get out there and do it *in situ*. Outdoors. Summer was not a time to stay inside. If we were meant to stay inside, we wouldn't have been given a summer, he reasoned.

Dad wouldn't dream of taking the boat out of the water before Thanksgiving, and that was still far away. Until then, they sailed on weekends. They would leave early on Friday afternoon and often not come back before Monday morning, with dad rushing off to the office.

With the water always warmer later in the season, this was the best time not only for sailing but also for swimming. The moment they'd drop anchor in any bay, Alec would dive overboard and spend practically all his time in the water. He loved swimming, diving, or just frolicking around.

***

This was by far the best time of the day. Perhaps wouldn't have been some years ago when, like his son, he'd rather race all comers trying to pick the best moments to execute a perfect tack, or jibe, to outwit other sailors along the length and width of Lake Champlain. And a most beautiful lake it was.

Still is, of course.

With islets and intimate coves along its length, offering hideouts to pirates and sailors alike, and mountain peaks reflected in often-flat waters at sunset when the wind died down, it was heaven on earth. Some of the hidden coves with narrow entries bore romantic names like "Smugglers' Notch" or "Pirates' Cove", which his son immediately appropriated as his own domains.

Once the anchor was down and checked for dragging, the sails secured and all was shipshape, father and son would dive overboard to cool down the heat of the day. Then Alec Junior, invariably wearing his snorkeling mask, would continue frolicking, sometimes as far as checking out the nearest shore, while Alex Senior would climb back on board, up the stern ladder, dry off, and flop down in the cockpit.

"Won't you join us just once?" he'd ask Alicia every now and then.

"If God wanted me to swim in the water he'd have given me gills," would be the curt reply.

After all, on her first sail, Alicia had only twice allowed the tepid waters of the Caribbean to touch her body above her knees. At least so, by the act of her will. Champlain waters were strictly for men, she thought. She'd tried. Alas, the last time she did she had slipped from the ladder and swallowed and mouthful of water. She preferred water in her Scotch, she affirmed, and stayed on board henceforth.

Soon Alicia, who also preferred to keep her hair dry, would emerge from the cabin, a large Scotch on the rocks in each hand. She'd give one to her husband, usually the much larger one, and spread out on the port of starboard seat, as far away from Alex's still partially wet body as she could.

And this is where he was now.

They chatted idly, about this and that, until Alicia would spot their son making his way back. She'd then go below and rustle something to eat for her two men. Alec Junior would soon join her, telling her of the wonderful things he'd seen above and below the water, while downing a large glass of orange juice.

It was that time of the day that Alex Senior liked the best. All engines were switched off, the sun was slowly sinking amid the tall pines, and the wind died down to a placid whimper. And don't forget the Scotch, he mused. Never, never forget the Scotch.

Sitting alone, ice cubes jingling in his glass, his mind would wander off. Sometimes he'd visit the old days, the days of his own youth, when he could only dream about owning a boat like the O'Day.

Just wondering…

Soon the sun would dive along the trees along the western shore, then behind the mountains beyond. Soon the moon would come out…

…in those days of yore, the moon was a call to action. To go out and conquer. Now…?

Now Alicia was putting together a light meal, with Junior giving her a hand. For a few moments he was free to sit back and remember. At home, in Montreal, and on all his jobs, he lived exclusively in the present. Here he was in his private dreamland.

He wondered what it would be like he were a young bachelor here, perhaps on this very O'Day, rather than in England trying to score a damsel on his scooter, or even in Mandelieu, by cajoling her into his tent.

Of course, even then, he would have been his son's senior by three or four years, but still, it seems that things in the olden days, were not as easy as they would seem to be today.

He would have given a lot to own an O'Day in those days. He would have scored a lot, too.

He looked down through the hatchway. There she was. As slim and beautiful as on the day they got married.

On the other hand, then, when youth measured achievements by desires, not by practicality, with Alicia at his side, he would have gladly circumnavigated the globe ten times over. And, it seemed to him, that even then he would not find another mate like her. Is it really possible to be in love for such a long time?

And then the bell rang for dinner and the chimerical images dissolved into, most probably, equally as enchanting reality. It was time to eat. Or, as Alex Senior liked to think of it, time to exchange his tumbler of a glass of wine.

***

Alec first saw her through the binoculars. She was slim, sun-tanned and had long golden hair. For just a moment he thought he was looking at the Princess. Not the little girl in the dungeons, and not exactly like the eighteen-year-old on the Home planet, but somewhere in-between. The instant he saw her, his heart missed a beat. Just one beat, and he had to drop the binoculars and pretend he was looking elsewhere. He was sure she was looking at him. Knew he'd been watching.

Later, it just so happened that she went swimming at exactly the time Alec felt the need to do the same. It was a coincidence that she was swimming towards the *Alicia*, while Alec just happened to be swimming towards her yacht, the *Princess*. It was also by chance that Alec, swimming his best backstroke, bumped into her. He apologized, of course. It doesn't matter, she said, it didn't hurt at all. Are you sure? Oh, yes. Perhaps I'd better look. All right. Let's get back to my boat. It's closer, he said.

And she followed him.

On board, he looked at the arm that he had struck with the back of his hand. It took a while to find the exact spot, but he was in no hurry. He never thought that examining a girl's arm could be quite so exciting. The other side of his brain was grateful that mom and dad had gone for a spin in the dinghy.

"My name is Alec," he said at last, releasing her slender arm.

"I'm Su. Suzy. Or Susanna, if you like opera."

"Opera?"

"In *The Marriage of Figaro*."

Mozart, Alec knew, but he didn't know the opera. Not yet.

"You sing?" he asked.

She laughed, her eyes sparkling, her long tresses already swaying as they dried in the gentle breeze... "I couldn't sing a note if you paid me," she said. "No, my father is an opera buff. That's why he called me Susanna, because he's mad about Mozart."

Alec wasn't sure what exactly was so funny. He would have been, had he heard her sing. No matter. They were talking, and Alec hadn't blushed even once. In fact, they seemed to be talking as though they were old friends. Well, almost.

"Do you sail a lot?" he asked.

"Not as much as I would like to, but I miss my friends."

She had friends. Alec had Pete, for tennis twice a week, and she had friends. Probably hundreds of them. All tall and slim, like herself.

"I'd better swim back," she said. "Mom and dad might be worried about me."

"I'll take you." Escort you, he had in mind, but it sounded too formal. "I'll swim with you, only not on my back," he assured her.

This made her smile. Girls sure look different when they smile.

Alec dived, she took the ladder. They swam without talking. Alec had to be very careful to make sure he wasn't left behind, but also not to show off and get ahead. Perhaps a stroke or two, but no more. Any more would be showing off. As they approached, a tall, heavy man stood towering over the stern pulpit. Alec wasn't taking any chances. He shouted a bubbly "so long" and beat a hasty retreat. He was glad that he was a strong swimmer. Suzy's father, for it must have been her father, was much too big for his liking. My name is Alec, not David, he thought, regardless of her father's size. He broke all speed records retreating towards his own yacht.

Goliath, Suzy's father, looked about twelve feet tall. On the other hand, Alec presumed that he swam faster than David.

By the time he got back, mother was already on the ladder, and dad was tying the dinghy to the pulpit. Alec got ahead of dad and managed to keep him relatively dry. Normally, boys are not very good at getting out of the water and not giving everyone within shouting distance a shower.

After lunch on board Alec asked if, by any chance, dad knew the *Princess*. Before dad could make some funny remark, Alec pointed to the boat some eighty or ninety yards on their port side.

"It's a Hunter, son. The older ones are OK, but the later models have too much draft for this lake. A good six feet. This one looks late seventies or early eighties. Should be all right."

Alec was still thinking of his hasty retreat. "I go, but I shall come back!" he muttered.

"What's that, son?"

"That's not quite what I meant, Dad. Never mind."

That was that. No contact. No follow-up. It was up to him. As usual.

He picked up the binoculars. For a while he looked everywhere except in the direction of the *Princess*. This was not like facing a herd of charging elephants. This required quite a different kind of courage.

She was waving!

Alec looked behind him. There were no boats anchored on his starboard. He looked at the *Princess* again. She was waving to him!

He waved back and quickly went below. He had to act quickly. There was the Goliath and there was Susan. You can only die once, he decided and climbed back up to the cockpit.

"Can I borrow the dinghy, Dad?" He tried to sound as indifferent as he could.

"Of course, son."

Since their return from Malletts Bay, he had been treated like an adult. Dad even asked his advice on some things, like which approach looked best. That was nice. Right now, he was grateful dad had not asked him to post a float plan. He wanted to just... He had no idea what he wanted, but he was going to do it, anyway.

"So there!"

"What's that, son?"

"Nothing, Dad." And he went off in the opposite direction from where the *Princess* was anchored. He needed time. What would he say? How would he approach the other yacht? How close?

Then he made the decision. He switched off the engine and put out the oars. Very gently, with an easy, relaxed stroke, he started circling towards the *Princess*, so that he would have to go by her to get back to the *Alicia*.

And then a strange thought came to him. He wondered if Sandra would approve of Suzy. He'd never thought of asking Sandra's approval for anything. Nothing he did or even felt. Sandra was... she was part of him. He felt that he could never do anything Sandra would disapprove of, but in a different way. It was—and this thought came to him for the second time—it was as though he and Sandra did everything together. Really as one. Funny that...

"How's your arm?" he asked after what must have been an eternity.

"Hi, Alec! Would you like to come aboard?"

What about the Goli-...

"Come on, lad. Susanna tells me you saved her life."

The Goliath wasn't nearly as big when he was sitting down. His voice was a lot deeper than Alec's father's, but it seemed to have overtones of humor. Alec was growing less apprehensive by the minute.

"Don't want to be any trouble," he wanted to add, "I've done enough harm already," but thought better of it. He much preferred the saving bit Suzy had made up.

"Nonsense. We're just having some juice. I'll get you a glass."

Suzy sat silently on the stern pulpit, an elfin smile playing about her lips. If Alec dared to look at her and if he were a poet, he would have said "full, ripe" lips. But Alec's attention was riveted on her father.

"That would be very nice, Sir."

He threw the line to Suzy, who tied it with the expertise of a seasoned sailor. She grew in Alec's eyes.

That evening, as he lay on his back in the fo'c'sle watching the clouds cut across the dark sky, he tried to make heads and tails of today's experience. He had met Suzy by accident. But her boat was named *Princess*. Her dad wasn't a Goliath at all and seemed to be, just about, in love with his own daughter. Whatever Suzy might ask, Mr. Norman, Mr. John Norman, would be sure to try and do. Suzy had asked him to meet Alec's parents and maybe sail in tandem, sometime. Like next weekend, for instance. A moment later Mr. Norman was on the radio, trying to signal the *Alicia*. Finding no success— dad never left the radio on—Mr. Norman borrowed Alec's dinghy, motored to the *Alicia*, and invited his parents for drinks that evening. Sailors are loners, by choice, but they can be really good company when they find out that you're human. I mean, really human.

All this was almost too much, and certainly too quick. Alec always expected the best from life; but hoping to meet someone, and to do so that very same day, was just plain silly.

And awfully nice.

And then the hair on Alec's neck stood on end. Sandra had said, "All boys will discover, sooner or later, their... other halves. And the girls, too. Only they will find their Princes."

Suzy had either just discovered her Prince or she hadn't. And there was nothing he could do about it.

Sandra never lied.

And not for the first time, nor the last in his young life, Alec felt completely lost.

***

23
The School Again

S chool can be fun at any time, but when you know that you are approaching your final year, it fills your heart with pride. You know that the next step is paramount to becoming an adult. By the time you turn sixteen, you will be getting your first driver's license; a while later you will be able to vote. For Alec, it didn't quite work out that way.

After his experience with his father's accident during the Malletts-Valcour crossing, Alec was determined to obtain a license to skipper a boat. After all, he'd already done so, and it was time the fact was officially recognized. He went about meeting his goal with the skill and guile worthy of a pirate of the seven seas.

He learned that he could not take part in any courses offered by the Royal St. Lawrence Sailing Club, in Dorval, just north of Montreal, for the simple reason that they were given exclusively to adults. Mature as he was for his age, no one would mistake him for one of voting age. Nor, for that matter, would he be allowed to make any purchase at Quebec Liquor stores for the very same reason. Yet, such trifles would not stand in the way of Alec's unbridled imagination.

He discovered that the Internet offers a number of coastal navigation courses, which award, upon successful completion, a skipper's license.

With his usual vigor and commitment, he dove headlong into the digital instruction. Within a week he could answer all the questions they could throw at him, as fast as he could read them. This was the prerequisite for passing the course. During the actual test, there was no time for cheating. The questions changed all the time, and if you failed to answer them quickly, you did not pass the test. After all, on board you often had but seconds to make the right decision. This was a practical, honest test of one's navigational skills.

RRR, Red-right-returning…
RRR, Red-right-returning…
RRR, Red-right-returning…

When returning from the sea, or going up an estuary or just entering a harbor, you leave the red buoys on your starboard side.

There were many such phrases that helped him to memorize the basic navigational skills. He also had to know on which side to pass oncoming ships, the regulations dealing with priority, right of way, and dozens of other practical bits of knowledge indispensable to safe sailing. Reading charts, compasses, calculating true north, setting course by the stars and suchlike were but a small part of the overall course.

GPS was just icing on the cake.

Within three weeks he received his diploma, his name displayed in elaborate scrawl on the document. His father's reaction was typical. Alex Senior stood to attention and saluted his son.

"I shall be proud to serve under you, Sir!" he said. He was only half joking.

Alec would not be able to drive a car for a little while, but he could skipper a boat. But what was even more important, Alec learned to accept responsibility not only for himself but for other people. Sandra will be pleased, he mused, his eye scanning the distant horizon. Half his mind was already circumnavigating the globe.

Alec had mixed feelings about being the youngest. It gave him an edge in some areas, but most of his classmates either resented his apparent precociousness or simply didn't want to have much to do with anyone his age. A fifteen-year-old is ages ahead of a thirteen-year-old, as it were. They shared the same textbooks but rarely the same interests.

This year there would be new teachers, and Alec was hoping that he would turn over a new page. If not, there was always Sandra. And... it was too early to talk about Suzy, but he had his hopes. Not too early to think about her... a lot, but not yet talk.

He'd seen her twice more on the Lake. They did sail the *Alicia* and the *Princess* in tandem, dropped anchor in the same bay, went ashore together, but... the water was already a little too cool for swimming. The sort of frolics one can indulge in when splashing and diving in cold water weren't quite what Alec had in mind.

Suzy's parents rented an apartment on the periphery of downtown, in Notre Dame de Grace, while Alec lived in Downtown proper. It was a longish bus ride, and Alec didn't really like NDG. There were no lakes, no canals and no real parks. From his house, Alec could walk up to the Park of Mount Royal or down to Lachine Canal all in twenty minutes or less.

If Alec had his way, he would live in the country, preferably by a large body of water. Lake Champlain would do very nicely. Or they could move to Ontario and settle somewhere within walking distance of the lake by the same name. Like outside Kingston, for instance. Or Oshawa. Or...

Only now there was Suzy, and that complicated things. A lot. "Why do women always complicate things?" he wondered. "First Sandra and now Suzy. Ah, women..." he sighed deeply.

As if living so far away wasn't enough, Suzy's schoolwork made demands on her time. Different schools have different agendas. But despite all that, he needed to see her, be in her company, her presence.

Soon Mount Royal and the Lachine Canal lost their appeal. And Alec found himself more and more often on the bus to NDG just to hang out with Suzy, anywhere, alone, sitting on the floor, talking and talking and... given half the chance—just being there.

His dad saw Alec sneaking in one evening close to midnight. He smiled sadly.

"Ah, yes, mother. Almost fourteen. That's what hormones do to a growing lad. Once awakened, they play havoc with your metabolism." Then Alex Senior looked at his wife already half asleep. "I remember..." he murmured, "it wasn't easy."

Alec's fortunes took an unexpected turn in the fourth week of the new school year. The "Entrance Tennis Tournament," started in the third week of the school year, had reached its finals. Alec lost in the semis to a guy twice his size, but he and Pete were the odds-on favorites to win the doubles. Imagine Alec's eyes when he, on entering the court, saw Suzy sitting in the front row of the bleachers, right next to her father. His knees almost gave way. He felt sure he would not be able to hit a single ball. They won 6:2, 6:4, after a tough second set. Alec couldn't help stealing glances at Suzy, who seemed to clap her hands practically each time his racket connected with the ball. If it weren't for her, they would have won both sets to love.

After the presentation, Alec's mom invited Suzy home for supper. Dad promised Mr. Norman, who had previous engagements for the evening, that he would drive Suzy home at a decent hour. After an early supper, Alec and Suzy went for a walk.

The first thing Alec noticed was that Suzy kept stealing glances at him. He was, of course, doing exactly the same.

"You really are very good," were her opening words.

"I presume you are referring to my tennis?" he countered.

It really was different on land. You had to know what to do with your hands, where to look, how to behave. It wasn't as natural. Even talking was different. And then they reached the water's edge at the Lachine Canal. They shared memories there.

"I really like the water." Finally he was close to his element.

"Me, too," she shot right back. "I wish my parents would move to the country, or by a lake or to Ontario, or something..." she caught herself. "Only... only now... it would be nice, though, wouldn't it?" Her voice lost some of its enthusiasm.

"Me, too," Alec affirmed with equal lack of eagerness. "It would be nice, though." And then he had an idea. "We could come visit you and go sailing on Lake Ontario!"

"We could race each other..."

"Or race together against other boats..."

"I'm sure we would win..."

"Every time!"

Alec stood, the wheel firmly in his left hand, his Suzy by his side wiping sweat from his brow. The wind whistled, the crests breaking on both bows, the sails billowing...

His right arm drew his sword, raising it above his head. He cast his eye with derision at the infidels cowering below the bridge. Let anyone dare to approach his lady. Anyone!

"...it would be nice, wouldn't it?" Suzy sat on the beam supporting the lock. She didn't look that happy at all.

"We can sail together next year, maybe... on Lake Champlain, I mean." Alec consoled her. "It's not so far away...?"

Everything on the tail end of the Canadian winter is always far away. It's almost in never-never land. They sat, side by side, in silence. After a while Alec picked up a stone and threw it expertly to skim over the water. It bounced and bounced...

"Seven!" she cried. "You did seven bounces. Oh, Alec, you can do everything so well!"

And the moment she said it, her head lowered to hide a deep blush spreading over her face and ears. She looked away, but not before Alec saw. Thank the lucky stars it's not just me, Alec thought, a strange relief filling him with great satisfaction... almost pleasure. I should go, he thought. I should leave her alone for a bit. I should go look for another stone. He knew she would be grateful.

It's not easy being a man, he thought. Not even when you're practically fourteen. Can't be that easy if you're a girl either. And on a sudden impulse he bent down and kissed her on the cheek.

"I like you, too," he said in the deepest tone he could master. To hell with skipping stones. He was ready for deep water.

That night he couldn't sleep. There was the Tournament, the presentations, but mostly it was Suzy. Su was everything a guy could hope for. She was shorter than he. She looked also around fourteen. Must have been. She was a good swimmer and could hold her own at the helm. And most of all, he knew she liked him. She was a real, flesh-and-blood girl who liked him.

It's quite different when it's your own girl. One can talk about other girls, but when she's, sort of, special, it's different. It's very different. You don't laugh at her any more. You don't make fun of her. You feel like you have to look after her. Protect her. A little as he felt about Sandra in the dungeons.

"Sandra!" he said out loud. I wonder what Sandra would say about Su. I bet she would like her. What was there not to like? She was pretty perfect. That's right. Pretty and perfect. Rather like... rather like Sandra that first time he saw her. But... it was different. With Sandra he was one. With Suzy?

He had no idea what he was with Suzy. But he was very determined to find out.

***

Almost as though he was a mind reader, Don called about eight, just after supper. For a moment Alex Senior had no idea who was on the line until he started speaking with his phony drawl.

"It's y'r ol' pal Dawn, Alex mah ol' frieeend."

"Don! How did you know that our own sailing season is over?"

"Ah read mah man. I noah all aboot y're poaliar reegion. Ah read books an' all sorts..."

"OK Don, cut the crap. How have you been keeping?"

"I just came down to Palm Beach from the Big Country. The hurricane season is over, so I can take a cruise or two. When are you and the young lady coming over?"

"I'm a working man, Don, I can't just pop over on the spur of the moment."

"Well, perhaps y'r young lady... no, scratch that. I'm too young to be a dirty ol' man." Don let out a doze of hearty laughter. "Although if you weren't my friend..." he left that hanging.

"She loves you too, Don. No kidding. I think you've got under her skin."

"I bet she says that about all the sailors."

They sparred men's doubletalk until Alicia who'd guessed who was calling signaled Alex. "I don't even know his name!"

"Alicia said that she can't be unfaithful with you because she doesn't even know your name," Alex said quietly but not quietly enough for his wife not to hear. She tore the tiny cell phone from Alex's hand.

"That's not true at all, Don. Just the contrary. I only sleep with strangers. Why, I hardly met Alex till I slept with him, only he already forgot."

"Alice my li'l young lady! Good to hear your voice!"

"And you, Don. What I was telling Alex was that, strange though it may seem, we don't really know your name. Even your email doesn't spell it out."

"Yes, you do, it's Don," Don replied surprised. Then he chuckled. "Don stands for DON, Donald Owen Nesbitt. On my li'l spread, before they found the gooey goo on it, there were two other Nesbitts and one extra Donald, so they started calling me Don, like an acronym."

"I see..." Alicia could hardly believe it but it could have happened, she supposed. Don was in a habit of pulling her leg.

"...and" Don continued, quite unabashed by the lack of conviction in her voice, "I told one guy that I'd make him an offer he couldn't refuse... He accepted. I got eleven more wells that way. It happened a week after the Goodfather premiered in our local movie house. You know, Vito Corleone... "

Now that made more sense. She could visualize Don as the Godfather. She also finally knew whom Don reminded her of. In certain light, towards the evening, he was a spitting image of a middle-aged Marlon Brando.

They chatted for a while. They were about to hang up when Alex came up with another question. "Just what was the offer you made the other man that he couldn't refuse?"

There was a momentary silence, then a chuckle then outright laugh. "So you're checking up on me, pal?"

"Just curious..." Actually that's all Alex was. Just curious.

"Well, in exchange for the patch with eleven wells, I left him two thousand acres and four thousand head of cattle."

"That's it?

"Well," Don said again, "he didn't like the gooey stuff and I didn't like the smell of cow's dung. I wanted to get away, out East, and smell the Atlantic, maybe Virgin Islands, maybe some other virgins... It seemed like a fair exchange. I recon he's got a good deal."

It did sound like it.

"You'll never make a real Corleone, Don. You're too soft."

"That's not what my wife... never mind."

Finally they agreed to speak again and, perhaps, spend Christmas together on Don's Catalina. There wouldn't be much snow, but there are worse things in life than carving a chunk of time out of Canadian Winter.

They hug up together agreeing to speak again soon.

***

24
Once More, My Love

The view hadn't changed from the last time. Even the enormous sun appeared not to have changed its position. The flowering trees swayed gently as though to fan them with fragrant, balmy air. Alec and Sandra were sitting on a deep window seat, the type you find in old cloisters or in medieval castles. Only the house was quite modern, as were all the houses on the Home planet.

It had been a while.

He and Sandra both seemed a lot older. More mature was, perhaps, a better word. They were wiser. Or at least Alec seemed wiser. Sandra had always been wise.

"We have to talk," Alec said after a prolonged silence.

Sandra said nothing. There was little point. She could read his thoughts; she knew what he was going to say even before he arranged his thoughts into words. She smiled her encouragement.

"She's very pretty," she said finally, when Alec remained silent.

"Am I in love?" he asked. It may have sounded ridiculous from a fourteen-year-old; but in the here-and-now, Alec looked a good twenty-five, maybe thirty. Sandra, as usual, matched his age. Earthly age didn't really matter, but it served to remind Alec that his present boyhood had nothing to do with his actual age. Also, that on Home planet you could be any age you wanted to be.

"Are you?" she asked.

"This is not a game, Sandra." Alec got up and started pacing the room. "I really do not know what a fourteen-year-old is supposed to do under these circumstances."

More silence.

"Why must you know in advance? Can't you just take it as it comes?" When Alec remained silent, she went on. "Imagine yourself to be an outside observer, who is watching a young boy's first love. It could be a beautiful experience."

"Is that what you're doing?" It came out like an accusation. It wasn't meant to be. Or maybe it was. He'd asked for help and wasn't getting any. "I'm sorry," he said at last. "I didn't mean that."

"You shouldn't be. In a way, you are right. As I am always with you, I can't help but be an observer. But I do not spy, if that's what you mean. You only share with me whatever you want to share... do you understand that?"

She knew the answer, of course. He did understand that but only vaguely. It wasn't easy to know everything and yet not spy at the same time.

"It's a question of where you, or I, for that matter, place our attention," she added.

This was a lot clearer. He could understand being in a crowd, among many people, but listening to only one person. It was a question of attention, and of intent.

"Precisely." That old smile was coming back. "Friends?" she asked.

He knew that she was right. The Suzy experience was a beautiful gift that had come his way. Every friendship is a gift. It is a foretaste of what it is like to be one. To lose oneself in the desire to please another.

He teased her by not answering, but letting her read all his thoughts and emotions. Assuming she wasn't doing that anyway. Finally they both started laughing. "I could no more be angry with you, Sandra, than with myself. Although with the latter I succeed, on occasion."

Once more they sat without talking. The sun seemed to stand still, and even the honeybees silenced their work. Time also stopped in its progression, but that was easy down here. You created your own reality.

"I suppose you were my real first love?"

"Thank you, my lord." Sandra bowed deeply. "But you know, my love, that you can only love me as much as you love yourself."

"And I can love others differently?"

"Of course. Love is the only commodity in the Universe that has no restrictions on variety or quantity."

"Some commodity," he pondered.

"It is quite inexhaustible. It is the very ground of being."

For an instant his last descent through the abyss hovered before his eyes. Then it was gone. But in that single instant he saw the immensity of potential created, ever ready, ever available to all who cared to take advantage of it. Free, with no strings. It was more like infinite love than anything he could think of.

"There is just no end to it, is there..."

"No end at all, my love."

"Can we ever repay such gifts?"

"By living them. By enjoying the gifts. By enjoying the greatest gift of all..."

"...life," he finished for her.

After some more silence, he asked, "Will I ever mature to the Next Step?"

He hadn't thought about it recently, but a sort of latent hunger had always remained at the back of his mind. The part of him that stopped his joy from being complete. Not that he had anything to complain about. But it was there, like a memory that he hadn't yet formed.

"We are a lot closer than you imagine," she whispered.

And this time he detected real joy in her words. It was as though she, too, needed to take that Next Step with him. As if she needed it for reasons of her own. His mind turned to all that had happened to him since he first saw the image of his Princess in the downstairs mirror. The early stages when he was, in a way, play-acting, like saving a Princess from the dungeons. Then the many talks and discussions they'd had, until he finally took the three trips to the bottomless pit on his own. Completely alone. He'd more or less figured out their meaning, although he still needed some help with the last one. He wondered if this was the right time to ask Sandra, or was he supposed to figure it out all on his own.

You have all the facts you need, her thoughts seemed to insinuate themselves into his mind. Her lips hadn't moved.

Am I reading your thoughts? he asked wordlessly.

And my state of mind, was her cryptic response.

But she was right. He heard her, and, to an even greater degree, he felt her presence. He was looking at her sitting opposite him on the windowsill, yet her voice and her emotions were mixed with his own.

"Is the Next Step death?" he asked, holding his breath.

"You couldn't be farther from the truth!" she said out loud, laughing a mixture of joy, of uncontrolled mirth, and just a little giggle thrown in. "You simply couldn't!"

Alec was a little lost. He was talking about a most serious Step, at least he assumed it was serious, and all he got was laughter. It may be easy for her, he thought, but it's eating me up inside. Well, sometimes. When I think about it.

"And when you're not thinking about Suzy?" she teased him.

"I thought you loved me!"

He tried hard to sound hurt. He didn't quite make it. She was right, of course. Wasn't she always? Since he had met Suzy on that sail in the middle of September, he'd hardly traveled the inner worlds, he'd hardly met with Sandra, he'd hardly done anything but think about that pixy.

Sitting here, on the windowsill of their Home away from home, Suzy took on a very different dimension. He was just as curious about her, but he was not as emotionally involved. Shouldn't he, in a world where imagination holds sway, be even more emotional?

"How come… how come I seem to be about twenty-five or thirty?"

"You are acting your real age, here."

"Here?"

"Here you cannot lie. Nobody can. When you reach certain maturity, it comes through. It doesn't mean that you look a hundred when you get to be old and gray. Just the opposite. Here, you always display your real age."

"It doesn't make sense. An old man looking young and a teenager old?"

"You know you are far, far older than thirteen when you are here." Sandra couldn't help smiling.

"Thirteen and a half," he corrected. "Hardly old."

"Here," Sandra continued, ignoring Alec's interruptions, "here, you might almost say you are an ideal age. Most men think they are at their best in a decade starting at about thirty-five. Before that they feel too inexperienced, later you're too... well, too decrepit, in a way."

"Decrepit at forty-five?!"

"I really mean set in your ways. Unable to absorb new concepts. New ideas. Unable to venture into the unknown. Older men seldom do it."

"But not never."

"I'm sure you will remain young forever, my love."

"Very funny. I feel old already."

"Ha, ha."

"I love you, too, Sandra. I love you very much." He just had to say it.

"I know."

Alec wondered how he could say such a thing to a girl. To a Princess. But she was more than that. She was neither young nor old. She had enormous knowledge, but she was not really a teacher. He could joke with her as with an equal, but she demonstrated concern for him akin to his own mother. She was neither a giggling teenager nor a wise old woman. She was none of these things, none of these people, yet, in a way, she was all of them at the same time.

They both gazed through the arched window.

The sun continued to stay still.

***

25
The Whirlwind

There is no other way to describe the first term in school. The Latin teacher, Mr. Thomas, had made it quite clear that anyone failing this year could say good-bye to the good life. They had to do well on the exams to enter the halls of higher learning. And the only way to finish well was to do well throughout the year. And that meant now.

Alec wasn't too concerned. A lot had changed since he was interested in geography to the exclusion of practically all other subjects. He was now fascinated by whatever he learned. And every year there was more to learn. It was as if the Universe were enlarging in parallel with his own body. And his body was definitely enlarging. The most recent mark on the doorframe was a good ten inches higher than the one at the beginning of the last school year.

By the end of the first term, Alec was well-positioned to be at the top of his class. And amazingly, in spite of his sudden academic achievement, the other pupils had not begun calling him 'square-head' or 'egg-head' or whatever else they could think of. It could have had something to do with his successes in tennis, though to most of them tennis didn't rate as high as baseball or football. The main reason, he thought, was Suzy. She was now officially his girlfriend, and she turned boys' heads whenever she came to see him.

And she came at every opportunity she had, parading on Alec's arm, holding on to him like a prized possession. The school play, the indoor tennis matches, the swimming championship, and even the concert that turned out to be a complete flop. The first violin broke a string, the pianist couldn't raise her stool high enough, and the drum player put his stick right through the tightly stretched skin. To be fair to the drummer, his instrument had been bought by the school some years ago, and the skin was probably a few centuries old.

***

The *vernissage* was tomorrow at 5 p.m. Not black tie, but on Sherbrook people seldom dressed as paupers. Alicia and both Alecs, more accurately Alex and Alec, were there at four, just in case some final adjustments were needed.

All seven of the artists were in attendance. So was the owner, who bowed and wiggled and kissed ladies' hands or whatever had been offered him. Monsieur Cellini was something between a libertine and a weasel. Middle height, made up by considerable shoe lifts. Tight fitting trousers, exaggerated shoulder padding, and a permanent smile that belied badly concealed concern for success.

The smile was the worst. It was cloy beyond need.

But, it seems he did his job with reasonable efficiency. Perhaps in a fluid fashion would be a better word. The only thing that Alicia found a little offensive was not the *Eau de Cologne* he was wearing, only the sheer potency of it. He must have bathed in it, in his underwear, and then forgot to dry himself. No matter, she usually managed to position herself with at least one other person between the Paragon of Perfume and herself.

Alex Senior was impressed. No, not with the host, the ladies were the true hostesses, but with the arrangement of artworks. Whatever Monsieur Cellini lacked in personal flavor, he certainly displayed nothing but good taste in the way the exhibition was arranged. Excellent lighting, spacious disposition, impeccable attention to detail.

Alec Junior stared at the seven nudes. Actually more then seven. On three out of seven oils and acrylics presented by Zaza, there was more then one. Zaza was a good painter if nothing else.

"She makes *Les Demoiselles d'Avignon* look like caricatures," Alex Senior remarked, not forgetting that originally the Picasso's masterpiece was titled "The Brothel of Avignon".

"Shhhhh," was Alicia's response. "She looks even better than she paints."

And there she was, hanging possessively on the arm of a tall young man with broad shoulders, a rich head of hair and a smile to melt an iceberg. Suddenly Alicia understood why Zaza was holding onto his arm for dear life. He was a rare find, if a bit young for her taste. She preferred, much preferred, maturity to boyish charm. Still… to each her own, she mused, taking another look just to make sure that she was right.

Alex took a bit longer to dismiss Zaza from his crosshairs, but only to be able to compare her to the nudes which, in spite of the various models Alicia claimed they employed, were apparently based on her own contours. After an in depth examination he'd decided that the young man in Zaza's harness wasn't doing too badly. There may have been a considerable difference in age, but here were compensations, which seemed evident even from a distance. He wished them both luck.

Alec Junior didn't know the intent of Zaza's masterpieces, but that in no way diminished his pleasure from examining her creations. She'd almost convinced him that he ought to chuck school and take up paintings as some people in Europe had done. After all, Picasso was only 14 when he'd painted the portrait of Aunt Pepa, which was admired by many.

"Do you think, Mom, that I might have a talent?" he asked when he got his mother alone for a moment.

"Of course you do, darling. You probably take after you mother," she assured him.

Actually, Alec Junior, a little like his father, was thinking more of taking after Zaza.

When the wine was drunk, and photos taken by the worthy representatives of the press, the artists were left alone. Alone except for their families. The exhibition would last for two weeks, but it was time to for the first, preliminary count of little red dots, which signified sales.

There were a few scattered around. Alex suspected that members of each family were obliged to purchase at least one. Alicia sold three without his involvement, the most she'd ever sold in her life.

And then there was Zaza. No. She had no sales. But each of her eight nudes had a little green dot. They were all reserved. Only the next day Alicia discovered what happened.

There was a man who was an interior designer for a brand new hotel just nearing finishing touches in the East part of Montreal. That was known as the French part. The West used to be predominantly English, though now it was almost equally divided between the English, French and the Others—the emigrants from virtually the whole world.

The young designer was not authorized to make actual purchases. He did the next best thing. He reserved every single one of Zaza's oils. The next day, early in the morning, he brought the checks. Zaza was in seventh heaven. She called each one of her colleagues to share the good news.

Alicia was glad for her. Zaza and herself were the only sales on the opening night.

"Poor Zaza," Alicia told Alex. "Her husband will never see the sixty-nine at home."

As usually Alex was lost behind his newspaper.

"What was that, dear," he asked.

"I was just saying that great artists never live to see old age. They don't live that long."

And she left it at that.

***

Sandra, **dear Princess Sandra**, must have been holding court elsewhere. She returned only when the first term had come to an end, and Mr. Norman took Suzy and her mother for a few weeks to their condo in Florida. Luckily, Sandra was not one to hold a grudge. He was studying French when she joined him. Not to speak French while living in Eastern Canada was almost like not speaking English in the rest of the country, or Spanish in Miami, and it was one thing Alec just couldn't seem to get right. He needed to catch up over the holidays.

"*Comment va tu?* " she asked innocently.

"You speak French, too?" Alec couldn't help smiling. Sandra was always a source of surprises.

"*Mais naturellement. Je parle presque toutes les langues. Couramment,*" she added.

"All of them?"

"I did say *presque,*" she repeated, and they both laughed. He'd missed that laughter. It was different from other forms of laugh. It was the type that makes you feel good all over.

"I missed you," he said at last.

"No, you didn't," she countered.

"What do you mean?" He tried hard to sound hurt.

"I'm always with you, remember?"

Despite his affection for her, he wished she hadn't said that. There were moments, when he was with Suzy, when such a memory did get in the way. He would have done, or tried to do, things, just things, which he could hardly do with Sandra around. Those other things were better left to such stories as *Catcher in the Rye*. Growing up was not easy when hormones started to interfere with a young man's brain.

"Perhaps you would like to review your regressions?" she asked.

Sandra never volunteered to discuss anything, and here she was offering help.

"You understood the principles, but not the intent," she added, reading his thoughts.

He'd almost forgotten how easily she did that. That's what happens when you go through a whirlwind.

The first trip down the abyss had obviously had to do with the beginning of the evolutionary process. It was meant to show him that nature worked on a trial-and-error method, rather than conforming to a preordained plan. Some people still think that there is a Big Juju, a Mighty God, somewhere, who does all the designing, and all nature has to do is to carry out His orders. This obviously was total nonsense. On the other hand...

"You mean there is no overall plan at all?"

"Depends what you mean by plan. There are laws that must be obeyed in every reality. As for a plan for the future, there is no such thing. There is a powerful plan for the Present, though."

"Just to live..." he interjected.

"That's practically all there is. But how you live in the Present, with what intensity—in fact, how much time you squeeze out of every minute—is entirely up to you. You know that already," she added, after reading his mind again.

Alec had never thought of squeezing time. But he was well aware how time dragged on when he did something that did not interest him, and how it flew when he was engrossed in whatever he was doing. He was also well aware how flexible time was on the Home Planet. Or in his dreams, for that matter.

"In fact," she picked up on the theme, "time is a characteristic of a manufactured reality, not the ground of one's being."

"Manufactured reality?"

"All reality is created by someone. Without people there is just a state of being," she said slowly.

"And with people...?"

"... and with people there is also becoming."

It was always strange talking to Sandra. Whatever she said always sounded familiar. Not really new, not a revelation, but an unfolding of his own knowledge. As if all she said were buried somewhere deep inside him, not quite able to come to the surface on its own. It was as if she were a catalyst, forcing him to face certain facts that, on occasion, were a little uncomfortable.

"How do you account for the mad scientist on my first ah... descent?" he asked.

"Regression," she corrected. "There is no up and down in time, just a sequence of events. As for the mad scientist, suppose you tell me..."

She stopped when Alec caught his breath. An idea struck him that was neither pleasant nor quite acceptable.

"You're right, of course," she said, a gentle smile accompanying her words.

"Was it simply my total lack of knowledge of biology and physiology?"

"What do you think? Things don't just happen. Someone had to do a lot of studying, a lot of work before reality reached the state of order you're enjoying today. And not just someone, but whole races, thousands of them. Past and present, and even, in a way you don't yet understand, the future."

"There must be an incredible number of dead ends in the course of evolution..." he mused.

"There would be fewer if people thought, read and studied more, and talked less," Sandra admitted.

Alec recalled vividly the two-ended grazing animals, the enormous behemoth stumping its way across the primitive, unpredictable and volatile earth. Vacuum cleaners indeed. His version of the food-chain. He went down there as a boy not quite fourteen, filled with desire for knowledge to the exclusion of any sense of responsibility.

"*Noblesse oblige*..." he whispered.

"Or even creative freedom must go hand in hand with responsibility," she added. "I'm glad you are getting the point. It is one of the most important lessons in the reality of becoming. It is on a par with free will, which is really another word for creative freedom."

"And the consequence of irresponsibility is mad science..."

He knew she was right, of course. What else is new? Yet he wondered how many people realized the full impact of introducing novelty into physical reality before others were ready to accept it with a sense of responsibility. He recalled what dad had told him about Hiroshima and Nagasaki. Was that responsible? Is there ever a justification for mass murder? Each one of those people who died might have had something to contribute to the totality of the human race... Something entirely unique...

It wasn't long before Alec realized Sandra was no longer present. Sandra had done what she came to do. Alec had done a lot of growing up in the last few minutes. "I will never be a mad scientist again," he promised himself. Not even in the murky past. Or distant future, whatever it might bring. With a sigh and a crooked smile he leaned over his French textbook.

"Maybe at least in French I'll make fewer mistakes."

"*Bonne chance...*" he heard a smile coming to him seemingly from a great distance. But in his heart of hearts, he knew that she was right here with him. Always.

***

26
The Middle Ground

Alec called it the middle ground, knowing full well that it was the wrong name for it. He was thinking of the green stew in the global witches' cauldron. 'Middle time' would probably be a better word for it. But now knowing that he was, in some mysterious way, the creator of the realities he visited, he was at a loss as to what he had to learn from his second descent.

Sorry, regression.

He wished Sandra would come back and explain the mystery. But Princess Sandra was not a messenger girl, and she did not answer a cell phone. The time had to be right, evidently, before he could learn his lesson for the second time.

After three days of fruitless waiting, he tried to dissect his own reasons for having created a reality, to teach himself a lesson. Put like that, it did not make any sense at all.

Unless there was a time loop.

Unless he, in some form or another, in some distant future, turned time on its head and decided to accelerate his own growth by offering his own earlier self the knowledge that would advance him on the ladder of evolution. If he could only translate this sentence into some sort of English, he was sure it would make some sort of sense. But even then, the only reality he could create at any particular moment of his own evolution would be one contiguous to the knowledge he possessed at the time.

Or something like that.

"Let's assume I'm right," he murmured under his breath. "Let's assume that I live, simultaneously, in different, ah... time zones. Like flying from Montreal to Vancouver in the same day. Or New York to Los Angeles. Only much faster, so that the slowing down of time would have an effect on..."

He suddenly realized that he had no idea what he was talking about. He knew that time is affected by the velocity at which any mass is moving, but had only the vaguest idea what this supposition meant. He had to try another tack.

"You are not so far out." Alec detected a familiar voice at the extreme range of his hearing. He smiled and said nothing. He even tried not to think. It didn't work. He knew that Sandra was listening; but, evidently, that's all she felt like saying.

"OK." He had no choice but to dip the ladle into the soup all by himself. At least he now knew that Sandra would not let him get too far off course.

So I have my being outside time, he continued.

"What?" Again he questioned aloud his own idea. Silence meant that Sandra didn't say 'no'. At least that's what he hoped.

So I have my being outside time, do I? And what else is outside time, I wonder. That reality, I suppose. Any reality.

No. That sounds wrong. Reality is exactly what finds its expression through time. And space, of course. The two prerequisites for reality: time and space. Or as Einstein put it, spacetime.

Now—how did I know that?

Curious, he looked up Einstein online. There were hundreds of pages dedicated to him.

By one in the morning, and after quite a few false starts, he'd learned that, according to Einstein, if you were to accelerate mass to the velocity of light, the mass would become infinite. In one direction, that is. At right angles to the direction of travel. And an infinite mass would require infinite energy to move it along. Ergo? No go. One would cancel out the other. And what on earth does this have to do with the Middle Ground? With the green slime? It had something to do with time. With the flexibility of time. Didn't something happen to time at the velocity of light?

I must be on the wrong track, he decided. Anyway, it was time to switch off and get some shut-eye. High time, he thought, and grinned from ear to ear.

"Thanks for trying," she said.

They were sitting, again, this time on earthly looking chairs disposed in the main chamber of their house, on the Home planet. The arched ceiling added an undefined dimension to the large room. Bit funny, he thought. The chairs appeared to be made from white marble, yet they felt soft. Dreaming is fun, he concluded, while duly noting, once more, that he looked close to thirty. Thirty years of age, that is. At least Sandra did, and here she was always about his age. "At least I have not slipped backwards," he mused.

"You'll help me?" he pleaded aloud.

Alec knew he was asleep on his bed at home, but this did not matter. The two realities seemed perfectly compatible. And he'd learned to distinguish the characteristics of his various bodies. They really did obey different sets of laws.

"You got side-tracked by the time factor, which led you to Einstein. Your lesson did deal with time, but from a different angle. In fact, you were very close to it."

Alec desperately tried to invoke the vision of volcanoes popping up in a sea of green slime.

"Forget the slime. You noted there and then that you had traveled in both directions simultaneously. Until that very moment, you were strictly a one-direction time-traveler."

"I knew that!" he said.

"Precisely. But you also learned, or at least it was shown to you, that you can actually learn in different—what you call—time zones. You also learned about the self-reproducing gene's being the building block of biological reality. And we can only experience the physical or material reality through a biological entity. Nothing else works."

"It has been shown to me...?"

"A turn of phrase. But you're right. Again, at the very ground of your being, you are the only reality. I think you should wait on this concept until we finish with the present one."

"There's more?"

"Just because I'm here, it doesn't mean that you're supposed to stop thinking, you know," she almost snapped. That is, as much as the most beautiful Princess in the whole world can snap.

"Sorry..." And after a moment's reflection he continued. "I've learned that time is flexible and that I'm not subject to it, with the exception of living in the physical reality. I've also learned that in the physical reality I must assume a biological form to gain any experience. I suppose that means to learn anything. But that's just about..."

He caught himself short. There was something else. It was so close he could touch it. Feel it. Smell it.

"No, Alec, you can't smell it." But this time her tone was amused.

He had it. "In my second, ah... regression, I learned that I am independent from both, from time and space!" he concluded triumphantly.

"Which means...?"

It means something? Isn't that enough? She wasn't helping.

"It must mean that, that..."

"That since any reality is, by definition, an expression of time and space, you must assume some kind of a body to experience the mode of becoming. Whatever the reality. In other words, there is no *experience* of being other than in a *mode* of being. But the modes are not limited to biological forms."

"And the mode of being in any reality is becoming. And becoming means change." Once again Alec missed the point.

"Get some rest, for a change," Sandra said and was gone.

***

It came as a delayed reaction. It's been more than two months since her first exhibition. Being the principle organizer, Alicia had to contain her emotions to make sure that all went well. With her husband at work and Alec busy on his computer, she was producing yet another masterpiece, to sate Monsieur Cellini's voracious appetite for her watercolor flowers, in all shapes and sizes. She left nudes to Zaza, and returned to her original love.

"There," she murmured. "I think I like that…"

She put her brush down, trilled it in a jar of water, and sat back. Smiling to herself, she recalled how it had all began.

Within the second week of the exhibition, she had sold two more paintings, making it five out of seven. Monsieur Cellini called her to advise her of the sale of her fifth work. She listened carefully, thanked him for letting her know and slowly, in perfect command of her senses, practically in a trance, she replaced the receiver. As she didn't have an exalted opinion about her talents, her apparent success came almost as a shock to her.

Within seconds Monsieur Cellini called again. This time he'd asked her if she'd agree to leave her remaining two works with him on commission. She nodded three times before swallowing hard and answering.

"That would be just fine, Monsieur Cellini. That would be just fine." And in case Monsieur Cellini might possibly change his mind, she quickly hanged up.

That was when it happened.

She got up and began to dance a series of dances, some of which she'd never heard of before. It was a goulash made up of Hungarian czardas, blended with a waltz, tango, a Russian troika and a few other rhythmic maneuvers she couldn't name but seemed strangely reminiscent of the jungle drums of the darkest Africa. If she were to define them all by a single word she would call it a dance of Joy. A completely unrestrained, uninhibited, devil-may-care whirl of Joy, with a capital 'J', such as she hadn't experienced since she was a little girl.

When Alex Senior came back from work that day, her cheeks were still flushed, her heart still beating a bit quicker than normal. She told him about the fifth sale.

Alex's reaction was more restrained than hers, but his pleasure was nearly as evident. He picked her up, swirled with her like a minor tornado, and put her down as though afraid of harming his precious cargo.

"I don't believe it," he uttered only then.

"I can't believe it either," she confessed also.

"And he wants to keep the last two on commission."

"He what?!"

"On commission!" she repeated raising her arms for another whirl.

Just then Alec Junior came through the door. He sensed something strange was taking place.

"What is it, Mom, Pop?" His eyes were wide open.

"We can't believe it," his parent replied in unison. "We just can't believe it," his mother repeated, looking at his father with true disbelief in her eyes.

They, all three of them, ate a celebratory dinner at *Che Grandpére*, in Old Montreal. Shrimp cocktails steeped in Amontillado were followed by *Canard á l'orange* washed down with N*uits-Saint-Georges* that even Alec Junior agreed had something he enjoyed, though he did prefer his own lemonade. They finished with coffee and Baba-au-Rhum— Junior's choice—just to catch up on his parent's alcoholic intake. He alone had two helpings.

Throughout dinner Alicia smiled left and right, as though returning glances that surely people must have stolen at her. After all, how often did they share a restaurant with a famous artist? Her imagination was confirmed when towards the end of the Baba, Alex Senior got to his feet, raised his glass, and proposed a toast to the greatest artist in Montreal.

Whatever you might deny the French Canadians, there is one attribute that you must give them. They like having fun. Every single man sitting at five or six adjacent tables rose also, raised their glasses and drank a toast to Alicia. Then they replaced their glasses and gave her a stormy applause. Alex had the good sense to raise the toast in French.

It bears mentioning that all men were total strangers.

"Ah, yes, I remember eet well," she mused, thinking of Gigi, and the array of aspiring painters on the slopes of Montmartre. Gigi still remained one of her favorite movies.

***

The whole of the next day Alec couldn't shake off the feeling that they had still left something very important out of the equation. He racked his brain. Surely Sandra would not have left if he were able to understand that missing fragment.

The day was sunny, so he decided to go for a walk. The Lachine Canal was frozen over. Not yet the thick, impenetrable ice of Canadian winter, but thick enough to support twenty or so ducks, which must have forgotten to fly south for the winter. Poor ducks, he thought. He made a mental note to bring some bread for them the next time he went for a walk.

But the real reason he went to the Lachine Canal was Suzy. This was where they'd said so-long just before she and her parents flew to Florida. She was the youngest of the four Norman children. The other three, all boys, men by now, had already left home. You could say that she was an after-thought. Perhaps that is why John Norman seemed so dedicated to making her happy. Alec knew he had retired two years ago, which made him about sixty-seven. The poor guy was probably a little afraid that he might not see her grow up.

Funny how different people manage to find different reasons to make themselves miserable. Mr. Norman wasn't really miserable, but he did spoil Su. All she had to do was to mention something, anything at all, and daddy—'papa' on occasion—would come a-running.

Then Alec managed to find a loose stone on the sparsely covered ground. There was no more than half an inch of snow, so far. It might disappear with the next sunny day. Probably by the end of today.

Then he flung the stone into the open water, right next to the locks.

"Good for her," he muttered. "Good for her."

***

27
The Missing Link

Alec decided to study his parents in the context of knowledge he gained on his inner travels. This was the second time he'd really tried to understand mom and dad. On both occasions his parents obliged by going out, and Alec became the sole possessor of dad's armchair. Somehow the two went together. The chair and thinking about his parents.

Neither mom nor dad gave any indication of unusual modes of being. They just lived, in the truest sense of the word. Mother was perhaps a little better than dad at extracting the elixir of life. Her ability to find beauty in just about everything was astounding. She could rave about the disposition of spots on a ladybug. She would get quite dreamy about the shape of a lonely cloud. As for Canadian autumn colours, well, there was hardly talk of anything else for weeks on end.

Dad was different. Men always are, Alec supposed.

Dad's work gave him a considerable dose of satisfaction, but not real joy. Work, for dad, was duty. Albeit very pleasant, interesting, but still an obligation. It was something he had to do, regardless of whether he enjoyed it or not. Normally he did, but there were times, occasions Alec noticed, that dad was ready to chuck it all, buy a bigger boat and spend the rest of his life cruising the seven seas.

Now that might not be such a bad idea, Alec mused with a grin.

The spark in dad's eyes when he gazed at mother in the cockpit of the *Alicia*, that very look seemed to explain the core of his dad's being. Alec loved his father for this almost child-like devotion to his mom, but wondered if this was quite the right way to live. He wondered if one had a right to live, well... at somebody else's expense, almost. In the emotional sense.

Dad appeared to derive joy just from watching his mother. His father wasn't so good at discovering the jewels haphazardly disposed on his journey, but seemed to breathe in the joy emanating from mom. She was his catalyst, his *raison d'être*, virtually his private Universe. A little like Mr. Norman in relation to his daughter Susanna. But not the same. Dad did not just love Alec's mother; he was in love with her. Although Mr. Norman may have, on occasion, created a comparative impression, the difference was obvious to anyone who knew them both.

But didn't one have to contribute a sort of intense act of living to the fabric of the world? To the fabric of reality? Not just rejoice in the fabric's being already there?

"True, I mostly contribute such intensity within my inner worlds. But, if Sandra has her way, I will eventually translate this intensity to the physical realm. Or, at least, I'll try."

He wanted to add, 'or I'll die trying', but thought that was pushing it. He did not think of himself as any type of martyr. Dying was not really part of his vocabulary. He just wanted to leave this world a more exciting place than it was when he was born.

"And that's precisely what I mean by just living."

"But don't you have to do something... heroic?" Alec answered before he realized who had spoken.

"It is often most heroic to do very little. To take on one's destiny and let it unfold as it should," Sandra continued

"That's just words..." Alec wouldn't give in so easily. "Don't we create our own destiny?"

"We do. But you have to define what you mean by 'we'."

"You and I?" And even as he said it, Alec knew that the two peas didn't seem to share their destinies in quite the same way. They were one, but... There was still that unexplained 'but'. Perhaps it would be resolved at the Next Step.

"Let's leave the concept of ego till later. There is a Chinese expression, *Wu wei er wu pu wei*, which means, literally: "taking no action, there is no not acting." This philosophy is attributed to Lao-tzu, but it was known long before that. I believe what the saying is trying to express is our attitude to reality."

"You sound as if you want me to sit back and do nothing."

"Not at all. But we must never forget that the bodies we occupy in any particular reality are only a means for our true selves to experience a mode of becoming. And it is almost impossible, due to the limitations that, for instance, a biological reality imposes, to encompass the full scope of free consciousness."

There ensued a prolonged silence. Alec was not very impressed with Sandra's latest offering. The concept of 'just living' had begun to take on a new hue. He would not have to struggle, fight, or conquer. He just had to be. It sounded dull. On the other hand, perhaps he would have to do all three, but...

Light was just beginning to dawn on him. Perhaps he might have to do all three, and much more...

For an instant of eternity he hung suspended in the most impenetrable darkness of nothingness; the pre-time potential Universe. Before he fully realized it, he was back, stretching on dad's chair, an aura of Sandra's presence permeating him.

Although it wasn't his first visit to such unfamiliar surroundings, for some minutes he remained disoriented. There was an element of shock in finding oneself confined to a body with such limited coordinates after experiencing...

...after experiencing what, precisely?

Sandra waited for Alec to find himself. Slowly, he did.

"T-t-time is a v-very funny thing..." he stammered at last.

"It helps to arrange experiences into a sequence. It stops them from happening all at once," she said gently.

"Ha, ha, that's funny." Alec was gradually relaxing. "All at once..."

But there was something more substantial in what she'd just said. If there were no time, and if all the realities already existed in their potential forms, then they *would* actually happen all at once. Rather like a seventy-piece symphony orchestra playing all the instruments and maybe all the notes at once. Simultaneously. Only the symphony of the Universe would be infinite and not just limited to our ears...

But even when we look at a painting of a beautiful landscape, we do seem to 'take it in' in a single sweep. All at once. So there are moments when we, even here on Earth, are liberated from the sequence imposed by time. But then... Alec cringed when he realized the immensity of the Universe, and again when the non-space of his last regression touched and almost overpowered him.

"What was that place?"

There was no answer. It wasn't a place, he answered himself. There were no places back then. Only, in a strange way, it wasn't back then. It was outside time, and therefore it was as much then as now.

As much then as now...

Slowly, very slowly, Alec was allowing the meaning of his last trip to penetrate his present resistance. He was beginning to appreciate the immensity of the responsibility of every human being, of every intelligent creature in the endless realities. If infinite potential was already there, we were the creators of realities. They were created from a bottomless fountain of infinite love that churned at the very core of our being. We—he himself—we all are fragments of that love that generates potential realities in which that which *is* regards Itself, as though in a mirror. Conversely, we regard ourselves, or can do so, in the mirror of our true Self.

"Each one of us...?" were the first words Alec uttered.

"Potentially. Each one of us has that potential."

"But how???" He knew it but he couldn't accept it emotionally.

"Because it is in our nature. We are indivisible parts of the Original State of Being. Through us, through the realities we create, the Becoming..."

"...is the mode in which that which *is* can experience Itself..."

Words seemed so inadequate. Poets have written thousands of odes, psalms, runes, yet none have done the concept justice. There is no way one can do justice to that which is beyond imagination, beyond definition. Beyond reality itself.

"The infinite potential..." he now talked in whispers. "So that is what is meant by infinite love... The infinite oneness..."

"Individual means indivisible. We all are." Sandra added. For the first time her tone was filled with as much reverence as his own.

When Alec's parents came back, he spent a few hours with them. It was amazing how very relaxing his parents were. They certainly didn't seem to require heroic actions to make their day. Nor were they in need of world-shaking achievements. Alec wondered if they were doing exactly what Sandra was talking about. He doubted he would ever find out for sure. It might be that no man is an island unto himself, but the water surrounding him or her created a formidable moat.

During supper, they talked about the film his parents had seen. It was good but not that good. It was, his mom said, an escape from reality.

Alec didn't say anything. He smiled and went upstairs.

He and Sandra talked and marveled well into the night. Alec was gaining a new sense of freedom. The type that comes with greater understanding of truth. Then they stopped talking and just were. They practiced *wu wei*. The action of not acting. Somehow, it now made a lot more sense.

***

28
Princess Susanna

Boys come of age slowly. They are awkward, get more awkward, and then return to being fairly awkward. A flimsy down suggesting its presence under their noses, their chins, and somewhat later along their cheeks accentuates the visible stages. The dawn of the down, his father once called this mark of pubescence. The aural change is defined by the ridiculous incongruity in the intonation of their voices, from a uniform *falsetto* to anything ranging from tenor to a sonorous *basso profundo*. Finally, there is a less discernible change that manifests in a man-boy's total inability to keep his eyes from anything attractive walking by. This last trait stays with men well into their nineties. Sometimes longer.

Girls come of age quite differently, and this change appears to be only loosely related to their biological age. One day they are cute little girls prancing from one uncle's knee to another, and the next morning they wake up as young women, full of allure, and apparently in complete awareness if not control of their power over men of all ages.

Suzy had come of age.

When Alec first saw her on Boxing Day, she literally took his breath away.

The cutest Su, Suzy or even Suzan, had turned overnight into Susanna. This was accomplishes by the invincible force which turns heads, makes men make complete fools of themselves, makes them act like the somewhat awkward males they are destined to remain for the rest of their lives. John Norman appeared to be the only male alive in and around Montreal who seemed completely unaware of what had happened. The transformation of his daughter into a young lady radiating the most enigmatic of all charms, the charm of youthful feminine innocence, seemed to have gone unnoticed by her father.

Le Nozze di Figaro notwithstanding, Alec was happy to play fiancé to Susanna any time, although he couldn't imagine Su being a maid to Countess Almaviva nor, for that matter, to anyone else. Rather, Countess Almaviva could pay court to Princess Susanna.

And what a Princess she turned out to be. Her long golden hair that she let hang straight down, as though carelessly, set off the dark brown of her skin, lustrous after her winter break in the South. Her pearly white teeth flashed irresistible smiles in all directions, while her eyes sparkled as only sixteen-year-old eyes can sparkle.

Alec was doing quite well in his own right.

The term exams placed him firmly at the top of his class. He was heading for academic *Primus inter pares*, as Mr. Thomas, who loved Latin, liked to say. His swimming had broadened his shoulders; his tennis added confidence to his demeanor. And in addition, his voice, turning, perhaps a trifle prematurely, into a pleasant baritone (with only an occasional high-pitched squeak), helped to create a masculine impression. He definitely had more poise than any fourteen-year-old he'd ever met, and radiated more confidence than many a man twice his age. Well, one-and-a-quarter... Anyway, he did not act like an awkward teenager.

And he would soon have the chance to prove himself to Susanna. After Boxing Day lunch at the Normans', Mr. Norman, with strange formality, asked Alec to escort Susanna to the New Year's Eve school Masquerade. This was no ordinary school dance. The theme broke with tradition. It was really a dress rehearsal, a smaller version of the debutantes' ball that would follow at the Ritz-Carlton later in the year.

Luckily, Alicia, when it had been her turn to be fourteen or so, had taken a number of lessons in ballroom dancing.

They started practicing just after breakfast on the 27th, broke for lunch and continued till supper. They did this for the next five days until, on the night of the Ball, Alec, dressed in a smart tux his mother had borrowed from a local theater company, felt ready for anything the band might throw at him.

"Would you care to dance?" he asked nonchalantly.

Instead of playing another ear-shattering tune, with the consequent disjointed jerking, stomping and twisting in tempo to the rhythmic noise generated principally by about ten drums of all sizes, the band had just struck up a tango. No self-respecting teenager ever learned a tango, nor would a self-respecting band play a tango at a school dance. This, however, as previously stated, was no ordinary school dance. It was a dry-run for the Ritz-Carlton. *The* Ritz-Carlton. The place where people still wore tails. Monkey suits. And, yes, they danced tangos.

As for the schoolboys, or girls for that matter, few had ever seen it danced. The dance floor emptied quite quickly.

Alec took Susanna's arm, wedged it in the crook of his elbow and led her practically to the center of the dance floor. There, with a simple pirouette, he spun her, ivory gown twirling, into his arms.

Although he had no idea what a natural dancer felt like, his dancing experience being limited to five days in his mother's arms, Suzy felt light as a feather and performed some steps he hadn't realized he had initiated. At one point he made a gross *faux pas*, only to find Suzy effortlessly turning it into a new step that looked and felt just right.

"I asked Daddy if they would play a tango for us," Suzy whispered in his ear. "You won't believe it, Alec, but very few people refuse father's requests."

Deny the Goliath—who would?

"Dad and I have been practicing all month, just in case you could dance it also," she confessed, the gentlest flush rising in her cheeks.

Alec felt drawn into a conspiracy in which he was little more than a willing pawn.

With a final *arpeggio*, the music stopped.

Apart from some polite clapping from his peers, and a bit more lively applause from a collection of parents sitting on the balcony, Alec, with Su firmly anchored to his arm, finally ceded sole possession of the dance floor. Then, when the young couple was about halfway 'home', John Norman single-handedly raised enough heated, sonorous "bravos" to rouse the other parents to a standing ovation. Frankly, Alec would rather have hidden himself in some secluded thicket, but he had no choice. He had to extend his arm to Susanna, who curtsied, repeatedly, with the proficiency of a well-established prima ballerina.

Yes. Susanna was definitely a Princess.

The rest of the dance was uneventful. Mom told him later that Mr. Norman was an awkward dancer; dad was little more pleased with Mrs. Norman. Alec did ask his mother to a dance. They spun to the strains of a Viennese Waltz, Alec preferring the counter-clockwise direction, which left his mother a little confused.

And then came the New Year's countdown.

The awkwardness, from which Alec apparently did not suffer, returned with a vengeance. What was he to do? Kiss Suzy in public? In front of her father? What the devil was he going to do?

As the clock struck midnight, Susanna waited until her father turned his back to take his own wife into his arms. Then, with the dexterity and speed of an antelope being chased by a hungry cheetah, she sprang into Alec's arms, planted a full, smothering kiss on his mouth, and withdrew before her father had a chance to give her mother a traditional peck.

Was Susanna a Princess or what?

The next morning Alec woke up a foot taller. Not physically, but his ego was bloated to within an inch of bursting. He had not only escorted by far the most beautiful Princess to his first ever Masquerade, but he had not tripped over his or anyone else's feet. Nor did he make a fool of himself at the stroke of midnight, and, all in all, he behaved as he thought a gentleman should. Mr. Norman actually came over to thank him for escorting his daughter to her very first ball.

Imagine? The Goliath thanking David?

**

There was one dream Alicia had that she'd never shared with her husband. And that was to spend the winter, or part of it, down south. A number of her friends had already retired and became, what is known in Canada as, Snowbirds. This term is not limited to Canadians, but anyone from U.S. Northeast, Midwest, or Pacific Northwest would qualify. Don, the sailor, would not. He was, as her husband would say, a very different kettle of fish. Although in Don's case, at least before they discovered the black gooey stuff on his li'l paaahtch, or was it spreeead, a "kettle of cattle" sounded more appropriate.

Still, what's in a name, she mused.

And here was her chance. It would be the last step to her complete happiness, her tiny nook of heaven.

Don must have been a pretty lonely man. Once the summer was over, he called every two weeks, with frequent emails attaching views of and from his yacht. If ever there were a way to tempt Alicia with anything, he'd become a master at it. They wouldn't make it for Christmas, but Alex and Don agreed that by 15th January they would be on board. And this time for a whole month of cruising. Maybe longer. Don said that in a month or two he could take them all the way to Trinidad and Tobago, and touch on every island on the way.

"And bring the young feller with you. It's not good to spend all the time in school. He might become a smart aleck," he tired hard to stifle a chuckle. "And we need someone to do the work, don't we?"

"Too late, my friend. He's got a girlfriend now."

"So? Bring her too!"

Alex had to laugh. Actually he could make arrangements for Alec to stay with Pete for a month. On the other hand he had grave doubts if John Norman would entrust his daughter to him and Alicia, with his son around. As for staying with Pete, next door, Alec had suggested as much himself, and Pete's parents agreed at once.

"He can stay as long as he likes," they assured him, "Go and sail, and don't worry about Alec. Pete will love having him over."

"Even for a month or two?"

"Enjoy yourselves," was the cryptic answer.

So that was that. On the other hand, Alex Senior very much doubted that his son would ever want to leave Suzy for that long. Not yet...

For Alex Baldwin, in Canada, winter was the slow season. For structural engineers work could go on but civil engineers dealt with bridges, dams, airfields and other megaprojects that involved vast outdoor works that could not be protected from the vicissitudes of climate.

Most of his work was covered by four or five feet of snow. It was the right time to get away. He could easily take a month off, maybe as much as two. It would be an incredible experience. And young Alec sounded as though he was looking forward to being alone. He seemed to have reached that age when a boy is just becoming a man. He was Coming of Age. Primitive cultures called it the Rights of Passage. It was the time when Jews had their Bar Mitzvah.

And young Alec?

Young Alec had his Suzy, as often and as alone as he possibly could. It would probably include late nights, or as late as they could getaway with. On the other hand, Alec was too young to do her much harm, and to mature to harm himself. And there was always John. John Norman. He'd keep an eye on both of them.

For Alex Senior it would be a dream-come-true, which began years ago between the Isle of Wight and the mainland of England.

For Alicia it was also a fulfillment of her dreams. After the first outing on Catalina, she'd gathered considerable experience on their O'Day. She could actually be useful. She would no longer be a wallflower, ducking under the boom each time they tacked. No. She could easily avoid it lying supine at the bow, converting her winter-bleached skin into a color that Alex would find much more palatable. As would she, not to mention Don.

For two or three years now, she dreamt of becoming a snowbird. Until now, she wouldn't consider leaving Alec alone; certainly not for a whole month.

As for the sail, it would be her final step on the way to heaven.

***

29
The Final Step

"It is time... my love."

Alec sensed a strange blend of joy and sadness mixed in equal parts as he heard the soft presence of Sandra's voice. He caught his breath.

"Sandra?" he whispered hesitantly.

"Do not forget my voice. Ever," she admonished.

"How could I? I couldn't forget you even if I lived to be a hundred."

There was a sense of confirmation in his heart. She agreed. What was more important, she believed him.

"It's time for what?" he asked, quite unnecessarily. He knew in his heart that the Next Step was his to take.

"Are you sure you want to take it?" It was she who was, in a way, dragging her feet this time. Rather as a girl would when faced with losing her virginity. Not just in the sexual sense, but, and more so, as if an important stage in her life was coming to an irreversible end. There was a 'never again' feeling permeating the air.

Alec remembered the many dreams and fantasies he'd had about the Next Step. It was the answer to his desires, the ultimate answers to all his unknowns. Now, somehow, Sandra's lack of enthusiasm was becoming contagious. It was like his coming of age. It was glorious to be a man, but... it had been such fun being a boy. He felt in his heart that the Next Step was the Final Step. It could not be undone. It was strictly a one-way trip. But... he was a man now. He had to face the future boldly.

"Like serving an AB...." Sandra added to his thoughts, reverting to the memories of his youth. Such a very, very short time ago. Just a few months... And, surely, he was still a boy in so many ways. He hadn't even decided yet what he was going to study. And here, the Princess, the Real Princess, was...

"Where are you taking me?" he asked.

Suddenly, for no reason he could explain, his youthful desire for the unknown came rushing to the surface of his mind. All his inner journeys, his dreams and fantasies forced themselves, *en masse*, to the forefront of his awareness. He was fighting the pirates in the Indian Ocean, wiping the sweat off his forehead in the sweltering heat of the Sahara Desert, and hunching his shoulders against the bitter cold on his approach to the North Pole. These and many, many other fragments of his imagination crowded and pushed out any and all the other, comparatively speaking, inconsequential memories.

Were they memories? Memories of memories...

"Memories of memories," Sandra repeated. "There is no end of memories. We live and dream, then live our dreams, then dream again..."

"But aren't any of these memories real?"

"They are all real. Whatever you dream you make real. By living your dreams you create reality. Then the reality dissolves, but the memories never die. They live on, intertwined into the fabric of the Universe."

"So even my life here-and-now, on Earth, is a dream?"

"It is, but it is also more than a dream. It is that of which other dreams are made."

Alec sensed the words 'for ever and ever' hovering at the edge of his awareness.

"So I'll never stop dreaming?"

"A wise man once said: 'I am but an actor and the world is my stage.' What else do you want, Alec? A greater part, a more important one? Then create it. It is yours to do as you wish."

"It is not in our stars but in ourselves that we are underlings," Alec quoted. Shakespeare had been one of the greatest dreamers of all time.

"We all create according to our ability. Mozart couldn't play tennis. Einstein couldn't maintain a happy family. There are different talents making up the Whole."

"So... I'll never have to stop dreaming?" He needed to be really sure.

"No more than we could ever be apart," she said. Yet, there was that smidgen of sadness again.

"Why are you sad?"

He sensed that Sandra wanted to say something, in fact to deny his question, but her inability to lie stopped her short. She smiled instead. "I'll miss you," she said.

"But you said that we shall..."

"I said that I shall never leave you."

This didn't make any sense. If she would never leave me... No. Never. It was not he who would leave her. NEVER.

"Shhhh… You're right. You will never leave me, either. But that which you are now will no longer be."

"But, but..."

"It is the way of the dreamers. But, for what it's worth, we shall be even closer together. Now close your eyes and let things just happen."

Even as she spoke, his eyelids grew heavy. His body relaxed on his bed. The house was very quiet. His last glance at his digital clock told him it was 1:30 a.m. The wishing hour, he quipped. But very quietly.

And he entered a silence more profound than anything he could hope for on Earth. He was in the Far Country, surrounded by the ocean of stars he would never forget. The diamonds, the fiery ice, the spellbinding beauty. Even as he opened his inner eyes to his surroundings, he felt Sandra's presence within himself. Not outside like on the Home Planet, but right there, within the body he couldn't see.

Some indefinable period later, on making a mental effort, he saw, once again, the mini-Universe filling the shape of his earthly contours. Galaxies joined by sparsely populated segments of space, individual stars hanging in the middle of nowhere, clouds and nebulas churning, gathering angular momentum, preparing for the stars yet to be.

"I am the Universe," he heard his own emotive thoughts. "I am the image and likeness..."

The trillions upon trillions of atoms of his mental body began to dissolve, once more, into the impenetrable darkness. It was sustained by his mental effort, but only for a little while.

He took his attention away from his astral body and waited for Sandra. He knew she was there, right besides him, right within him, like two peas in a pod. Then, even as he smiled at her first simile, the darkness of the Universe around him began to fade.

"Is it over? Is that all there is?"

The Universe became much brighter, painfully so to his unaccustomed inner vision. The light, heretofore only individual points from stars, was bathing him from all sides with ever-growing intensity. As he waited suspended in a realm wherein time and space had no meaning, he no longer saw his body but some inner presence within himself beginning to attract, or absorb, the radiation all around him.

No, it wasn't that. It was... could it be?

It was he. He, himself, was beginning to shine, as though all the galaxies within him were emitting their own previously constrained radiance. For an ephemeral instance he saw himself as though from outside. He saw a brightness of a thousand stars... a billion points of light dancing a dance of celestial harmony. In the essence of this brightness that burned his eyes, he saw Sandra. Just as he saw her on the Home planet, only made up exclusively of light. Purest of all light. In the next instance he merged with this radiant phantom. He and Sandra no longer shared the same pod. They were fused into a single entity.

"I love you, my Prince."

He detected the very last emotive thought as if coming from the outside of his own being. And as he consolidated his oneness with the glorious being of light, he whispered with the same ardour, "I love you for ever more, my Princess. You are my life."

In the next segment of eternity they became one.

Days passed before Alec's mind could absorb the immensity of that last Step. As far as he knew, the Final Step. What else could follow a total fusion with that part of him which was before he came to be, which will for ever continue, long after his contribution to the fabric of the Universe would be long past. He suspected he would never see Sandra again, although he was intensely aware of her presence. More so than ever before.

He would no longer have to wait for her, nor call out her name. They were a single entity. They occupied the same space-time. Even as every drop in an ocean is one with the ocean, so he felt at one with the infinity welling within his inner self. This awareness also transmuted all time into a single instant. The instant of the never-ending Present. He also felt a unity with the endless ocean. Not of the transient, ephemeral oceans of the planet Earth, but the ocean of stars, within and without himself, ever vibrant, ever expanding, forming new stars, generating new life through which he could behold himself.

He would never, ever be the same.

All thanks to Sandra, his Princess.

***

EPILOGUE

Alexander

Susanna remained for another year in her school in NDG, and then John Norman moved his family to Kingston, Ontario. He bought a 38-foot sloop with a cutter rig, on which Alec was always a welcome guest. Once Su learned of Alec's true age, the passion she had displayed at the New Year Eve's ball waned somewhat. She'd learned the truth from Alec himself. At the time, he didn't think it would make any difference.

He was very wrong.

But they remained good, really good friends. And the truth came out, but not before Alec had learned a great deal about growing up and about the requirements and secret desires of a young lady. He had always been an avid learner, and Susanna, though almost his chronological peer, had a lot to teach him. Alec didn't mind at all.

After the first intense twelve months or so, they saw each other no more than three or four times a year. Each time they met, it was as though a long lost brother and sister were finally getting together. The days were invariably on the *Suzy*, as the new yacht was named. Yet, even as time passed, when their meeting took place on a starry night with moonlight highlighting the gentle ripple on the great waters of Lake

Ontario, they were apt to forget about their newly found understanding. Her eyes shone with the old sparkle; Alec's admiration born at that Masquerade surged back with the intensity of a rising gale.

But these were fleeting moments. Few and far apart.

Two years after the Normans left Montreal, Alec was entrusted to take the yacht under his own cognizance for a longer tour. He took *Suzy* from Lake Ontario all the way to the Georgian Bay. Most of the way, Alec was the skipper, with Su acting as his number one mate. All four of their parents took turns joining them periodically along their route. Not so much to chaperone their children—they probably thought it was too late for that, or possibly they were hoping that it might be. I guess, we may never know. They joined them to bring provisions by car and to spend a day or two on board. By then, although Alec looked like a presentable young man in his early twenties, he still counted a mere seventeen springs. Su, by then, was a very mature nineteen-year-old.

Back home, after a lot of soul-searching, Alec decided to study physics. Eventually—theoretical physics. He thought that, with his experience of the inner worlds, he might be in a position to cast the Universe in a different light. He always thought that Einstein's theories were not the result of the genius's mental deliberations but the consequence of his unique view of reality.

There was one other reason why Alec chose an academic future.

Since the Final Step, he was free to venture to the Home planet almost at will. I say almost, because he had to be in the right state of mind, one could say of spirit, to succeed. On one occasion he thought he needed to learn something about quantum mechanics that had been nagging him for some time. He entered the abyss momentarily and emerged with a spark in his eye he hadn't had since he first saw Sandra. He had glimpsed his future. He saw himself in Oslo, waiting in line to receive the Nobel Prize for some aspect of Theoretical Physics. He did not discover what he wanted to know about quantum mechanics, but he was nudged in the direction where the answer might be found. There were no real shortcuts in the continuum. The Home planet was there to enhance his life, not become a substitute for it.

"Just live..." he remembered her words. "Just live."

Alec didn't share his reasons for his choice of studies with anyone. Not even with his mother, who, he learned later, was hoping for a more artistic venue for his future. He compensated greatly by joining his mother's painting class. He actually discovered he wasn't half bad as an artist. It helped considerably that he no longer felt compelled to turn his head each time a model divested herself of her gown.

There is little to add to this story.

Alec already had one Princess engraved in his heart. In the meantime, the earthly, the very human Princess, continued to generate a warm glow in his libido. No longer sleepless nights, nor pangs of anguish, but a pleasant glow that Alec found quite comforting.

At a certain point along Alec's studies, for reasons unknown to himself, some of the powers he had acquired under Sandra's guidance began to grow exponentially. He found himself doing things he never before thought possible. Things that earlier in his life he would have found frightening. This, however, is quite another story. A story a long, long time into the future. Or into the past. Depending whence you are looking at it.

But one thing is certain.

All fables, tales or stories worth their salt, or writer's ink, must end with the Prince and Princess living happily together for a long, long time. And this was never more true than of Alec and Sandra. Not since they became one. Later, even as

Su blossomed into Susanna, Alec became known as Alexander; only in his case, Mozart had nothing to do with it. And you know something?

They really did live happily ever after.

Well....?

So Long...

If you enjoyed this novel, please don't forget to write a (brief) review on the Amazon.
I'm interested in your thoughts.

Part two of the Trilogy continues in
ALEXANDER

Acknowledgments

I would be remiss were I not to thank Bryn Symonds and Madeleine Witthoeft for their diligent editing, each in his and her inimitable way. I am indebted to my many friends for their meticulous proofreading, with particular thanks going to Kate Jones, who took great pains to perfect my manuscript. As always my gratitude to my wife, Bozena Happach, who put up with being a grass widow for weeks on end and then offered me her inspired insights.

Second Edition was studiously examined by Ronald Piecuch, assuring the continuity of the previous work. My thanks to all of them.

Sincerely,
Stan I.S. Law

A Word about the Author

An architect, sculptor and prolific writer was educated in Poland and England. Since 1965 he has resided in Canada. His special interests cover a broad spectrum of arts, sciences and philosophy. His fiction and non-fiction attest to his particular passion for the scope and the development of Human Potential. He authored more than thirty books, twenty of them novels.

Under his real name he published seven non-fiction books sharing his vision of reality. He also composed two collections of poems in his original native tongue in which he satirizes his view of the world while paying homage to Bozena Happach's sculptures. His poetry in English, as well as a number of articles and short stories, can be seen at Authors Den: http://www.authorsden.com/stanislaw

The story continues in
ALEXANDER
Part Two of the Trilogy

INHOUSEPRESS, MMONTREAL, CANADA
http://inhousepress.ca

www.ingramcontent.com/pod-product-compliance
Lightning Source LLC
Chambersburg PA
CBHW031313170626
46807CB00001B/412